Channel

"Effortlessly, the narrator's story becomes one with the stories of the women in prison. Rarely do we encounter a perspective clear as glass, through which the characters look back at the narrator without mirror or microscope, false hierarchy or romanticizing. Brava!"
—TONI MORRISON

"What really powers this prose is Muske-Dukes's own magical ability to channel this excellent story about reality and the imagination—and the truth that resides safely in between."
—*Time Out New York*

"Muske-Dukes uses her poet's gifts to turn real life into powerful and exploratory metaphor. . . . *Channeling Mark Twain* is an unerring celebration of the power and utility of the poetic in our complicated world. It is also an extraordinarily empathetic portrait of the artist as a young woman. Like the greatest fiction, it provides a window onto a world most people would never dare cross into."
—*San Francisco Chronicle*

"A *wonderful* book . . . I can't get it out of my mind."
—LIZ SMITH, *New York Post*

"An elegant piece . . . rich in both ideas and prose . . . Muske-Dukes's triumph lies in building a discourse on the nature of language, of poetry, of its small sucesses and inevitable limitations in the midst of ruinous lives. Lovely, original writing on the unlikely romance between prisoners and poetry." —*Kirkus Reviews*

"Intriguing . . . intensely and poetically written."
—*Chicago Tribune*

"Carol Muske-Dukes has concocted a riveting story about women in prison, with language that scorches the page and characters you won't be able to live without. The woman at the story's heart goes on a quest that has all the fresh resonance of a truth never told before. The complicated issues of race are handled with a poet's lapidary precision. In an antiheroic age, she's given us a true hero in Polly, who's as unforgettable as Huck Finn. Send up a flare!"
—MARY KARR

"Elegant . . . Muske-Dukes is such a wonderful writer."
—*The Hartford Courant*

"Rueful yet affirmative . . . radiant with feeling yet chastened by experience . . . Art has the last word in Muske-Dukes's impassioned narrative. . . . If art cannot change the world, Muske-Dukes suggests, then at least it can change us, open us to the hearts of others."
—*Los Angeles Times Book Review*

"Known for the beauty of her writing, both in prose and poetry, Muske-Dukes may have written her best book with this one. . . . The narrative is filled with tension, humor and realism."
—*Deseret Morning News*

"A compassionate poet as well as a mythically inclined novelist, Muske-Dukes is spellbinding in her precision and invention as she pays haunting tribute to women who hold fast to their humanity under the most barbaric of circumstances, while celebrating poetry as a liberating force." —*Booklist*

"An unforgettable cast of female characters . . . Muske-Dukes delivers an exquisite story about poetry, prison and empathy."
—*Edmonton Journal*

"[Muske-Dukes's] literary endgames display a versatility rarely practiced in today's highly specialized world of serious writers. . . . The character of Polly is . . . wildly unique, and complex."
—*Poets & Writers*

"Muske-Dukes proves . . . that nobody's tougher or more tender than a hard-core poet with a social agenda."
—*O: The Oprah Magazine*

"Fiction with a political conscience often sacrifices craft in favor of driving home a message, but Muske-Dukes pulls it off."
—*Publishers Weekly*

"[The characters are] painted with brutal candor but sympathetically, rough edges clearly visible, so that you see and hear and smell Rikers. . . . In the end, it's the indomitable human spirit that shines through the grit and despair, making this a novel to remember."
—*The Roanoke Times*

"After reading Carol Muske-Dukes's *Channeling Mark Twain* you might decide her protagonist, Holly Mattox, is the woman you'd want on your Conestoga wagon. You can speculate that Carol herself has obviously been There (yes, capital T) and having been There she has written the bravest of novels. The book challenges on various levels—intellectual, emotional, physical—and when you put it down you want to sing. Better still you want to tell the world: Read this book. It will lift your heart."
—FRANK McCOURT

ALSO BY CAROL MUSKE-DUKES

FICTION

Life After Death
Saving St. Germ
Dear Digby

POETRY

Sparrow
An Octave Above Thunder
Red Trousseau
Applause
Wyndmere
Skylight
Camouflage

ESSAYS

Married to the Icepick Killer:
A Poet in Hollywood

Women and Poetry:
Truth, Autobiography, and the Shape of the Self

Channeling

MARK TWAIN

Channeling

MARK TWAIN

a novel

CAROL MUSKE-DUKES

RANDOM HOUSE
TRADE PAPERBACKS
NEW YORK

The standard disclaimer familiar to most readers of fiction, to the effect that characters, places, and incidents depicted in a novel are either products of the author's imagination or are used fictitiously, is appropriate to *Channeling Mark Twain* but not *entirely* accurate in identifying all of the inspiration for this book. *Channeling Mark Twain* is indeed a work of fiction, yet some of the locales, characters, and events have been suggested by events of my own life and by people I have known. From about 1972 through 1983, for example, I taught poetry at the Women's House of Detention on Rikers Island, and I directed a prison arts program I'd earlier founded called Free Space/Art Without Walls; I also worked for a rehabilitative program called AfterCare. To some degree, this teaching experience and other actual events and relationships in my life provided the catalyst for this novel's narrative. Some of what appears in these pages is indirectly autobiographical, yet every event and every character portrait is highly fictionalized—and most of what happens here is invented. To my mind the novelist's rendering of the world is essentially no different from the poet's: I believe that the nature of the imagination is transformational—everything in these pages has been transformed in portraying fictionalized "truth."

2008 Random House Trade Paperback Edition

Published in the United States by Random House Trade Paperbacks,
an imprint of The Random House Publishing Group,
a division of Random House, Inc., New York.

RANDOM HOUSE TRADE PAPERBACKS and colophon are trademarks of
Random House, Inc.

Originally published in hardcover in the United States by Random House,
an imprint of The Random House Publishing Group,
a division of Random House, Inc., in 2007.

Portions of Chapter Eight were originally published in different form in the Fall 2000 issue of *TriQuarterly*.
The poem "Twin Cities" by Carol Muske-Dukes was originally published in the Fall 2004,
Number 5, issue of *Hunger Mountain*.

Grateful acknowledgment is made to Alfred A. Knopf, a division of Random House, Inc., for permission
to reprint "Final Soliloquy of the Interior Paramour" from *The Collected Poems of Wallace Stevens,*
copyright © 1954 by Wallace Stevens and copyright renewed 1982 by Holly Stevens. Reprinted by
permission of Alfred A. Knopf, a division of Random House, Inc.

LIBRARY OF CONGRESS CATALOGING-IN-PUBLICATION DATA
Muske-Dukes, Carol
Channeling Mark Twain: a novel / Carol Muske-Dukes.
p. cm.
ISBN: 978-0-8129-6749-4
1. Nineteen seventies—Fiction. 2. New York (N.Y.)—Fiction.
I. Title.
PS3563.U837C47 2007
813'.54—dc22   2006049174

Printed in the United States of America

www.atrandom.com

2 4 6 8 9 7 5 3 1

Designed by Stephanie Huntwork

To my unforgettable students,

the members of the original

Free Space/Art Without Walls Poetry Workshop,

Women's House of Detention, Rikers Island, 1973–1983

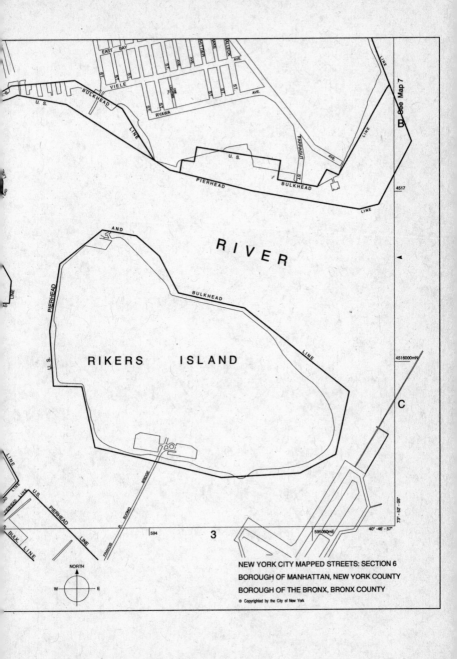

NEW YORK CITY MAPPED STREETS: SECTION 6
BOROUGH OF MANHATTAN, NEW YORK COUNTY
BOROUGH OF THE BRONX, BRONX COUNTY

© Copyrighted by the City of New York

The difference between the almost-right word & the right word is really a large matter—it's the difference between the lightning-bug & the lightning.

—MARK TWAIN

There is no point in tempering your convictions this side of the prison wall, because you might find yourself behind it. . . . Though hope is indeed what you need least upon entering here; a lump of sugar would be more useful.

—JOSEPH BRODSKY

PART I

T he pimps got on the bus at the stop just before the end of the line. The end of the line was Rikers Island and the stop before was just at the foot of a very long bridge. I'd read somewhere that the Rikers Island bridge was over five thousand feet long and before it was built the only way to reach the island was by ferryboat. Now the bridge connected the island with the City, but the largest penal colony in the United States was still remote. *But not so remote,* I wrote in my notebook, *that pimps couldn't manage to slouch out past the great glittering skyline, hats on their heads, to haul in their booty.* I added an exclamation point, then glanced out the window. Here the East River swirled up into a curse from the days of the Dutch: Helegat, *bright passage,* anglicized to Hell Gate—*sinister waters.* Hell Gate: *where killer currents swirled out from under the Triboro Bridge* (I was scribbling again now) *and swept around Rikers Island where it lay, between La Guardia Airport and the Hunt's Point sewage treatment plant, between sludge pumps and the rolling sky. Between shit and heaven.*

We were all riding the Hazen Street bus, which stopped daily in front of Bloomingdale's, in Manhattan, where I got on—then crossed the Fifty-ninth Street Bridge and trundled out through Queens, all the way to the foot of that mile-long span. Cars were not allowed on the Island, only Corrections vans, work vehicles, and prison shuttles, which looked like golf carts—and the daily bus. As we crossed the bridge, planes skidded through the clouds above us, above the flat-topped cellblock buildings—nine jails for men, one for women.

I stashed my pen in my pocket, then pulled it out again. I'd noticed that, as always, the pimps had left their Cadillacs and loaded Lincolns gleaming in the lot on the Queens side, or near side, of the bridge, parked next to the Hondas and Pintos of the corrections officers, below the twenty-foot-high posted sign: YOU ARE NOW ENTERING RIKERS ISLAND PRISON COMPLEX and THANK YOU: NEW YORK CITY DEPARTMENT OF CORRECTIONAL SERVICES. They lounged in the front of the crowded bus, in the entry well near the hunched-over driver. I watched them tapping the floorboards with their metal-tipped walking sticks. Their faces were grave under their plumed hats. This gravity was shaken as we crossed under the flight paths of the jets taking off and landing at La Guardia, just a few hundred yards across the water. The bridge rose up high enough for ships to pass under, and it stood directly in front of Runway 13. Landing approach lights were hung beneath the bridge roadway. I'd read somewhere about the bridge and its history, though I couldn't remember where—and I doubted that the pimps or my fellow passengers would be very interested in any case to know what I knew about it.

The pimps tried to maintain their solemn, sinister expressions, though their faces began to vibrate slightly, then steadily, as the roar of a descending plane shook the bus. They looked as if they were going to fly apart. I envisioned jagged pieces of pimp-face: stud-ringed noses and shrewd, cash-quick eyes swirling out the grimy bus windows into the breath-colored suck of a jet contrail. I wrote all this down, struggling to keep my handwriting steady. The bus, which had been noisy, smoky, and rocking to ghetto-blaster favorites all through Queens, fell silent. I glanced out at the expanse of oily water as the prison buildings came into view. *So close to the airport,* I wrote, *that a prisoner peeking through a mail-slot casement could see the heat waves shuddering above the tarmac; a prisoner could sniff the breeze and smell jet fuel.*

I closed my notebook as the bus parked outside the Reception Center and the pimps eased out through the hissing doors, their walking sticks hooked over their shoulders. The rest of the passengers got off hurriedly, pushing a little, obeying the overhead speaker's commands to form individual visitor lines for the Adolescent Remand Shelter, C-76 (the Men's House), or finally the House of D, the Women's House of Detention.

The pimps didn't form lines—they remained outside the Reception Center in a cluster, smoking joints and talking. Whenever an unescorted woman passed them, they would sing out: "Hey mama, hey mama? Whatjoo do for, bitch! Come here, girl, you hear? You hear me?"

They shouted at me and I ignored them. I knew why they were there: they had business interests on the Island, vested and new. The hooker who'd served her short sentence or been bounced out of court would be coming out through the Reception Center doors, ready to go back to work. But the New Interest was the releasee who'd never been in The Life, never whored before, never known that a woman fast on her back could make seven hundred dollars a night. I knew that the New Interest would be dropped by a Corrections vehicle on the prison side of the bridge where the bus rolled in. I knew that the New Interest would be wearing ill-fitting rumpled clothes and shoes too large for her feet. The New Interest would be carrying five dollars of good-luck money from the City of New York in her jacket pocket. Nestled in that same pocket would be a hot tip scribbled on a folded bit of paper—a possible position at the phone company, one hundred dollars a week. That job tip might have come from me, after all—I knew everything I knew because I had been working for the summer in a spectacularly ineffective rehabilitation program called AfterCare. *As a writer-spy,* I told myself, *a writer-spy.*

I had been employed for a few months now at the Women's House as an AfterCare worker, and now that I knew a little bit about how the system worked—I had a photo ID pass in my wallet and I'd survived Civilian Orientation—I'd asked a favor of the warden. I asked her if I could teach an evening poetry workshop at the Women's House. I stood in front of her desk, revealing myself, my passion for words, my desire to share this passion. I hastened to add that I'd been to graduate school in creative writing and that my first book of poems was about to be published. I felt I was qualified to teach. I had a lot more to say, but she raised her hand and nodded at me, glancing up over her glasses.

"Yes. Fine, Miss Mattox. Talk to the Dep."

"Great," I said. "No other questions, then?"

I was a polite young woman, but my one-note politeness hid a mob of angry contradictions. For one thing, I was angry because I was polite. I wanted to be an unconventional woman, I wanted to be tough, taken seriously, worth the trouble I'd cause. It happened that I was pretty and didn't want to be. Yet did. I longed to erase my looks even as I glanced sideways at their effect. I wished to be invisible but *seen.* I announced myself a Free Woman, identified myself as a radical feminist, but flashed a smile I'd hidden behind since I was a toddler; I wore lipstick called Moon Sugar and let my light hair grow long and streaked like Gloria Steinem's when she went undercover as a Playboy Bunny.

I was here at the Women's House, I told myself, because I wanted to know what it felt like to be a woman living outside the law. That was it: Jesse James as a streetwalker, Annie Oakley gone bad, shooting up the church picnic. I wanted to know what it was like to be a poet whose words could break open the bars—I wanted to know firsthand how adversity could make a woman utterly fearless.

Tonight was my first workshop meeting at the Women's House.

As I got off the bus, I thought about what I would say to the women, my students. Usually I walked fast, usually I hurried—but tonight I was moving a little slowly, preoccupied.

The pimp stood right smack in front of me. I hadn't noticed that I'd veered slightly out of my usual beeline path to the Reception Center and he had, of course, like a shark sensing flailing in the water, picked up on my momentary hesitation.

"Hey bitch—look here in my eyes."

I tried to move around him but he glided ahead of me, blocking my path. He was tall, hatted and plumed like all the rest, with a cigarette half smoked hanging from his lips. I tried again to step around him in the other direction—but he blocked me again. As he moved in front of me, I took in a quick series of impressions: lavender-tinted aviator glasses, bell-bottoms, a velvet frock coat, and high-heeled snakeskin boots. He smiled. A diamond glinted in his front tooth. For all his attempt at badass drag, for all his attempt to look fly, he looked prissy to me. Beneath his wide cruel mouth, his chin receded, turtle-like; his features appeared undeveloped, like a child's. He took the cigarette from his mouth and held it delicately between his fingers. Then he put it back between his lips, inhaled, removed it again, and blew smoke in my face. I was aware suddenly of the planes stacked overhead in their holding patterns—I wondered how many people sat up in the clouds above us, holding cigarettes and drinks in their hands, smoke in their eyes.

"Blondie, I'm talkin' to you. You hear me, Blondie? You see me, Green Eyes? You speak, girl?"

We stared at each other through the blue drifting exhalation. The river breeze picked up his cologne—a greeny bog-waft of Paco Rabanne. I said nothing.

"You a social worker?"

The eyes behind the tinted lenses were meant to be menacing, mesmerizing: slap-you-around-then-fuck-you eyes. *Jesus, what an incredible moron,* I thought.

I smiled at him.

"I'm a poet. I'm here to teach a poetry workshop at the Women's House."

He blinked: a crack in his veneer. He looked confused. Was I making fun of him? Then he threw back his head and laughed so loudly that it attracted the attention of a couple of his lounging comrades, who cocked their heads and began to sidle over.

"I got a poem," the first pimp announced, never breaking eye contact with me, still blocking my passage. He was speaking very loudly now, almost shouting—so that his community could hear.

"I got a poem," he repeated, smirking at me. Then he struck a pose, gesturing with his right hand as if declaiming, and recited, half singing: "Got me a slash called Dime a Time / Slap her ass and she do the grind—"

He pumped the air with his pelvis. "Like this."

Then, "You like that poem, Blondie?"

"Not really," I said. "It lacks metrical assurance and doesn't take risks, diction-wise."

He stared at me, then shook his head, truly rattled.

"Bitch!" he cried. "What the fuck you talkin' about?"

He gestured toward me, calling the pimp-collective closer to witness.

"This bitch crazy out her head!"

Out of the corner of my eye, I saw two male corrections officers coming toward us. They were walking slowly, I noticed. There were a lot of pimps gathered around us by now: a veritable panderers' convention.

What sense did it make to alienate a flock of pimps? Even at a distance, I could read the C.O.s' expressions. They were irritated that some fool girl had gotten herself mixed up with the jackals, maybe caught in cross fire.

But I was driven, by a lifelong near-diabolical desire to make all things right. I'd believed, growing up, that my mother was the living human embodiment of Justice, and her passion for completely subjective fairmindedness had flowed into me, her daughter. I'd overcome my politeness now—and I desired to show my tormentors a better way. They would see it somehow: there were other worlds for women—intellectual, imaginative, spiritual. A plane screeched through the air above us on its descent to Runway 13, flaps up and landing gear extended.

"There's also"—I raised my voice over the engine noise—"the matter of credibility. If the poem's subject only makes ten cents each time—then what do you, her . . . the speaker of the poem, make?"

I noticed suddenly that he was sweating—looking at me with the same irritation I'd seen on the faces of the C.O.s, and other men before this. Stronger than his desire to humiliate me now was a pure high-register annoyance that had settled like a migraine behind his eyes. We could hear the plane decelerating as it cleared the bridge and zeroed in on Runway 13. Then the jet roar softened to a whine and evaporated into the breeze.

The pimp pushed his great hat back on his head, mumbling to himself. Then he lunged at me suddenly, his face in mine, nose to nose. I took a step back.

"I get it *all,* slit. I get the whole *all.*"

"Come on, girlie, this way," a C.O. called from a few yards away.

"The whole *all,*" he repeated, recycling his single insight. His eyes were cranked wide, staring into mine.

"Nothin' go to a ho but what her man give. You see that back?"

I glanced at one of the C.O.s, a tall, worried-looking man with a shock of white hair, who shook his head at me. *Don't answer,* his eyes said. He held his hand out tentatively, politely, as if he were asking me to dance.

I reached out to take the hand and felt a grip on my arm, spinning me back around so fast that I lost a breath—we were eye to eye again.

The pimp spoke very softly now—leaning in to me, a gaze depthless as tin.

"I'm talkin'. To you. Bitch. I'm sayin' to you: You see that back?"

He drew out each syllable. I flinched out of his grasp and grabbed the C.O.'s hand.

"I see it," I said, as convincingly as I could. "I got it."

Under my breath I added "asshole," and the C.O. shot me another powerful warning look.

As I walked away with my escorts, the crowd parted and there was a grumbling chorus of jeers and threats—and above all that, one shout: "Hey Blondie! Stick with the *po*-tree! You ain't shit good at anything else!"

"Great," the C.O. on my left growled. "Way to go. They sit out here day and night, calm for them. Then you come along and get them all riled up. Let me tell you, the last thing you want out here is an alert pimp."

The other C.O. turned to me, raising his voice as another plane roared in over us.

"You work here, right? What were you thinking there, Miss? Talking to that sleaze? They're *carrying*—a lot of these guys."

I looked at him.

"They're packing guns and other weapons. The one talking to you? Did you see the firearm?"

"He had a gun?"

"Miss. We can't do anything as long as they keep their distance from the entrance and keep order. As long as they don't bring their piece inside. But they're just lookin' for opportunities, you know what I mean? When you see them? From now on? You need to just keep on walkin'."

"Right," I said. "I'm sorry."

But I wasn't sorry. For some reason, I felt ready now to teach poetry at the Women's House.

* * *

*I*nside the Reception Center doors, the C.O.s stopped lecturing me and turned away, ignoring a pitched battle over the pay telephones at one end of the building. I glanced at the crowd of relatives and other petitioners filling the huge waiting room, hoping to be called for Visitor Clearance. They were seated on row after row of hard, scuffed, dull-red plastic chairs—languishing, smoking, crying, complaining—sometimes for hours before they were bused to the individual prisons for their visits. There were babies in soggy diapers and screaming hyperactive children, lounging, drugged-out teenagers and beaten-down adults playing cards. Spanish, Haitian, Spanglish, and borough New Yorkese, with a sprinkling of Long Island, all shouted in the thick smoky air. I hurried toward the checkpoint turnstile at the rear exit, holding up my photo ID card. Most of the guards recognized me now—when I arrived for AfterCare work, they nodded and waved me through. Some even smiled at me. I'd found it amazingly simple to smuggle in contraband items.

In my large brown Danish schoolbook bag, I lugged all that I could: copies of *On the Barricade,* a leftist newspaper (unapproved reading matter), chocolate candy bars and chewing gum (impressions of locks could be made), and tonight, the forbidden items I felt were necessary to teach a poetry workshop: spiral-bound notebooks and ballpoint pens (wires could be straightened into weapons, criticisms of the institution could be written down).

It had grown late enough, while I dallied with the pimp, for the shift to have changed: different gatekeepers were in charge. I didn't recognize the jowly heavyset guard with dark sweat circles in the armpits of his blue uniform at the exit checkpoint. His name badge read "C.O. Janowitz." He raised his hand like a crossing guard, stopping me just past the turnstile, and then motioned for me to hand over my bag. He shook everything out onto the counter between us:

my leather wallet, keys, a single owl-shaped tortoiseshell barrette, a clear plastic swizzle stick from the Algonquin Hotel bar, a silvery packet of Violet gum, eight Snickers bars, *The Bean Eaters* by Gwendolyn Brooks, *Ariel* by Sylvia Plath, *The Voice That Is Great Within Us,* six subway tokens, a tube of strawberry lip gloss, five copies of *On the Barricade,* a pack of clove cigarettes, and pens and a pack of small spiral-bound notebooks.

Scornfully, he shook free a notebook and the packet of gum and waved them in front of my eyes. Then he tossed things one by one into a large metal tub behind him. I watched him snag a couple of Snickers, slipping them into his breast pocket. He stared at the clove cigarettes, sniffed them, looked at me, sniffed them again, then threw them into the tub.

"You went to Orientation—right, sweetheart?"

I nodded. I had actually enjoyed the orientation classes—particularly when the lecturer had held up a thick copy of *Great Expectations* as a prime example of contraband. The title's irony, given the setting, made me smile, then laugh out loud as the lecturer opened the book with a flourish, revealing its hollow interior occupied by a .45 automatic.

The lecturer had frowned at me. "Actual recovered contraband," he noted in a hushed, triumphant tone.

C.O. Janowitz spoke to me now in a similar tone.

"I'm a stickler," he said. "Too much trouble walkin' through here on two legs. Everybody sleepin' at the switch, but I'm not sleepin', I'm a stickler. You bring in bubble gum and cute shit they can make weapons out of—you take the rap for what happens. You follow me, sweetheart?"

I said I followed him. He reminded me again that he was a stickler.

After he let me go and I'd walked outside through the rear exit to the shuttle stop for the institution vans, I checked my bag. The Stickler had removed all the contraband items except for the copies of *On the Barricade.* Its threats against the fascist establishment, its maps and strategies, its pages praising the triumph of the Revolution, hadn't qualified as dangerous to anyone at all.

Just inside the entrance to the Women's House, I waved to the C.O. in the glassed-in control room. She pressed the button that buzzed the moving wall. It opened and I stepped into the between-chamber as the wall slowly shut behind me. Posted over the check-point window was a large sign: NO FIREARMS BEYOND THIS POINT. I held my ID card up to the glass, and the C.O., a bored-looking woman with an institution-approved tamed-down Afro, nodded at me and pressed another button. The inner door very slowly slid open. I stepped through and was Inside.

*I*nside it was Friday night, just like outside. But Friday night—just like every other night Inside—was a whole other universe. Inside it was hot, very hot—eighty, eighty-five—a temperature that laid sticky palms on the body, slowed it down, drew sweat. Security Inside knew that the sluggish body (and its hazy overheated brain) would follow orders. The shrieking plane vibrations that shook the foundation every four minutes or so were nearly drowned out by New York City's black radio station blasting over all the speakers, its sheer volume a kind of sedative: "Papa was a rolling stone, wherever he laid his hat was his home . . ." This could have been Friday night at a youth center, roller rink, or church basement—but this was Friday night in prison. Despite the heat and the echoing mindless pumped-up baying of radio deejays, the screams and laughter echoing up and down the halls reverberated with the boundless defeated energy of the caged.

The prison was L-shaped, and I stood just at the angle of the L. On my left was the Watch Commander's office, where the master console was housed: the institution's brain. Inside the glassed-in office was a huge lit-up panel with rows of red eyes that blinked every time a door opened within the walls. The commander sat with her assistants at the console, talking by phone to the officers on the floors or intoning P.A. announcements. At the beginning and end of each eight-hour shift, the prison population count had to be verified. Tonight the count had been off. C.O.s were just getting off from the earlier shift—they hurried past me, shouting to one another, loosening their jackets and white blouses. I knew that when the count could not be confirmed there was immediate lockdown. No one, C.O. or civilian, was allowed to leave the institution until The Count was retallied for an all clear, and now the all clear had just sounded, half an hour late.

Around the corner from the Watch Commander were the superintendent's and deputy superintendent's offices. In front of me were client/lawyer interview cubicles and cubicles used as confessionals. I turned around and noticed C.O. Aliganth bustling up the hall on my right. C.O. Aliganth was a tall skinny Olive-Oylish figure, her conked hair bunched into a furious French twist and her large mouth moving lickety-split as she conversed with herself. Unlike the other C.O.s, she maintained no distance at all with civilians like me. She had been assigned to guard the poetry workshop, much to her chagrin. She'd told me earlier in the week that attention to the "ladies' poetry society" was, from her point of view, a waste of valuable personnel. I couldn't hear what she was saying, but she was shaking a finger at me as she approached.

I glanced down the hall to the first set of electronic gates, where inmates swayed and finger-popped near the gate stations. The C.O.s were tipping back now on their stools, pulling out their shirttails and shooting the breeze with their charges. There were inmates in threes and fours, line dancing. There were a couple of "penguins," inmates snowed out on Thorazine or chloral hydrate (the other heavily administered "diagnostic"), waddling, nodding to no one in particular. Marvin Gaye sang on about the grapevine.

Aliganth landed, swinging her big silver ring of keys and calling: "You close up on breakin' my balls, Mattox."

I looked around. I hadn't been aware that she had balls, but then you could never be sure at the Women's House. There was, for example, a person of mysterious gender who chose this moment to appear before us, pushing a mop, rolling his/her pail on wheels in front of the lawyers' cubicles. "Gene/Jean Keeley. She called Jean for her *female* inclinings, Gene for the other," snorted Aliganth. I remembered her case suddenly from the files in Social Services. Gene/Jean was a woman who was becoming, operation by operation, a man. So far she had not acquired completely convincing manhood—which was why s/he had been housed in the women's prison—yet s/he was given work duty in the open areas of the facility, where his/her actions could be closely observed. Given her thick hairy legs, bad tattoos, bright red crew cut, goatee, and unreliably baritone voice—and given the intense level of testosterone providing her with a big new libido (the reason she'd propositioned an undercover cop and landed here)—s/he bore watching. She leered at me now and Aliganth reared back and shouted at her.

"Captain told you she want that floor shine enough see your ugly-ass face in it!"

Gene/Jean smirked and when Aliganth turned back to me, held the mop handle between her knees and waved it lewdly back and forth, winking at me. When Aliganth whirled around, she was back at work.

Aliganth glared at me. She liked me, I thought, and I liked her too, but there were the inflexible demands of our setting.

"What can I say here? Not a damn thing. They give you a classroom right next to the Dep's office. And I got to sit there waitin' on you all night. And you breeze in here late."

"Sorry I'm late—everyone's late tonight," I said, and smiled at her. "And you don't have to stay here the whole time with the class. Really."

"Right," she nodded, shaking her keys. "That's right. You know best, Miss Ann."

The "Miss Ann" part was barely audible, but I heard it, as I'd heard it before.

"It's so damn hot in here," I complained, but she ignored me.

Before she unlocked the classroom, Aliganth helped me phone up to the floors from the Watch Commander's office, making sure each floor C.O. would announce the class. Then the Watch Commander cut into the music and made it a general bulletin. I watched Gene/Jean through the glass—she looked up as the voice floated out over the thick air. "Ladies: poetry class tonight. If you're serious, ask for a signed pass and come down directly to the Dep, no stops on the way." Gene/Jean leaned against the mop, stroking her goatee, ruminating.

The first two students arrived together. Aliganth stood just inside the door of the classroom like an enraged butler, her hand held out for the handwritten passes that the women carried, muttering the women's names to herself as they arrived.

The first was a pale frightened-looking young woman with light brown braids carrying a large plastic Bible Studies prayerbook. On its cover was a glossy three-quarter profile of Jesus Christ, his melancholy eyes upturned as if drawn by the magnetic force of the Halloween-orange halo floating above his brow. On his neck Jesus wore an adhesive-backed name tag: DARLENE DENISKY. Accompanying Darlene was a pixie-faced, golden-brown young woman with a dancer's body and the sly cheerful look of a hooker.

I got up from my chair at the metal table in the center of the room.

"I'm Holly Mattox," I said. "Pleased to meet you."

They nodded solemnly and the pale girl introduced herself, then ducked her head and mumbled something. The other woman winked at me.

"Sheree Mason," she said.

They sat down at the table as two more women stood in the doorway.

"Ladies, sit yourselves down. No shufflin' around in here, you follow?" Aliganth shook her head at me.

The women chose chairs at the table. One looked like an extremely thin Liza Minnelli; her dyed hair fell to her shoulders in a dark brown shag and she wore bright red lipstick and thick mascara. Beside her was a Puerto Rican woman, pretty and sturdy, her hair pulled back primly in a bun. They sat down next to one another, repeating their names.

"Roxanne Lattner," said Liza Minnelli.

"Never Delgado," said her companion, then smiled at me sweetly, apologetically. "I was born Flor de Navidad Delgado," she said, "but I am now Never."

"Never do this! Never do that!" threw in Roxanne. She folded her hands in supplication, turned, and mock-bowed before her sweet-smiling friend. "And do what her Ladyship tells you or she will *never* watch your back again!"

"She be Never, and I Baby Ain't!" Sheree Mason cried suddenly, waving her hand in the air to get my attention. She pushed back her chair and stood up proudly, as if she were about to recite something.

"After the dirty deed, one hunnert per-cent say to me: 'Baby Ain't Nobody Better!' "

She fanned the air in circles with both hands wide, like a Holy Roller testifying to the Power, then waggled her rear end and cackled with enormous pleasure, openmouthed, the way a child laughs. Her laugh was contagious and seemed to perk everyone up a little, except for Darlene and C.O. Aliganth.

Gene/Jean sidled in without the mop, striking a manly pose in the doorway, flexing her biceps—and began introducing herself. Aliganth stopped her cold.

"Everybody here know your ass. Show me your pass or you out."

Grinning, Gene/Jean pulled a crumpled piece of paper from her sleeve. Curly red hair peeked out of her blouse top.

"Cap gave me time off. I finished up the floors pretty good."

Aliganth frowned at the pass, then pointed to a chair.

"Sit down. You look sideways at a fly, you out the door."

Gene/Jean dropped clumsily into a chair next to Roxanne as Aliganth turned away to greet newcomers in the hall. Gene/Jean leaned in close to Roxanne and leered at her.

"You got some hot pussy for me?"

"You so much as breathe one of your stinking breaths on me and I'll chop off whatever it is you're calling a dick today," said Roxanne with formidable Long Island aplomb. She shook out her shag cut and peered at her nails.

Gene/Jean jumped up, hands fluttering, her voice suddenly female.

"I'm sorry, I'm so sorry. I really am. I can't believe I said that."

Roxanne rolled her eyes and moved away. Sheree, a.k.a. Baby Ain't, winked at me again.

"Jean on the *rag*."

"Praise Jesus," mumbled Darlene.

There was commotion outside, and more women entered. One of them I recognized from newspaper photographs. Her name was Akilah Malik, formerly LeeAnne Kohler, one of the leaders of the Black Freedom Front. I'd read the headlines: she had felony charges, including one involving her role in the shoot-out murder of a New Jersey state trooper, a charge to which (it was reported in the press) she intended to plead not guilty. She was quite beautiful, with high cheekbones and fierce light eyes. I knew she'd given birth in prison and that her baby had been taken away. She carried herself like a gift, with a fuck-with-me-if-you-dare dignity—even Aliganth had backed away from her. She stood outside the door, looking off into the distance, jangling her keys.

There were two others behind Akilah Malik, and I asked them all to introduce themselves.

Akilah sat down carefully, far away from Gene/Jean.

"Akilah Malik. My slave name was LeeAnne Kohler."

The two other women waited in the doorway. I looked at them expectantly.

"I'm Billie Dee Boyd," one of them said. She looked a little crazy to me. Her hair was standing up, uncombed and wild, and one of her eyes rolled around like a marble. When she smiled, I noticed that she was missing a few teeth, yet somehow her expression was endearing.

"I'm Polly Lyle Clement. I come from the river," said a wiry girl. She was a light bisque color with stringy platinum hair and bad teeth (she flashed a shaky smile) and the odd masked expression and pigeon-toed walk of inmates overmedicated with Thorazine. Her left cheek looked smudged. Perhaps, I thought, it was scar tissue from a burn. I had a swift, unmistakable sense of her fragility—strange because I also sensed her strength. She bowed stiffly, formally, in my direction, and sat down.

"And here now we got Sallie Keller," announced Aliganth.

I nearly gasped as Sallie came in. She stood staring at me and I tried to meet her gaze, but her eyes occupied two different levels on her face. Her face looked like a cubist baseball—or a hot dog split open on a grill. Her mouth was smiling and she carried a piece of cardboard on which she'd printed in big letters with bright red marker: SALLIE KELLER! WORLD'S GREATEST POET!

I asked her to sit down. I wanted to ask her what had happened to her face, but I was afraid. Aliganth shot me another inscrutable look.

Sallie turned her strange stare on the other women, twisting her head to the left, then to the right, like a barn owl.

"Every flatback here know my face," she said. "So quit starin' up. Nothin' goin' to change nothin'."

She strutted over to the last free chair and sat down, folded her WORLD'S GREATEST POET sign, and propped it up like an official place card at a diplomatic dinner. Then she nodded at me as if she were giving me the signal to begin. I took a deep breath. I folded my hands, which were shaking a little, in front of me.

"Welcome to you all," I said. "I'm Holly Mattox. I guess we will get to know one another better over the next few class meetings. I'd like to ask each of you to write a poem for me—a poem of your own, in your own words. But unfortunately, the notebooks and pens I brought with me for you to use were confiscated at Reception."

There was a knowing groan.

"Still. I'm wondering if C.O. Aliganth—to whom we are so indebted for guard duty tonight—I'm wondering if C.O. Aliganth would mind borrowing some pencils and paper from the Watch Commander's office for us. C.O. Aliganth?"

Aliganth looked at me with a kind of startled regard—I'd one-upped her so early in the evening: she had to respect it. She mumbled something about Miss Ann and who-in-charge-here, but after a quick slap to Gene/Jean's chairback, she wandered off down the hall, shaking her head and bitching to herself halfheartedly.

When she was gone, I pulled out the *On the Barricade* from my bag and quickly passed them around.

"Some political reading matter," I said, "sent to you by friends on the outside."

They looked skeptical.

"Praise Jesus," whispered Darlene, then scribbled something on a tiny piece of paper, folded it, and pushed it across the table to me. I opened it. It read PLEASE CALL MY KIDS—HERE IS THE #. I nodded at her and put the note in my pocket.

Someone asked if the paper had personal ads.

"I think so," I said. "But there's also a book review section."

"How about them horo-scopes?" asked Baby Ain't, and I shook my head.

No one seemed particularly impressed by *On the Barricade*. Baby Ain't glanced quickly through it, then used her copy to fan herself. Only Akilah nodded as she scanned a few pages. Sallie Keller stared at me disconcertingly. It hurt me to look at her.

"If you wouldn't mind," I said, "if you could put the newspapers away somewhere before the C.O. gets back—that would be good."

Instantly the papers vanished into blouses, socks—into who knew.

Then Aliganth was at the door with a handful of Rainbow tablets and some chewed-up pencil stubs.

"Thank you, Officer," I said.

"You way too cute, Mattox," she snapped, and threw the tablets and pencils on the table.

I waited for a few seconds, then faced the women again. They'd opened the tablets and chosen pencils. Gene/Jean was drawing what appeared to be a humorous portrait of C.O. Aliganth. Before Aliganth noticed, I held up my hand for silence.

"Does anyone," I called out, "have any idea what a sonnet is?"

*L*ater that night, on the bus back to Manhattan, I thought about what a sonnet was. Fourteen lines, ten syllables per line, iambic pentameter, rhyme schemes a-b-a-b or a-b-b-a: Shakespearean, Petrarchan, Spenserian. I thought about my mother in the kitchen, some long-ago suppertime, turning from the stove, where she was stirring a beef stew to death and steaming the life out of a green vegetable. "Do you know what a sonnet is?" she asked. Her glance was riveting, bright blue and full of apprehension, as if my answer would forever influence her opinion of me—perhaps force her to disown me. I swallowed hard and tried to remember my sixth-grade English lessons: I saw the word "sonnet" printed out like a subtitle, the way I always saw words typed out and running beneath the sounds of spoken language. "Sonnet" appeared, then more words, unraveling like a ribbon: " 'Shall I compare thee to a summer's day?' " I opened my mouth, then looked at her face and stopped.

She narrowed her eyes and took an audible breath just as two of my brothers came roaring into the kitchen, shooting suction-tipped darts at each other from plastic guns. One dart-sucker adhered to a cheek, another to a forehead, another smacked the kitchen wall and stuck in place, vibrating. I watched her consciousness divide before us: she seemed to increase in size, drawing the poem and maternal admonition out of the same omnipotent address:

"The world is—*Put that down right now!*—too much with us!"

I listened, slowly grasping a revolutionary variation on a poetic form, one that I would remember forever.

"Little we see in Nature—*Shut that door!*—that is ours."

The world is too much with us, I thought. *So put that down right now! Though (confused, heartbroken, lamebrain) I shall still compare thee to a summer's day.*

two

There was a meeting of the Women's Bail Fund the next day. I
arrived late, and a familiar argument about raising money was
in progress as I came in the door. All of the Fund's project
cash flowed from general contributions and the occasional bake sale
or bike wash—or the odd embarrassing trust fund. The apartment
where the meeting was held faced west into the sun setting slowly over
the Hudson River. The windows and walls blazed with bright red
light spilling over onto the earnest faces of the women of the Fund. I
had not been a member of the group for very long, but I'd closely
studied my fellow Bailers' severe yet comradely demeanor. As I came
in the door, I adjusted my expression to conform to the topography of
the faces turning toward me. Each face seemed custodian of a guarded
yet enlightened look, sprung from our ideology—which itself sprang
from a synthesis of dialectical materialism and a hand-cranked pop-
cultural nationalism: a critique of Pink Floyd, a "symbolic" recipe for
black-and-white cookies, a review of our commitment to mobilizing
the U.S. proletariat and freeing those whom the courts had wronged,
victims of racism and injustice.

The apartment was on the twelfth floor of a Columbia-owned
building and looked out over other buildings landlorded by the
university. Many of the Bail Fund members were grad students or
alumnae of Columbia, unlike me. I'd gone to grad school in San
Francisco—but I was from the Midwest. I had not yet lost my Min-

nesota combination of overenthusiasm and shyness; to my chagrin, I often blushed. Yet during the years I'd lived in California, I'd acquired what I liked to think was tough-mindedness. Enthralled by words, by everything literary, I had worked against my own elitism, studying Marcuse and Fanon and Ortega y Gasset. I'd arrived at San Francisco State and Berkeley the year after the San Francisco Tactical Squad beat up and gassed students on campus, and later I had marched at People's Park. I signed up for a course in the Revolution taught by a radical Berkeley professor. But the professor had laughed bitterly as he looked out at our faces.

"There will never be a revolution here in America," he'd begun, and smiled at our shocked expressions. "And why? Because everyone wants the next rung up in the middle class—a better car, a bigger barbecue. They want automatic garage door openers, do you follow? Television clickers and remote-control bombs. Marx tells us that in order to live we must enter history. But America no longer lives in history—America has acquired remote access."

I glanced around. *Remote access.* Usually I felt comfortable at Bail Fund meetings, but not today. Usually the level of attention of the Women's Bail Fund to the suffering world, manifested as passionate concern and compassion for lost causes, for the oppressed, made me feel at home. Today I felt, with terrible inevitability, the argument about funds exhausting itself and beginning to turn, gradually, to me.

Remote access. To appear close but to remain removed while effecting change. *Like the Bail Fund,* I thought disloyally. Money raised in safety for our idealistic anarchical purposes: wrinkled bills and sweaty coins slid under a barred window, quick metal-tipped counting fingers drawing the blood-price in. Then a stranger, an unknown woman, slumped in a cage, tapped on the shoulder and beckoned to. *You free, bitch.* I believed that each of us desired justice, even if it was random unexamined justice. Yet I could not turn away from images that popped uninvited into my thoughts as I glanced around the room. Some of my fellow members looked peculiarly revved-up, even blood-hungry. *Liberty in a mobcap, brandishing a pike,* I thought—brandishing a popular Bail Fund motto: "Death to the Fascist Insect that Preys upon the People."

I heard (again) my mother's voice, quoting this time that mad mystic poet, William Blake: "For mercy has a human heart / Pity, a human face!" And I had been reading Blake myself. I had come across, just the day before, a bit of his political advice: "He who would do good to another must do it in Minute Particulars. General Good is the plea of the scoundrel, hypocrite and flatterer." So said Blake, who etched his politics into the minute particulars of his words, the minute particulars of his hallucinatory copper engravings.

General good. Remote access. I focused on the Venceremos and SDS posters on the walls. There was a huge, deeply depressing black-and-white photo of Attica, D Yard: the prisoners huddled in blankets around a small dugout fire, their heads shaved, holding hand-lettered signs: WE ARE HUMAN BEINGS. One inmate slumped, sleeping, against the shoulder of another. A few hours later they would be shot like animals in a pen, with expanding bullets outlawed by the Geneva Conventions. What Blake the engraver would have done with that scene! Next to the Attica photo was a poster of Pearl: Janis Joplin onstage at the San Francisco Fillmore. She held a flask of Southern Comfort in her raised fist, her head flung back with its electric mass of pale-sugar waves, her eyes half closed in an ecstatic squint, the phallic mike gleaming before her openmouthed wail. For one non-sequitur second I thought about blow jobs. I wondered if any of my fellow Bail Fund members practiced fellatio. I looked around at the serious inquiring faces. *Probably not,* I thought.

About fifteen women were sitting there in the red sun of the living room. Some were folding and collating *On the Barricade,* listening. Others sat straight up and took turns addressing the group, then examining their own statements, accompanied by the steady *crunch-crunch* of staplers. The Women's Bail Fund was a Marxist/

Maoist "cell" and we practiced Mao's criticism/self-criticism approach, which took a significant amount of time and uncomfortable probing. "Slow boat to China," a smart-ass might have joked. Because I was a natural smart-ass, I tried to curb my joking. Everyone except me wore sweatshirts and jeans. I was dressed in a long skirt and a turtleneck and boots—I was due at a dinner party after the meeting.

The imposing woman guiding the discussion, Corinna Firestone, wore jeans and a down-to-her-knees sweatshirt with SLUMLORD stenciled across its Columbia University logo in dripping-blood letters. We were supposed to be an egalitarian group, but Corinna was clearly our leader, our chief, enforcer of broad ideological insight. When I'd first noticed a Women's Bail Fund poster on a kiosk downtown at the New School, where I'd been hired to teach a beginning poetry workshop, it was Corinna Firestone's name that was listed as "contact." When I called the listed number, she seemed happy to hear from me. They'd been looking for someone new to work with them on a special project, she said. And that project turned out to be bail mule: taking the trip across the bridge to Rikers Island with a cache of dollar bills and coins, carrying the freedom money. And I'd been proud to do it for a while—until I realized that no one else was inclined to take a turn at it.

Abruptly Corinna crunched a Dr Pepper can flat with her hand (*wham-clack!*) to close the money discussion—and looked directly at me.

"Holly," she said. "We'd like to be hip to what's going on with you."

I felt the attention of the room, heads turning toward me. I nearly reached for my notebook. *Like a shudder of wind through wheat.*

"What's going on," I said, "is that I'd like to request that someone else try handling the bailouts of women at Rikers from now on."

Corinna stared at me and smiled. She had black hair that was big and bold and frizzy like Janis Joplin's, but without the erotic voltage, without the wicked shimmer—and her broad-toothed smile was oddly grim. She seemed solidly intact, but too solidly. I could sense that she was secretly off-kilter—as if she were a house of cards or pick-up sticks, as if, tapped lightly in a hidden place, she would collapse all over the floor.

She cleared her throat. "Patty told us that you'd called to rap to her about this. Just like that—you're saying that you're no longer committed to the women Inside?"

"I am still committed to the women Inside. It's just that I'm doing other things out there."

I looked at the faces, all turned toward me now.

"I've been hired as an AfterCare worker and I'm . . . teaching." I decided to go for broke. "I'm teaching a poetry workshop at the Women's House. It's really interesting."

Someone repeated "Poetry?" with parrotlike bewilderment, and then there was complete quiet.

Corinna snorted. "Your interests," she noted scornfully, "are not the point. *They* are."

"I know," I said. "I know that. The women: they are the point. And there are Our Priorities."

I looked out the windows for a long minute until Corinna coughed loudly and rolled her eyes, impatient. I smiled wanly at her and shrugged: I couldn't help myself. I kept falling into reveries lately. I wrote down each daydream, each random floating interruption, in my notebook, hoping the collection would make profound poetic sense as I reviewed it in some distant literary future.

"Holly!" Corinna murmured reprovingly. She recited the Bail Fund Priorities for me, gesturing for the others to join in: "Pregnant women, political prisoners, sick women, women whose children are about to become wards of the state and sent to foster homes."

She nodded accusingly at me. "We gave you the names."

"Sorry," I said, sitting up, waking up. "But Our Priorities take in just about every woman at the House of D." I considered Akilah Malik, a famous "political" prisoner, but I said nothing about her presence in my poetry class. I considered Billie Dee Boyd as well, but I didn't mention her either.

"Good grief!" I cried, aware of the rising pitch of Minnesota in my voice. "It takes so little money, you know? We could bail out the whole place with one day of Columbia library fines. Twenty-five dollars for shoplifting Kotex. Forty dollars for jostling."

Vicky Renslauer spoke up. She was a scholarly young woman who was forever reading Mao or books about him. She had recently tried to interest me in a volume about China's barefoot doctors called *Away with All Pests*. I'd promised to read it at some point, along with Mao's poems, although Mao's literary gifts had not so far engaged me. Once Vicky had cornered me after a Bail Fund meeting and read me these lines from a poem by Ho Chi Minh: "Calamity has tempered and hardened me / And turned my mind to steel."

"How could a human mind be turned to metal?" I wondered aloud. "A person's resolve might be steely," I suggested to Vicky, "or their stance straight and steel-like, but a mind? Turned to steel?"

Vicky had narrowed her eyes at me. She asked me if I was sure that I was a poet.

"You keep missing the point of advanced *metaphor*," she said.

Yet Vicky possessed a very sunny temperament and had forgiven me not long after that exchange. Now she was looking at me with a kind of distracted fondness.

"Then it doesn't sound like it would be that difficult to keep on truckin', Holly! Right on! We can keep covering the small bails. We can get down with the struggle from day to day! We've got the bread, man, and we're setting our sisters free!"

She grinned at me. She turned her head and her thick glasses snagged sunlight. They glowed violent pink, then grew transparent again as she nodded at me. She radiated the breathless distracted energy of a tourist arriving at a destination—a tourist from somewhere not very interesting or far away, I thought irritably, though her mind was always in China.

"I've done it for six months. I think it's time for someone else to take over," I said. "You could go, Vicky—or you, Corinna. Or you, Martine."

Corinna offered criticism/self-criticism on my behalf. She said that because I was from California, I represented no "risk"—unlike other Bail Fund members. She knew for a fact that she and others were on the FBI list and would be immediately arrested if they ever set foot on the Island.

"I don't think so," I said. "They're not all that efficient out there. Really."

I hesitated. "Though undoubtedly you're right at the top of the FBI list."

Corinna scowled at me. Was I being sarcastic? I refused to meet her scowl. I looked around me, trying to fathom the response of other members. Everyone else was, it seemed—like Corinna—high on an FBI list, or too busy or committed to other projects. Still, I was surprised by the amount of resistance to my mild suggestion that the job of bail carrier be shared. The time for me to move on had come: Why was no one else willing to take over?

A spirited debate ensued about how to demand one's individual file from the FBI through the new Freedom of Information Act. There was consideration of what would happen if the "long-term" Bail Fund members showed up on Rikers Island. The discussion gradually turned to me again, and I reiterated my desire to try something else at the Women's House. It was then finally, crankily determined that Vicky Renslauer would make the trip to the Island with the bail money the next time, the trip I'd been making every week. It was further decided (though I wasn't named directly this time) that one of us was being "uncooperative," "bourgeois-neurotic," and "counterrevolutionary," and that a lesson could be learned from these reactionary attitudes. Much criticism/self-criticism bubbled up from a deep caldron of steeped implacabilities and appeared to refresh and calm everyone. Each dipperful from the ideological vat diluted the group's tensions: the red sunset war paint gradually faded from each troubled face, and one by one lamps were turned on and a soft dusk-gold, color of appeasement, suffused the room.

I listened with a kind of masochistic interest to my condemnation as it turned to slow exculpation and then realized suddenly that I had to leave. It had grown late. I picked up my bag and stood up, then sat down again, pulling the strap over my shoulder as Corinna turned back to me, still smiling her grim smile, and inquired where I was going. Before I could answer, she shook her head at me again:

"By the way, what the hell is AfterCare?"

"It's a program for women who are being released. They're called *ex-offenders*, which I think is pretty funny."

No one laughed.

"Anyway. The idea is to find jobs or job training or get them back into school. That kind of thing."

A tall nervous long-faced woman in a frayed blue-striped poncho whom I hadn't seen at our meetings before (though I'd heard it whispered earlier in the evening that she was a member of the Weather Underground) observed that I was playing into the hands of the System and was I aware of this? How did it feel to be made a pawn of the Establishment?

"Hey, sister," she called out to me, her expression stony and contemptuous. She squinted at me as if she were half blinded by my sellout clothes and hair. "How naïve can you get?"

I stood up. "I have to go," I said. I felt completely reckless now. "I'm expected at a dinner party."

There was that straight-man silence, quite a long one—then Vicky offered the inevitable: "Mao said it perfectly for us, Holly: 'A revolution is not a dinner party.' "

. . .

I learned to teach creative writing by comprehending without a doubt that it could not be taught—the approach I acquired by default in graduate school in San Francisco. One of our writing professors, in an attempt to teach us craft, noted that the most difficult things to describe were the familiar objects of every day.

"This chair, for example," he said, hauling an empty straight-back to the front of the classroom. "How would you go about getting it on paper?"

We stared glumly at the creaky four-legged polished wooden seat, its sweat-stained, scratched back, and its single flappable wing, which was crisscrossed with scratched graffiti, designed to serve as a rickety desktop. How indeed?

That workshop was followed by a seminar with Dimitri Hajikakis, a Greek surrealist. He liked to reminisce at length about his years in Athens and Paris before he "broke with Breton." An earnest student with waist-length hair, dressed in a shaggy sheepherder's jacket with splinters of mirror stitched into the hide, reported to Prof Haj that we had spent the previous hour attempting to capture the essence of a classroom chair.

Prof Haj smiled ruefully, hoisted his shaggy eyebrows, and gazed out the window for a loaded second, then winked at the student, who smiled lazily back, shrugged, and shook out his hair, his mirror-shards catching the light, sending tiny prisms spinning about the room.

"But what would happen to your description," Prof Haj asked, drawing out each word, his expression impish, "if the chair suddenly sprouted wings and flew?"

The bemirrored student laughed approvingly and the class members sat back in their indescribable chairs and also laughed, a little nervously, "Right on, Prof Haj!"

Professor Haj had taken an interest in me for some reason. He invited me to his office, where he reminisced at length about European literary capitals, shaking his head and laughing to himself. Later that year, near graduation, as I was preparing for a backpacking trip to Paris and beyond, he called me into his office and offered me two formal letters of introduction he'd written on my behalf: one to the French actress who was subletting his apartment in Paris (the apartment included an atelier, which he thought I might be interested in renting) and a second letter, to the underground filmmaker Maurice Girodias. I blushed with gratitude and embarrassment as I held the letters in my hand. An atelier in Paris was a gift beyond reckoning—and though the little I knew about Girodias fixed him in a category slightly above an artsy porn-flick director, I felt a hot shiver, a little red frisson of vanity. Was I really pretty enough to be in a French film? Then it struck me that I might be asked to take off my clothes for the camera. Maybe Prof Haj thought of me as a whore?

He raised his great eyebrows as I reddened before him.

"The reason I'm recommending you to Girodias is because I think you'd be perfect in his films."

He looked out the window, his famous sly gaze in place.

"Because," he said, "you walk around with no expression on your face at all, then suddenly that face bursts into emotion. Very peculiar. Right for Girodias. Just odd enough."

After graduate school, I went to Paris and beyond for four or five months. I never phoned Maurice Girodias. I stayed odd enough, with my face lit by no expression except in those bursting emotional moments peculiar to me. *At least,* I thought, *he didn't think I was dumb enough to take my clothes off for a goddam underground movie.*

Still, there was a footnote: in Paris, I somehow ended up in the cast of the rock musical *Hair.* It was easy to see why, in a way. I looked like an American hippie, I could sing—but when it came to nude scenes, I was completely uncooperative, and unsurprisingly I was not invited to accompany the troupe when it moved on to Belgium.

Back in Prof Haj's class, I put down my pen and I too stared reflectively out the window. The day before, we had spent time with another professor, who had asked us to rate our writing, brought in for discussion that day, on large cue cards, on a scale of one to ten.

"Dynamite metaphors but needs more energy—I give it a seven!"

The one-to-ten professor and his wife had lost a little girl to leukemia that spring. His wife had been grieving for the child, depressed. He told us that her shrink had recommended that she write a story about blood, as a connection to the child's fatal disease. As we sat in class rating our poems, she was at home constructing the tale of a vampire who had lived for hundreds of years, a story that would eventually haunt national consciousness. I caught myself thinking of her in her ordinary chair, which morphed into a flying chair. She'd circled above us in the room, where we sat in place, holding up cards with numbers on them, then winged off again unseen.

I shook my head, trying to dislodge all the sevens and nines and twos. I tried to remember what the poet Theodore Roethke had said about writing and pedagogy. Something like "We do not teach writing, we insinuate it."

Teach what you read, I thought, *the great haunting voices. Teach what stays in your memory. What runs in your veins.*

Outside the window, under the trees, there were groups of students gathering with placards emblazoned with large scarlet hand-drawn peace symbols and the raised fist of Black Power. The familiar smells of buckskin and marijuana wafted in on a breeze. It was almost time for our college president, R. H. Wattlinger, to begin his daily tour of the campus. Since he'd invited the Special Services unit of the San Francisco Police Department (called the Tac Squad) on campus to spray mace and rough up students, his popularity had hit an all-time low. He'd once ridden around campus perched on a sound truck, urging, in amplified tones, "cooperation with authority," till a student leaped up on the truck and pulled out the speaker wires. The professor slid the windows closed as the first catcalls and cries of "Establishment lackey!" signaled the arrival of the president's vehicle.

I thought about how the Season of Dreams had changed. The Haight-Ashbury district, where the Summer of Love had originated, had been remade, even in the brief while since I'd arrived from Minnesota. Only a season or three ago, flower children had floated about, beatific, high on mushrooms, wind chimes, Jefferson Airplane. Now speed (methedrine and STP) contorted face after face in Golden Gate Park and the Haight—hippies slumped against buildings in the foggy sun, panhandling, holding mirrors up to the gawking faces of tourists pressed to the windows of their buses as they lumbered slowly through the neighborhood. I glanced at the protesters outside, milling about, their mouths moving. Someone held up a sign, bobbing around with the other NO MORE WAR placards. It read WITHDRAW DICK.

Later, back in the Chair Workshop, we tried an old familiar writing exercise designed to help build imaginative muscle, called Where I Come From.

"Write what you believe to be true," the teacherly voice intoned. "About your roots, your background, what makes you you."

There was a derisive chuckle or two. It was warm in the room. Someone had dabbed on way too much patchouli and the scent suspended itself in the classroom atmosphere like an aerial oil slick.

"I come from the sticks: Thai sticks!" someone snickered. Some of us rolled our eyes.

But I gave it a big overblown try. I ended up not bringing my effort to class to be read aloud, but I did turn it in to the professor, who wrote "Look homeward, angel!" and "A stone, a key, an unfound door" at the top of the paper, and then, "Give it another whirl, retaining the refrain, but fewer modifiers!" Still, I kept the first shaky attempt in my notebook for a long time:

> *I come from the prairie and the north woods. My parents: children of the Dakotas, children of that huge mindless sky going nowhere. Red "Depression glass" in the china cupboards,*

a vellum-bound anthology of poems, the Harvard Classics *1932 reprint—in my hands, held in my hands: willed to me.*

I come from thwarted dreams, amended expectations: their two-year college instead of his law degree, her literature degree, her ambition to be a writer. But their gradual ascent to the middle class, then a little higher—in the city to which they'd moved after marrying, the city where I was born, named for the saint struck by lightning, Saint Paul. His real estate business, their children, six in all. Her tears, her furious face, her recitations of poems like pure seizures of delight and alarm. Her declamations—condemning all that she found inhibiting or pretentious: "Let me not to the marriage of true minds admit impediment." But impediment there was. No one knew her mind, she cried. The world was "too much with us," getting and spending, yes. Yes, but the poem made sense to me. It was the everyday words we were required to speak to one another in order to know one another—that was, for her, for me, for all of us, an impediment. I come from that.

I come from growing up thinking that she was Beauty remade through loss as Truth. I also come from fearing her pregnancies, one after the other. Fearing her inhabited, imprisoned body. Hating sexual references. Fearing the female body as destiny.

I come from thinking myself religious, then knowing I was not. Not in the way of the so-called Holy Book. Who made me? Longing made me, longing and wonder—those entwined gods: Blake's universe.

I come from Fritos in a clear glass bowl, hard candies, sourballs, in a fluted red dish. Cleats on oxford shoes, black hockey tape and padded shin guards and skates on the scarred mudroom floor. Icicles, roof-high snow. Wet scratchy wool scarves drawn ice-tight over the mouth and nose like purdah veils, protecting the lungs against forty-below temperatures. I come from

*mowed lawns and barbecues and rec rooms, from lake cabins,
water skis, and speedboats. And poppy-seed kolachy cake, but-
tered figured scrolls of krumkake, popovers, lutefisk, lefse, Ole
and Lena jokes, Czech self-deprecation, Norwegian stolidness,
oyster stew on Christmas Eve. I come from that constant sense of
deprivation emanating from them, children of deprivation—
though the rewards of the material world were now theirs.*

*I come from defying the Baltimore Catechism, then the Index
of Forbidden Books (reading, though not understanding, Boc-
caccio's* Decameron*). From the notorious but get-it-right tute-
lage of nuns, from John Keats, that pagan poet, read at night
in my bed by flashlight. I come from alliance with my Jewish
neighbors, the Golds, who moved in next door after the neighborhood voted on their presence on Pascal Street. I come from
babysitting their children, then later, sitting at their dinner
table—I come from those shouting, debate-filled meals, so unlike
my family's repressed repasts, learning from those exchanges to
have an opinion, to think on my feet. I come from waving to
Mr. Gold, the kosher butcher, as he stayed up late every night
reading—as I read—my bedroom window across from their
kitchen window, where he sat turning pages till three A.M. His
hand lifted in response, his kind smile and tired lidded eyes, the
thick book open under yellow light. I come from that comradely
figure reading till dawn in the window, the same window where
the candles were carefully lit on Friday nights—I come from
wanting to be a Jew.*

*I come from Christmas, the holiday for which I was named.
Carried home in a swaddled bundle on Christmas Eve, little
Holly Ann, laid down under the spreading boughs. How I stood,
reciting, singing carols before that magical tree, year after year.
I come from understanding that one can be named for something
larger than the self. I come from prairie, woods, Twin Cities, the
Mississippi as divide—as I am divided: into dust storms and un-*

touched plains of snow, bad jokes and Keats, a babysitter's Ju-daica and The Lives of the Saints, *sarcastic affection for my sib-lings and battering political arguments with my father, a "self-made man," a Republican. Totemic struggle—all of my life divided into fear and unbelieving joy.*

And through it all, that voice—her voice, reciting the canon of poems. She sang of Arms and the Man, Fruit of the Tree and Man's Fall, of a flower in a cranny wall, of Death, who would kindly stop for me, of the village smithy, of O Captain, My Cap-tain and the Children's Hour, of Hiawatha, laughing waters and one if by land, two if by sea, the Highwayman Riding Up to the Old Inn Door, the moon a ghostly galleon: its light filled with the sorrows of her changing face—Wandering Lonely as a Cloud. That's where I began—that cloud, that wandering— O that's where I come from: I come from that.

W e were deep into our first workshop meeting at the Women's House, and I attempted to establish ground rules. I looked around at the expectant faces.

"The way the workshop is set up—each poet writes a poem, then reads it to the group. After that we talk about it and try to improve the poem. Make it better. That's it."

There was a long pause.

"Look," I said, "the idea is that you write about what you know. Something you know."

Baby Ain't glanced around at the others, her clown face in place. "Say we all know this poem."

She stood on her tiptoes and began to recite. Everyone but Aki-lah, Aliganth, and me joined in.

One fine day in the middle of the night
Two dead boys got up to fight.

Back to back they faced each other,
Drew their swords and shot each other.

One was blind, the other couldn't see
So they chose the sun for a referee.
A deaf policeman heard the noise
And came to arrest the two dead boys.

If you don't believe this story's true
Ask the blind man, he saw it too.

We talked for a while about "Two Dead Boys." Nearly everyone seemed to know it, but no one knew where it had come from or who had written it. I decided to look it up later in the library.

I tried again. "What I meant was a poem that you write yourself. Something you remember from your childhood—or maybe something you saw once. Write about someone in your family. Add your words to a memory. You can rhyme or not rhyme. It's up to you."

"From each according to his abilities, to each according to his needs," quoted Akilah—then crossed her arms over her chest and leaned back in her chair, her fuck-you gaze on me.

I was pretty sick of Marx. "Sort of," I said. "But a little more like *The Price Is Right*."

Much later, on the bus back to Manhattan, I pulled from my bag the poem that Billie Dee Boyd had written in response to the assignment. It was printed in pencil in big tumbling hard-to-decipher letters on ruled Rainbow tablet paper. Beneath the printed words was the tentative signature: "Billie Dee Boyd, Poet." I'd helped her correct the spelling errors because she said she wanted me to have a "keep clean" copy. I read the poem slowly, carefully—and then I read it again.

. . .

Why was it, I wondered, as the bus lumbered along, that I suddenly envisioned my mother, pregnant, in a pale lemon-yellow sundress, on a humid early summer day, in our backyard on Pascal Street, hanging wash? Fastening wet laundry to the line with wooden clothespins—clutching one or two pins in her teeth like a war hero unpinning hand grenades with her incisors, grimacing like John Wayne. A heaped-up wicker basket lay at her feet. Sheets bellying up a little, damp underwear and baby diapers, dozens of them, then my first brassiere: undergarments as personal history. That early summer air suffused with the scent of orange blossoms, dark pink peonies, white and purple lilacs, a cascade of bleeding hearts and little white bells of lily-of-the-valley, exhaling atomized fragrance out of their hundred flower-mouths, insisting on themselves, jostling in a swift breeze—a tribe of blossoms, circling the house.

I could see her more clearly after the laundry filled the line, standing near the breezeway, by the sandbox where the red swing hung on its doubled rusted silver chains. She shook her right hand (a nervous habit) as if she'd just run out of a burning house with her hand on fire, flapping away the flames. I watched her there, sensing suddenly as I stared into memory that I was there too, in the picture. I could see myself then—looking at her and holding something in my arms: a big diaper-heavy baby, yet another bed wetter, sack of piss and whine, against one canted hip. A sibling, just up from a nap, mouth slack, drooling forthrightly on my neck. I did love babies, loved their soft powdery smell and trusting fat faces, but the drool and the poop convinced me: there were too many of us.

My mother looked up and smiled at me and my burden.

"No rest for the wicked," she called. "So I guess I've been bad!"

How had she been bad? I'd wondered. She was unpredictable and sometimes mean, unsparing—but always truthful, righteously angry, compassionate. Raised by immigrant parents, "full-blooded Bohunks," as she described them. She mingled a little Czech with her everyday exhortations: "Pick up that chupeek, you doosk!" A *chupeek*, we learned, was a small thing, a button or pin or unnameable widget (also a belly button). A *doosk* was a dumb oaf. My mother's family was Catholic and my father's Norwegian Lutheran. His family was a bit glacial, tall and blond and reserved. My father "turned," as they said, for her—converted from Lutheranism to Rome, with its painted images and gold vestments—and his mother never forgave him. Or her. She came to their wedding and refused to drink the wine (she was a member of the Ladies' Temperance Union) or dance with her son, the groom.

I took a cab from the Women's Bail Fund meeting at 117th and Broadway, down to Sam Glass's place. When Sam Glass gave a dinner party, it was a literary event. Sam Glass was a self-created phenomenon, editor of *Samizdat West*, which some wags thought should be called *Sam Is At. Sam*, as it had come to be known, was underwritten by Sam's patron, the water-softener heiress, guest of honor at tonight's dinner party.

Sam Glass lived in a midtown building designed by a famous architect, in the penthouse-apartment-with-terrace. The place looked Moroccan, especially at night. The walls were blood-colored and covered with photos of the Blue Men, the Tuareg nomads of the valleys of the High Atlas Mountains—the fire-walkers who stepped high over burning coals, exhaling kif while praying to Allah. And hard by: a photo of the forbidden—a woman in a veil, in burka, her wild eyes taunting above the dark cloth. There were also framed shots of famous expatriate writers whom Sam had met in Tangiers and who were now his friends and contributors to *Samizdat*. I slipped in through the open front door. The air was heavy with incense and with the aroma of the main course, a tagine: chicken slow-baked in a bath of red wine, prunes, and onions.

I slid into an empty chair, waving to Sam, a dark-haired, magnetic presence at the head of the table. He lifted his wrist and pointed to his watch. *Late,* he mouthed, then mock-frowned and turned away. There were only ten of us at dinner, and I found that my place at the table was next to Baylor Drummond, the former poet laureate who was famous for his strong jaw, rangy height, and sterling blank verse. He was also famous for his cruel sense of humor. He liked me, for some reason, which was why I'd been seated next to him. I was considered accept-able by the Sam Glass crowd. To them I was a plucky, sometimes feisty young woman, and a decent conversationalist. I'd been seated next to Drum before at dinner parties. He was between wives at the moment, and he appeared to crave pluck. Though I had learned that (like so many men) he didn't like his pluck revved up to the smart-ass level.

Drum didn't acknowledge my arrival. He was engaged in passion-ate conversation about fund-raising for the arts with the water-softener heiress, who was seated across from him. He did, however, pat my hand as I sat down. The heiress noticed this gesture, stopped midsentence, and glanced at me.

"I know you," she said.

"Hi. I'm Holly Mattox. We've met before."

"Is that Missoni? That you're wearing?" she asked. Then shot a quick flicker of a look at Drum.

"No," I said. "I don't think so."

I looked down at my napkin and thought ruefully, furiously, that my awkwardness came from having been a tomboy, from fighting with my brothers as I grew up, from living in my head. These were all rea-sons for my disconnection from my body, my looks. I knew that I was clumsy, yet, for all my embarrassment, somehow insistent on myself. My parents sent me money, I could buy what I wanted. But I didn't know what I wanted. I knew I did not want to be a capitalist pawn, but I also did not want to be thought of as an unsophisticated oaf. A doosk, my mother would have said. I knew I didn't want a Missoni skirt, but I wouldn't have minded knowing who the hell Missoni was.

I stood on one foot and then the other in my mind. In the physical world I was half there. I walked a herky-jerky walk, my hands flew up and around my face as I talked, I had nervous tics. I would occasionally stutter, then rush to the point in argument, startling my fellow conversationalists. No thanks, can't dance—but may be heard later over the band, arguing about Equal Rights.

The heiress looked away, as did Drum, neither interested in my existential fashion dilemma. Then she lifted her pale beringed right hand heavenward as if she were bearing witness to something.

"I want you to remember what I'm saying."

"There's no forgetting," said Drum.

She frowned. She couldn't tell whether he was being sarcastic— and neither could I. Then Drum patted my hand again, and I understood that he was putting her on.

I stole a glance at her as I ate my chicken. She was gilded with the roseate glow of the spa devotee. Her creamy breasts gleamed, and her hair, which I admired, was twisted lengths of glossy chestnut held by glittering combs. I rarely noticed jewelry, but tonight I was struck by how her fingers and neck and bosom were engemmed and how the gems imprisoned the light. Jewels were her theme.

She swallowed her wine and smiled dreamily at Drum. I found myself smiling dreamily back at her, though it was clear that her affection was not for me. I had no interest in the fact of her wealth (though I was fairly sure she assumed that her wealth drew people to her). I stared at her, charmed by her elegance, her aura of romance, the graceful attitudes she assumed, unself-consciously. She was lovely and utterly at home in her body.

So far I'd found the cultivation of beauty embarrassing. The female body, adorned, simpering, suspended helpless in the male gaze—I'd refused all that. So why was I now, briefly, stupidly, transfixed? Was it because I spent so much of my life wishing to be invisible? Here was visibility, here was a woman who liked to be seen.

She continued to smile luminously, at Drum.

"Do you know that when we were out on the terrace, looking down on Fifth and then over to Madison—I had a poetic moment?"

Drum's arm brushed mine.

"I looked down at the traffic moving uptown and downtown—coming and going—and I said to myself: Look! Diamonds coming toward me, rubies going away!"

She nodded twice, satisfied, and held out her glass, and Drum lifted a bottle of Bordeaux near his glass (a very good year, and a good buy, I'd heard someone next to me observe) and replenished hers. Then he leaned toward me and refilled my glass.

" 'Diamonds coming toward me, rubies going away.' So painterly," he murmured.

"Well, I have these moments."

"And you share them."

"I'm going to visit the powder room," she said.

While she was gone, Drum quoted the diamonds-approaching, rubies-receding line more than once—deadpan—with cruelly accelerating relish.

"Okay, Drum," I said. "I got it. A taste of the *poète-manquée*."

A fluted green glass dish bearing a pear poached and gleaming in liqueur appeared before me. Drum was often vicious, but he was also often right—therefore I knew he'd give me some version of the truth. There was something I had to know. I began by telling him that I'd been working in a women's prison and had started teaching a poetry workshop there.

"Stop right there," he said. "You're teaching poetry *where*?"

"Rikers Island. The Women's House of Detention."

He laughed loudly, pushing his poached pear away with a flick of his wrist. He looked down into his wineglass, swirled the dregs, and smiled slowly.

"I'll bet you're getting some killer literary work out there." He laughed again, nudging me to be sure I got the play on words.

"Better than the diamonds-and-rubies reference."

"She should be prosecuted just for coming up with that line."

We both laughed, though I didn't think much was funny. Then I set my wineglass down, carefully. I felt a little drunk.

"I smuggle in . . . things," I said. "I take in a magazine called *On the Barricade* and instead of reading the political articles, the women like the personals. They believe that there's someone out there—an SWM or SBM or GWF or GBF—who will fall for an ex-offender female, an XOFF FEM, who needs TLC.

"Most of them want to write romantic or rhetorical poems," I added. "With a couple of exceptions. And there are real exceptions. I mean, of course, no works of genius, but . . ."

"But that's the question one has to ask oneself, isn't it, my dear?" His tone was very amused. "How good are these poems?"

"They're not what you yourself might call good. Though I'm not sure," I said. "But there's one I can't get off my mind. It's . . ."

"I sense that you have a copy—am I right? Read it to me now?" he asked, as I'd known he would.

I was indeed carrying Billie Dee's poem in my bag. I'd read it over and over, until the middle fold was a little frayed. I wanted Baylor Drummond's reaction to the poem, but I also didn't want it. I wanted him to be stunned into silence, I wanted him to be confused by the poem's simple dramatic power. And then I wanted him to—what? Offer to lend a hand teaching in prison? *Sister, how naïve can you get?*

I reached down and pulled the folded piece of tablet paper from my bag. I cleared my throat twice. I could see the heiress talking to Sam Glass at the other end of the table. She'd be back in her position across from us soon.

I felt uncertain for a moment, as if I might be betraying Billie Dee's trust, but I decided that having a great poet's thoughts outweighed the question of violating confidence. Drum lit a cigarette and leaned back in his chair.

I read the poem aloud, quickly, trying to do justice to the words. When I finished, I put the poem down on the table and looked over at him. He sat up suddenly, blew smoke through his nostrils, then winked at me, waving away smoke, shaking with laughter.

"Terrible," he gasped. "Just goddam awful."

At the door, after dinner was over, Sam Glass kissed me and asked if I wanted to go with him and a couple of others to hear Mabel Mercer at the St. Regis. Her voice, he said, was like blackstrap molasses over gravel. He croaked out a few bars of "All the Sad Young Men." Sam Glass always dressed entirely in black, and his great ram's head was covered with wild curly hair. He was a renegade kisser, but he couldn't sing for shit. He was in his twenties, like me, but he seemed older.

"It's the Age of Aquarius." I backed away from him. "The rest of the world is listening to Jimi Hendrix."

I looked into his half-lidded hazel eyes, trying to gauge how drunk he was.

"See, you've got that frozen-steppes look on your face again," he said. "Try not to concentrate so hard. You look like you've spent too much time milking reindeer. The problem with you, Heidi, is that you fail to appreciate the diamond of decadence."

"Anyone who comes up with a phrase like 'diamond of decadence,'" I shot back, stung, "has his own problems, specifically Catholic or Jewish. Too bad you just can't be convincing as a Bad Boy."

"The diamond of decadence," he repeated, and moved in to kiss me again. I backed quickly out the door and turned toward the elevator.

"Ask your devoted patroness," I said. "About the diamonds, I mean. And the rubies. The diamonds moving toward us and the rubies going away."

He shook his head at me. "Wait—what the hell are you talking about?"

It occurred to me, as the elevator doors closed on his confused face, that that question was fast becoming my personal anthem. *What the hell are you talking about?* Sam Glass, I'm talking about prison. All of our cramped migraine-bright cells in the day-to-day House of Detention. *Diamonds coming toward me, rubies going away. Uptown, downtown. Midnight/dawn.* "How I may compare / This prison where I live unto the world," quoth the tired king. Then, too, I'd wanted to be one of what Lear called God's spies, seeing it for myself: I longed to perceive how the ordinary boring suffering world turned into a story, a poem, from which I could learn. *Describe this chair, class. Then, please—describe the light on its wings as it ascends. Describe the real and unreal worlds in their Minute Particulars. The last thing you want here is an alert pimp. Two Dead Boys. You way too cute, Mattox. From Helegat, bright passage, to Hell Gate, sinister waters. Is that Missoni? Describe the faces of the dead, who are with us always. The chair opens its wings, rises. A revolution is not a dinner party.*

What was it that I actually aspired to make of myself, I wondered. A poet or a so-called revolutionary? Someone intent on restructuring society or a word-dreamer, reseeing, reimagining beauty or truth— from a prison cell or the back of a motorcycle? "Truth is Beauty and Beauty Truth," the poet said. Why then did they seem so far apart to me? Worlds apart. Perhaps, I thought, I was just trying to do what everyone else was doing, struggling to make sense of each stumble, each loss of the gradually disappointed heart. I had experienced that in the Bail Fund meeting as well as at Sam Glass's table—how it felt almost to be able to express, then to lose irrevocably, a precious insight—sudden illumination flashing up into rhetoric or social cliché. "SBCB," Sam Glass sometimes called me—Serious Blonde in a Che Beret.

But Sam Glass, I knew, did not really understand my conflicted heart. It was true—I was an idealist, I was of my generation. I thought one could work toward what we termed *the healing of class and eco-*

nomic wounds. And so what if, along with this, I wanted occasional romance? Not fashion-magazine romance, not an heiress's Diamonds Coming Toward Me, et cetera, versus fucking in the shadow of the barricade—rather, the sudden rightness of knowing how to love, let go my ruinous anger. No, I didn't like the way the world had been treating me: I was not some shiny accessory—but I was readily lumped into that category. The way I appeared to be drew unwanted assumptions about the way I was. Finally what I wanted was to come from Somewhere Else, some dream country, capital of reinvention, the fun-house mirror rippling me into a true reflection.

A little bit of *The Ballad of Reading Gaol* popped into my head as I walked toward a cab parked at the corner: "I never saw a man who looked / with such a wistful eye / Upon that little tent of blue / which prisoners call the sky."

Dear Oscar Wilde: I'm just a wee bit fried.

I looked up at the sky over Manhattan, pitch-black except for one lonely star. It was time to go home.

Taneesha

I say to you how my baby
Could fly. Two year old
And I seen her go way up
At my cousin's. When they
All in the kitchen. She go up
On the ceiling all by herself.
My neighbor on the 12th floor
Told me I was a lie. I told her
That Taneesha could fly any day.
They come to spray roaches and I
Put Taneesha out the window for
Good air. She could set fly, but
This old woman scare her, stickin'
Her head out. Taneesha went step by
Step screamin' Mama where I put her
On the ledge. I told her, Fly! fly!
But she kept on screamin' till she
Took a step out down. See I say that
Bitch next door, There she go. But
Taneesha didn't fly that time.

—BILLIE DEE BOYD, POET

three

The cab took me home to the West Village, to Kenneth Brown Severn, my husband—also known as K.B. K.B. and I had been married for just over a year, but we hadn't announced our wedded state to the world at large.

We'd been married in Minnesota, on impulse, during a visit to my family. In two weeks, we'd put together a hippie wedding ceremony that featured Handel's *Water Music* and (as if to ensure lifelong embarrassment) "Morning Has Broken" by Cat Stevens. We recited poem-vows taken from T. S. Eliot's "Ash Wednesday" ("Because I do not hope to turn again") looking into each other's eyes. We did "construct something upon which to rejoice." K.B.'s father and stepmother flew in from San Francisco. We pledged our love, we were declared man and wife.

We were the closest of friends—so close that we'd mistaken our sweet intimacy for grown-up committed love, or a reason for marriage. We just wanted to be together, the world be damned. We didn't need to tell anyone about marrying each other, it was nobody else's business, we said. Still, it gave our lives a kind of mystery, a mystery I hadn't lived long enough to recognize as pure unarticulated doubt.

K.B. was a doctor completing his training. He was a brain specialist, a resident in neurology at Columbia-Presbyterian. His "areas"—ataxia, aphasia, coma, and stroke—were a chain of horrors, yet he made his work in his threatening specialties somehow full of hope. His interest in stroke and coma took him uptown to Harlem Hospital, where he ran a weekday clinic.

K.B. was the noblest person I had ever known in my life—I adored him. I adored him the way people who believe they see angels adore each manifestation of winged travel and light. I'd once accompanied K.B. to Harlem, on the way to his clinic. As we climbed up out of the subway, heading toward 135th and Lenox, an elderly black woman approached us.

"Say, Dr. Severn," she cried. "I been walkin' out here, waitin' for you. I got something here to show you."

She parted the gray frizz on top of her head, then ran her fingers along her scalp, describing the pain. K.B. reached out and put his hands on her head.

"Okay, Mrs. Turner, you need to get this checked out. Come by the clinic later and we'll X-ray. And, Mrs. Turner? You have nothing to worry about, okay? We'll take care of you."

I watched him, his hands on her, blessing her, and I thought: *There is some good in the world and K.B. is that good.* I knew there were so many doctors in the world whose hands would never have opened in that way over her bowed troubled head. And so many people who would never know a doctor like K.B.—hands like his held above their heads: a halo made of healing.

He was the one who had gotten me the job in the prison—he himself worked (whenever he could find the time) as a physician at C-76, the Men's House on Rikers, where he had been working on improving basic medical care through his organization, Radical Health Watch.

How would I explain my feelings for K.B. to the Women's Bail Fund? They didn't respect anyone who worked in the System. It was true, we struggled against Patriarchy—there was a poster of Gloria Steinem on the wall of the apartment where the meeting had been held, up there next to wailing oversexed Janis. Beautiful Gloria with her square jaw, flashing aviator glasses, and long frosted hair, an arm thrown up in the feminist solidarity salute. Beneath her image was her famous quote (which much later I'd learned had originated with an Australian feminist): "A woman needs a man like a fish needs a bicycle."

Right on, I thought. Those words had been my motto—until my impulsive marriage. But when I was honest about my own situation, I realized that I did need K.B. I needed K.B. because he was true to himself. K.B. was a bicycle, like other guys, but he was what he was. Unlike me, the unreliable fish-on-land, fish-on-wheels. *I was unreliable,* I thought again—because although Sam Glass ridiculed me, I realized finally that I had secretly acquired a taste for the Diamond after all. I longed for the literary life: I felt that I was ruined for the life K.B. represented. The literary world asked, it seemed to me, exactly what K.B.'s world would never ask: that everything be fuel for the fire of the imagination. That the imagination be the god of the self.

Still, if it was true that I was ruined for a life of political action—I thought a little drunkenly, fumbling with my keys at the door of our apartment on West Twelfth Street—then I was ruined for the inward-turning life of letters as well. I was, quite simply, fucked up.

The lights were on inside the apartment and Procol Harum wafted from the stereo: *Her face, at first just ghostly, turned a whiter shade of pale.* Unbelievable—K.B. was home early from the hospital. His schedule was so demanding that he sometimes had to crash in one of the hospital beds.

"Is that you?" he called from the bathroom. I could hear the shower.

"I'm fucked up," I called out, by way of hello.

He told me later as we sat eating Frosted Flakes and drinking hot cocoa with marshmallows that it had been a slow night, not too many admissions. Even the terminal patients were sleeping calmly. Even the babies with Tay-Sachs disease and the grandmothers with dementia—the No Cures. As a resident, he didn't have to do what the interns were required to do—he wasn't obligated to stay all night.

Still, he looked exhausted as he sat there in his boxer shorts and faded sky-blue scrubs-top eating cereal. He was tall and thin and pale with medium-length reddish-blond Prince Valiant hair and a smile left over from childhood. His hairline was just beginning to recede. A striped towel was draped over his head and occasionally he rubbed his damp hair with it. He smelled clean, like the bright green soap in the red plastic frog dish in the shower.

I told him about the Women's Bail Fund meeting at some length. I didn't go into my dinner party experience at all. K.B. knew a certain amount about Sam Glass and hadn't much enthusiasm for him, so I didn't spend time there—certainly I didn't go into Sam's random kissing style.

"Corinna Firestone got after me because I want to move on from doing all the actual bailing out."

I put my spoon down and stared into his eyes, eager for his approval.

"I can't do it anymore," I said. "It's so random, you know? I can do a lot more good working in AfterCare."

I heard the defensiveness in my voice, and I realized that I really had felt lonely on my forays to the Island. I did want the others to know what it was like—riding the bus, facing the bail window all alone, piping up with the names. Having to repeat them, again and again, as the surly shaded presence behind the tinted glass claimed not to have heard correctly.

"I go out there, I'm carrying dollar bills and quarters and dimes in a brown paper lunch bag or whatever they've collected the funds in. I end up in front of the window and I read off the names and they check them off. It takes hours for the women I've bailed out to be processed. So I always have to leave finally—without ever seeing one of them." I laughed ruefully, and he smiled back at me. I thought for a minute.

"Actually," I said, "I waited once, one time, for someone I'd bailed out to appear. And a woman eventually did show up. Her name was Carmen Reyes, and she was grateful to be out, but not interested in who made her bail. She was nice, but she looked pretty butch. We rode back into Manhattan together on the bus and then we got off and she shook my hand and said, 'We go different ways now.' And just vanished around a corner. Couldn't wait to lose me." I shook the cereal box. "Other than that, I'm a hit-and-run bailer."

"Then let somebody else hit and run for a while," K.B. said. "Time for these serious bailers to check out the House of D."

I laughed. "Hey, I joined the serious bailers because it seemed so simple, so realpolitik—whammo, just getting people *out*!"

I took a sip of hot chocolate, then sat back. The towel slid from K.B.'s head and he ran his hands through his wet hair.

"And okay, it's not like AfterCare is such a huge improvement over random bailouts," I said. "But at least you feel connected, at least you feel like you know the stakes, who you're working with."

K.B. pushed away his cereal bowl and drank the dregs of his cocoa in one long gulp.

"Speaking of which," I added, "how can you stand working with some of those incompetent doctors they hire out there? There's a guy at the Women's House who calls himself a psychologist, Dr. Vincent Bognal—have you ever run across him? The women call him The Bog. He calls the women 'hopeless cases.' He'll yell out, 'Here comes that loudmouth from 3 Upper—Hopeless Case Number Twelve!' I mean, who is this guy? Where did he train? He couldn't get a job anywhere but Rikers—he admitted that to me once. He believes that all the women are retarded or regressive or he says that they hate men because of penis envy. Not because they have pimps who are beating them or stringing them out on drugs. It couldn't be *that*."

K.B. shook his head and laughed. He had grown so pale with exhaustion that his washed-out freckles stood out suddenly like a flurry of rust-red raindrops on his face and arms. He ran a quick hand over his eyes and shook his head again.

"Listen," he said. "Then there's the other extreme. Some of the guys from Radical Health Watch just got back from China. . . ."

He got up and poured himself more cocoa and held out the china pot to me. I shook my head. Our kitchen was tiny, barely there, but it was friendly, with dirty blue-and-white tiles around the stove, some broken, interspersed with empty gaps like missing teeth. Neither one of us really knew how to keep house, but we cheerfully indicated it, I thought.

"They were in Peking visiting some major neurological/psychiatric hospital there—and had been welcomed by the staff as the young radical American docs, blah blah. Tom and Vanner and those guys had decided not to wear their white coats or carry stethoscopes—they thought that that would be an elitist statement in the land of free universal health care—so they were in jeans and sneakers. So then they see that all the Chinese doctors are in starched white coats with name tags: very formal. The Chinese docs start their presentation: the group observes a few psych patients first. The Chinese very politely ask our guys what their diagnosis would be in each case. Tom tells me that once again they didn't want to be 'traditional medical establishment'—so they say they're not sure, though they're looking at, for example, a classic case of, say, manic depression or paranoid schizophrenia. They tell the Chinese that they're not into Freud anymore—they give them a kind of R. D. Laing creative interpretation rap—I think they suggest that maybe the patients are having a *shaman* crisis. The Chinese docs start looking at our guys like *they're* fucking crazy. Through the interpreter they say, 'Hey, you guys can't tell a classic case of schizophrenia?' And they pull out their textbook—it's Freud. Every goddam clinical description of symptoms is right-on accurate, they say. They use him all the time."

K.B. laughed wearily. He rubbed his hair with the damp towel again, then bunched it up and lobbed it in the general direction of the bathroom.

"So fuckin' much for R. D. Laing."

Conversation had wound down. We both stared, flagging, at Tony the Tiger boinging up and down with ghastly energy on the Frosted Flakes box: an orange-and-black-striped hypnotic, flashing his big atavistic tiger grin.

K.B. yawned, then I yawned in response.

"You know," he said, "I was thinking that we might ask a few people over and announce our . . . wedding. What do you think? Serve some champagne—like that? Just Rick Myers and maybe Tom and also Sasha Brownstein and a couple of the other residents . . ."

I kept my gaze steady on Tony the Tiger.

"No," I said. "I mean, like, maybe *not*. I just think it would be really hard to squeeze it in right now. There are so many things going on, you know?"

I felt K.B. trying to get me to look at him, but I extended my moment with Tony.

"What things?" he asked.

"I don't know. You're at the hospital or the clinic all the time and I'm running around. Besides which, I couldn't invite the Bail Fund women. They disapprove of bourgeois capitalist mergers."

I laughed and looked at him at last. He didn't laugh.

"We wouldn't want them here anyway," he said.

There was a silence. We listened to the sirens outside and the clang of garbage cans, the roar of a sanitation truck, a shout in an airshaft somewhere close by. The crank-up and shuddering synapses of the City's huge brain, the city-brain in the body of America, the great orange-and-black-striped grinding rumination—tigering on all day and all night.

"My mother," I said, aware that I was changing the subject, "wasn't all that happy with the poetry we recited at the wedding."

K.B. lifted his hands, palms up, and closed his eyes.

"She didn't like the T. S. Eliot?"

"No," I said. "She thinks he's a surrealist."

He laughed and I quickly ducked away to the bathroom, where I brushed my teeth and commented loudly, cheerfully, on the paucity of fresh towels. Then, despite the towel situation, I turned on the shower. Under the pouring hot water, I told myself I should seriously contemplate why I didn't want to lift a flute of champagne to toast our new marriage. But I didn't listen to myself—my mind strayed to the poetry we'd spoken at the ceremony—and then I thought about my mother.

*M*y mother was of that last generation of Americans who had learned, in their youth, poems and orations, by rote, in classes dedicated to the art of elocution. Out on the prairie, in the 1920s and '30s, in the obliterating dust storms of the Dakotas, she remembered writing her name in the dust on her desktop at school. She spelled out ELSIE K. TALLICH, 192– Then the dust stirred and her name sifted upward into the air. I saw her name floating before me in the mist of shower steam. I shook my head, shut my eyes, let the hot water erase me.

She was taught Aristotle and the classics, and in English and American literature my mother read Alfred, Lord Tennyson; Byron and Shelley; John Greenleaf Whittier; Longfellow; Dickinson; and Whitman. The students of Elocution held the books in their hands as if the pages were spun from gold: they memorized poem after poem, solemnly, joyfully. They stood up and recited, then bowed their heads for the wreath of laurel.

She lived in a world where ordinary people "quoted" from scripture and inspirational thought, a world in which they recognized rhyme and homily and lines from the great odes. They nodded and smiled in recognition as they called up Shakespeare or Milton for one another in farmhouse parlors or town meetings, at funerals (most held at home, after the body had been "dressed" and laid out on a table covered with flowers) and weddings and births, at the schoolhouse or the local bar.

There was a quote for every occasion, ordinary or exalted. People knew this, relied on it. Standing in line at the post office or somewhere, desperate and bored, I would look up at my mother—and she would glance down at me, raise a finger, arch an eyebrow, and intone: "They also serve who only stand and wait!" When I refused to eat an overboiled vegetable: "How like a serpent's tooth, an ungrateful child!" Or when the alarm clock went off at six A.M. and I burrowed back down deep under the quilts, dreading dressing and pulling on high boots and sinking deep into the snowdrifts—she would appear, luminous, in my doorway: "Let us then be up and doing, / With a heart for any fate!"

She had to kind of rear back before entering a conversation, because she was always readying quotes from her arsenal, her great personally inflected canon. This gave her a preoccupied aura, which turned into steady distraction. She rode roughshod over meter and breath stops, yet never failed to convey, reciting, the mysterious powerful thrill of a poem's emotion.

I reached up and turned off the shower stream, shook my hair out of my eyes, and felt around for the one remaining semi-fresh towel hanging on the rack. I dried myself, hearing my mother's marginal shouts interjected into the body of a poem ("Do not go gentle— *Don't sass me!*—into that good night"), adding a curious secondary weight to the lyric, as if the announcement of a country's decision to go to war bled into another, less portentous radio broadcast. When I learned to read, I discovered, for example, that the line "Shall I com-

pare thee to a summer's day?" did not include the observation
"You're going to put your eye out!" I noticed that I felt a little sad
abandoning my mother's version—and a little disappointed in the
original.

I turned and bumped against a cabinet door, which yawned open.
How she would appear in doorways or turn swiftly from the stove,
hawklike, her eyes alight, her hair in disarray, her index finger pointed
skyward, shouting: "Sunset and evening star / And one clear call for
me / May there be no moaning of the bar / When I put out to sea!"

It had taken me a little while to understand, as a child, that poetry
was not a cause for panic. Poetry, I gradually came to believe, was a
kind of salvation. I peered into the still-steamed-up mirror. Poetry
was indeed, I thought again, a kind of salvation. It had not occurred
to me yet—standing before the opaque mirror, holding my breath—
that in saving yourself, you might betray your past. The mirror still
resisted me, my image. It had not occurred to me how it was also possible to betray the present.

I found a clean knee-length T-shirt in a cupboard. I pulled it over
my head and opened the bathroom door.

Not much later, K.B. and I were in bed, nearly asleep, nose to
nose. My WAR IS NOT HEALTHY FOR CHILDREN AND OTHER LIVING
THINGS T-shirt and his shorts and scrub-top were cast off on the floor
by the bed. We had made love, quietly, as always. As quietly as if we
were a pair of teenage lovers in the bedroom of parents, the house of
elders. Perhaps this near-soundless lovemaking triggered, in its
tamped-down style, the dark heat and confusion of my dreams that
night. The last thing I remember seeing was the round phosphores-
cent glow of my diaphragm case on the bedside table. I closed my
eyes. Later a vision of the pimp's piratical eyes behind his tinted aviator glasses rose up, leering at me, then gradually morphed into
Corinna's sour expression, then another face, resembling that of Sam
Glass, grinning at me ironically, holding up his wrist, pointing to his

watch: *Late.* His face receded into a red sky filling with planes—descending, ascending—as I stepped off the gritty ledge on the twelfth floor of the projects (or was it Sam Glass's penthouse terrace?) trying to catch up to a baby with wild clear telegenic eyes, holding in her small hand a small glass of champagne, spilling it glittering out and away as she dropped it, screaming *Mama, Mama,* and fell suddenly, just beyond my grasp. She held out her hands to me, pleading, as she dropped downward swiftly away from me—just one small length of quickening breath out of my reach.

"See, Billie Dee wrote this poem about what she knew, in her own voice," I said at our second meeting. "Which is why it works so well."

Roxanne–Liza Minnelli made a face at me and chewed the pink eraser on her pencil.

"So Billie Dee *does* know she's fuckin' crazy?"

Billie Dee looked up from doodling on her Rainbow tablet. She was sketching many smiling toothy rabbits with large collar bows, I noticed.

"Who's sayin' I'm crazy?"

Sallie Keller laughed out loud.

"You think your baby set to fly out the window? You throw her out like you throw out dishwater—and girl, tell me—you *normal*?"

Billie Dee crumpled up the page before her and shouted, "My baby fly, I told you! You sayin' Taneesha don't go up like I said?"

I heard Sallie muttering under her breath, "Taneesha done gone the other direction."

Darlene began repeating her single prayer under her breath: "Have mercy, Lord Jesus; Lord Jesus, have mercy."

I touched Billie Dee's arm and she turned to me, her terrible loose eye rolling, her breath ragged.

"It was true in your poem," I said. "In your poem it was true."

Sallie, and the others, all looked unconvinced. Aliganth had stepped away for a minute and I felt bold. I gathered up my strongest arguments for the mystery of art.

"Poems are about what you *think* is true. What you *feel* is true. They make emotional sense, they are emotional truth—they're about feelings as much as thoughts. In poetry there is no One Truth. It's good, as I said, to write about what you know—but sometimes what you know is *what you don't know*."

Billie Dee put her head down on her folded arms, panting. Baby Ain't patted her back, then pointed at me.

"Billie Dee," she said, "don't *know* she don't know."

"That's exactly what her poem tells us," I said. "That a poem can know more than a poet. And communicate that."

Skeptical looks again. Billie Dee began to cry softly, slow tears rolling down her face. Her quiet grief-heavy exhalations became counterpoint to Darlene's steady repetition, "Jesus. Jesus."

What, I wondered, *am I going to say now?*

Suddenly Polly Lyle Clement, who'd been completely silent, sat straight up in her chair as if it had zapped her with Death Row voltage. Up till now she'd seemed lost in a drugged haze of Thorazine, "penguined," as they said, walking the walk, her face a dull mask. But now she looked lit up, her odd light hair framing her strangely radiant face as her eyes glittered.

"Taneesha had nothing to eat—her brothers and sister neither. I see now clear that you couldn't feed those children, Billie. I see them eatin' paint off the walls. Peelin' paint and chewin' it. Those your children? Eatin' paint off the walls?"

There was a long silence. Even Darlene slowed down, then stopped, her Jesus prayer.

"I see that *clear*," Polly Lyle Clement repeated, then smiled oddly and lowered her head.

Billie Dee pushed away a tear and nodded at her slowly.

"Social Service come up, but they don't give enough stamps for four my baby mouths—and then they start talkin' about takin' my Tyrone and Janeel. Takin' Taneesha. Take my babies to Foster."

There was a low murmur of recognition: *Foster, Social Service, food stamps.* Billie Dee leaned over and touched Polly Lyle's arm and Polly looked up into Billie's rolling eyes. They sat like that for a minute and then Polly said: "And I see you sometimes raisin' your hand against your babies, Billie. Your little boy in his blue pajamas, just got the bottoms on there—and the other? Sometimes you come to that."

Billie's hand twitched but stayed on Polly's arm.

"Sometimes," Billie Dee repeated very softly. She and Polly stared at each other.

There was another pause. Sallie Keller pushed her ripped face toward Polly Lyle. "How you see what you see about Billie? How you do that? Girl, you got the Sight?"

Polly turned very slowly away from Billie Dee—so slowly the move seemed menacing. She drew herself up and looked straight and steady back at Sallie.

Billie Dee smiled beatifically to herself. "The day Lady die, the night before, I dream a white dress. You know how they say *Dream a white dress mean a funeral*?" She nodded to herself. "My mama name me for her, for Lady Day, sweet Billie."

She sat up straight and began to sing in a low Mahalia Jackson quaver as Darlene mumbled backup. The song she sang seemed to be of her own composition. There was a refrain: "I fly up, I fly down—they give me poison and call it sugar—yes, they surely do."

Polly and Sallie had still not broken their odd locked gaze, but Baby Ain't shook things free at last.

"Let's go back to how you say you sometimes up to write what you don't know."

Never Delgado, seated next to Gene/Jean, who was breathing heavily on her, asked, "Could Gene make a poem about why she don't know how nasty she is?"

Gene/Jean waggled her tongue at Never, then belched loudly.

Baby Ain't tried again. *Acting fast,* I thought, *reversing the mood.* A sweet-faced courtesan, used to pleasing drunk or stoned or angry men, used to cajoling them out of their cruelty, their violence, their impotence. I marveled at her deftness, her backhand diplomacy—I'd never sipped champagne from that ballroom slipper. I'd never acquired a minute of that cynical grace. *Not,* I thought, *that I'd wanted to.* Still, it was undeniable Baby Ain't had real left-handed power.

"What I can write strong about is how I be in The Life. Look at this: I be in a bar with a john and he know I'm a ho from the giddyap. So that part I got down. But my poem now is got more strange and different. I ain't writin' the love or cuss stuff I wrote last week."

Billie Dee resurfaced, smiling a wan toothy smile at me. She'd begun to look like one of the rabbits she'd been drawing: she was all ears as she began listening again.

I put down the copy of "Good Times," by Lucille Clifton, that I'd just passed out and read aloud. The workshop had been going pretty well; it was the second Friday night we'd met. Was it because things had been going smoothly that I blew it, that I lost my focus? Because I couldn't leave a good thing alone? I knew it wasn't considered proper prison etiquette to ask an inmate why she was incarcerated— yet all at once I couldn't stop myself. Aliganth was back in the room, but even her presence didn't hold me back.

"So the only thing you're locked up for is prostitution?"

Aliganth had been sufficiently relaxed to nod off a little, leaning against the wall by the door. I noticed that she opened her eyes at my question and glanced at me, then at Baby Ain't.

"I met up with a cop need his quota—so I come in, Jump Street, on a pros collar. But then, 'cause they say drugs involved, I miss to have a date set and I fall off the calendar. Now I gone zip to two hunnert fifty days."

"She's a Detention inmate. She has been charged with no crime at this point. Because the pigs say their courts are backed up, women who come in on a nothing arrest end up without a fascist-pig court date listed on the calendar. They rot here innocent. Sometimes for years. Till they rise up. Till they won't take it anymore and they tear the walls down. Or the System destroys them completely. Like Billie Dee."

This information came from Akilah, who as usual had seated herself across the table from me, staring at me in a manner that I sensed was meant to unnerve me. She sometimes smiled a mysterious smile or snorted at something I said. I appeared to amuse her. I now wished I'd never asked the question about Baby Ain't's charge—there were, obviously, reasons for not inquiring in front of others.

"Miss Kohler, you been requested not to proselytize anywhere within the institution walls. You havin' a little lapse in memory?"

Aliganth was standing up very straight now, her chin jutting forward, in charge. Akilah half closed her gamin light eyes and peered out from beneath her long lashes. Darlene kept spinning her wheel, her voice barely audible. "Jesus. Jesus."

"Screw, I believe *you* the one having a memory lapse: Kohler was my slave name? It's *Akilah Malik* now, it's Islamic, my name—think you can get your ofay mind around that? You got yourself a civil service job out here, monkeyed up in a uniform—oppressin' your own? While the white man pull your strings from Downtown?"

"You sure seem to enjoy appearing before the Disciplinary Board, Kohler. I can set that up for you again right now."

Aliganth stepped forward, her keys clinking. Akilah slowly pushed back her chair, starting to get up, her eyes still amused. I looked over at Darlene. Her praying had become white noise, I realized—I'd finally stopped hearing it, like the planes overhead. Akilah stood up.

"You may need the assistance of a few of these bulldaggers to get me to lay down, Screw."

Suddenly Gene/Jean pitched forward, then back, then heaved

over the side of her chair, vomiting violently. A thin string of green bile dangled from her mouth, dripping from her goatee.

Everyone jumped up from the table, backing away. A chair fell backward with a crash. Gene made horrible gagging sounds.

Aliganth went into action, directing the entire class, including Akilah (who for some reason acquiesced), to back up against the wall. A thought occurred to me: perhaps Gene/Jean's episode had given Akilah an out? Aliganth nudged me into place behind her, putting her body between me and Gene/Jean and the rest of the class as she examined the slumped figure—pulling a cloth from her belt, wiping Gene's face. Then she dropped the cloth on the small splat of vomit on the floor.

"Are you done now, tell me, are you done? Where the hell this come from? You been to the Infirmary? You steal shit from the med truck?"

Gene/Jean groaned. Gasping for breath, she told Aliganth, in her inimitable way, that the "male and female sides" of her couldn't stand confrontations. The male side got hugely aggressive and the female side filled with fear and desire for compromise. The result of this internal imbalance was that Gene/Jean got nauseous—it was like being seasick, she cried as she rocked back and forth. "Jerkin' me two ways at once," she yelled, then lowered her head again and gagged, but nothing happened. I watched Aliganth push a button on one of the keys on her ring.

I wondered if Gene's reaction could be patented. "Hey, this might be a way to end world wars!" I called to Baby Ain't across the room. I still hadn't grasped how close we'd come to an Incident.

Baby Ain't flashed me a V sign and called to me in a mock-whisper.

"She stand up to piss. That why she seasick, it put her off her feed—she always got that one wet leg, poor Jean."

A heavyset sour-faced C.O. I'd never seen before appeared in the doorway. She picked up Aliganth's cloth from the floor and put it in a plastic bag, produced a small spray bottle, spritzed the floor, and righted the fallen chair. Then she, along with Aliganth, helped Gene/Jean to her feet, her head lolling a little on her neck, and led Gene away, coughing. Aliganth ordered everyone to return to their seats.

"Gene just got a little confused—maybe at the Infirmary earlier. She be back."

We sat down again and Aliganth stood at the head of the table, behind me—directly across from Akilah—and said that she was going to let things "return to normal." She would allow "each member of the class" to continue. For now. If there was any further questioning of authority, there would be "repercussions." Akilah's face remained unchanged, a steady dead-calm hate-glare radiating back at her. I couldn't tell who, if anyone, had backed down earlier. After a long minute, Aliganth moved away from my chairback and returned to her place at the door.

A change of subject seemed in order.

"Okay—I forgot to tell you that I looked up the history of 'Two Dead Boys,' " I noted brightly. "I looked under Folklore and Folk Songs of the British Isles at the Forty-second Street library and I found out that it comes from a tradition called Impossible Ballads or Miracle Verse. You know, where blind men see and deaf people hear and the dead get up and fight. 'Two Dead Boys' was sung by children on playgrounds all the way back in the nineteenth century in stanzas like the ones Baby Ain't recited."

I looked around at their unreadable faces.

"Anybody else have a poem to recite? Then we'll go back to our own writing."

Dead silence. I was losing them. Darlene wasn't even calling on Jesus. Akilah's eyes were on me, mocking.

Suddenly Billie Dee piped up, singing out a non sequitur, her version of a poem—a sexist airline commercial jingle in her rock-back gospel voice.

"Fly me! Fly me do: I'm Billie Dee!"

Her jingle turned flat in the dead air. A plane ascended overhead, suddenly loud. Then Polly Lyle Clement began to speak. As she spoke, her voice changed tone and accent—it sank lower, and a Southern drawl crept in.

"Well, I do know that song you mention there. It just slipped my mind. I damn near forgot to own up to it!"

Everyone turned to stare. She was so very peculiar-looking, with her very light brown skin and her white hair. Scrawny but muscled. The left side of her face was smudged with a slight reddish shadow, a rose-colored blotch, as if she'd been burned once, long ago. Her eyes were piercing and gold-flecked, like a bird's. Roxanne frowned at her.

"So what does that have to do with anything?"

Polly smiled back. A very sweet smile.

"I sang that poem 'The Two Dead Boys'—or one just like it— back in my schoolyard days, far away and long ago, children. And that ain't a lie."

She shifted in her chair and chuckled a little.

" 'Course, the strikin' difference between a cat and a lie is that a cat got only nine lives."

She laughed to herself again. "Got it? A cat only got nine lives and a lie can live forever."

Then she looked directly at me. " 'Course you can't pray a lie, that's true!"

I must have looked back at her strangely (Why was the phrase "pray a lie" ringing dimly in the back of my memory?), because she smiled indulgently at me and straightened up even more, as if gathering, clarifying, her thoughts.

"I can offer you a poem of my own composition and I can speak it from memory, I believe." She rubbed her eyes.

"I been given soporifics," she confided, suddenly whispering.

"But now I'm wakin' up. I've taken to hidin' them under my tongue, then tossin' them down the drain later."

Aliganth leaned in to listen more closely, but someone had been shouting in the hall and luckily she'd missed what Polly had just said.

I felt a slow chill ripple through my blood. Polly's weird abrupt animation seemed to be giving everyone else the jitters too. Even Akilah raised an eyebrow, and Baby Ain't glanced around from face to face, smiling nervously. Sallie Keller turned her sad split owl's face to stare at Polly.

"Would you all like me to recite my poem?"

"Sure," I said. "Let's hear it."

What next? I thought. I noticed that Aliganth was back on alert. She had a look of seriously exaggerated patience on her face. I knew she'd have a whole lot to say to me after class. We listened to Polly as her voice deepened and drawled. Darlene was mouthing her Jesus prayer now, her lips moving soundlessly.

"Well, here it is, an ode. It was actually written by a person I made up in a little book of mine. Her name is Emmeline Grangerford— a melancholic eulogizer, quick on the draw. Nobody could write heavenly farewells faster than Emmeline. She hung about the funeral parlors and graveyards, mainly for inspiration."

Ode to Stephen Dowling Bots, Deceased

And did young Stephen sicken,
   And did young Stephen die?
And did the sad hearts thicken,
   And did the mourners cry?

. . .

No whooping cough did rack his frame,
   Nor measles drear with spots;

Not these impaired the sacred name
  Of Stephen Dowling Bots.

Despised love struck not with woe
  That head of curly knots,
Nor stomach troubles laid him low,
  Young Stephen Dowling Bots.

O no. Then list with tearful eye,
  Whilst I his fate do tell.
His soul did from this cold world fly
  By falling down a well.

I flashed on my mother in her apron, standing in the kitchen, reciting Milton and Tennyson as the dog and I sat listening attentively—then I remembered how she would pull up a funny poem for us, her flour-covered hand on her hip, laughing, her other hand flapping nervously. *Emmeline Grangerford. Stephen Dowling Bots.* A boy on a raft floated up before my eyes. I lifted my hand to stop Polly mid-line.

"Wait. Emmeline Grangerford is not somebody you made up, Polly. She's a character in *Huckleberry Finn.* By Mark Twain."

"A book steeped in racism," noted Akilah.

I blinked at her.

" 'Nigger' every other word."

"Jesus. Jesus have mercy."

"I got no problem with the word 'nigger.' Hey, nigger, y'all, all you niggers, hey up! You listenin', niggers?"

This from Sallie Keller. Akilah opened her mouth to answer Sallie, then closed it. They stared at each other, not with hate but a fierce reluctant regard, weighing each other's resolve. Sallie's ravaged face was alight with a weird look of triumph. Then Akilah laughed, a short bitter sound.

I noticed that Aliganth had moved just a fraction closer to the table.

"Polly," I said. "You recited this poem brilliantly, but it's not yours. It's by Mark Twain."

"I have to plead guilty to writin' that claptrap myself. Though I admit that Emmeline got a habit of takin' things almost entirely into her own hands when she got the chance."

Suddenly everyone was talking at once.

"That's a lie she's tellin' about writing!" cried Darlene, suddenly abandoning her prayer. Her high thin voice cut through all the others.

"Look," I said. "Let's deal with the Mark Twain thing later. Why don't we just focus on the poem about Stephen Dowling Bots for a second? Tell me something: What makes it funny?"

"No," said Sallie. "That ain't cool. And anyway, what so funny about some stupid honky fallin' down a dark hole? Baby Ain't told out 'Two Dead Boys' and everybody know she didn't come up with it by her own hand. Now you sayin' we can boost any poem we want and say it mine?"

Aliganth had stopped zeroing in and had been prowling aimlessly around the room. Now she stopped, her head cocked, listening to what I would say.

"Boosting poems," I said, "is not cool, and no, you shouldn't do it. I wasn't saying that. Stealing someone else's words is wrong."

I had a sudden surreal image of inmates lifting poems from typewriters and unbound manuscripts, stockpiling them for later reference, filing them in their underpants.

"You take someone else's words, you be blessed by them—by the one who's gone on. The words keep goin' on by themselves. Anyway, children, we don't need to fall down a well over this point of difference," said Polly suddenly. "You were sayin', I remember, that poems tell not only one truth, am I right?'

"Right," I said uncertainly. *Very strange, this Polly Lyle Clement.*

"Well, what I put before you is the truth but, as the fine poet Emily Dickinson says, it's Truth Told Slant. I wrote down Emmeline Grangerford, but it was my great-granddaddy who wrote it first and I took it up."

"What are you saying?" I asked.

Darlene revved up her prayer again.

"I'm telling you the truth a bit slantwise"—she smiled at everyone around her and twirled a strand of her white hair—"that Mark Twain is my great-granddaddy and that he speaks through me."

Snow

Snow is just dead rain—
I walk slow, like a bride train.
A hooker is like dead rain—
No Snow-White—but a slow cold pain.
No man ease her walk in fear—no gun.
She pay him to strut in the sun—
But she shines in the dark, she falls slow—
Like dead rain, like icy snow—
She stays out, she keeps comin' down.

      —BABY AIN'T MASON, POET

four

Sam Glass touched my shoulder, then ran his fingers quickly down my forearm. I was wearing a Rolling Stones T-shirt and jeans, he was dressed in a sort of smoking jacket and loafers. We were in the audience at the reading of a rather prim nature poet, Frances Beatrice Francis, at Chumley's, a literary pub in the Village. The reading had gone on for nearly an hour and we were seated on hard wooden benches. I looked up at the walls covered with literary graffiti. I did not brush Sam Glass's hand away.

> *Pastoral crows leave furrows in the sky*
> *Above the bright-leaved box elder trees*

the poet intoned, adjusting her granny glasses, stepping back dramatically from the mike, then returning, clearing her throat:

> *I imagine Wordsworth calling out to them,*
> *Plow birds! Plow birds of the clouds!*

Sam Glass leaned close and whispered into my ear:

> *I imagine Farmer John*
> *Plowing through the muck of*
> *Cow turds! Cow turds among the clods!*

"Shut up, Glass."

He didn't really annoy me—what threw me off balance was how he just presented himself to me like a fact of my life: *Here I am. You dig me, of course.* And the sexual charge: maybe I felt it, but did not want to acknowledge it. At last I pushed his hand away. He grinned and winked at me.

The poet at the lectern shook back her hair and smiled out at her restless audience. I'd heard that she'd once been bitten in the nose by a badger while taking notes for a poem. How *had* she gotten that close to a badger?

"For my next poem, I'll read a sestina which takes its six repeating end-words from a Yoruba chant about tree frogs and also from words used in classifying types of protozoa."

I'd met Sam Glass at the New School. He was teaching a course in Editing the Literary Magazine—just down the hall from the personnel office, where I went to apply for my first teaching job in New York City. I had my graduate degree and a forthcoming book of poems, but I was wildly nervous. I dropped my manila-folder dossier, papers fell to the floor and scattered everywhere. The dean-type older woman who had come out to greet me in the outer office looked impatient as I knelt down to pick up my file. Just then a tall figure appeared in the doorway, grinning.

"Well, hello! How are *you*?" he boomed. I nearly spoiled his effect: I hurriedly looked behind me, thinking that he was addressing someone else. Luckily, I was crouching, picking up papers below the eye-line of my interviewer, and she didn't see my confusion.

Sam turned his smile on the impatient administrator.

"You're interviewing her? What a stroke of luck!" He glanced downward at me, hazel eyes amused.

I stood up slowly, a little shocked, a lot embarrassed, fighting against a feeling of vertigo, a slow downward spiral, as in a dream. It was crazy, but undeniably thrilling. He went on and on, singing the praises of a person he didn't know. Finally the dean, smiling, shaking her head, told me she'd call me the following day after looking over my dossier (now reassembled) and consulting with other personnel administrators.

"Don't take too long, Mrs. Parteman." He bowed to her and she actually tittered a little.

"I'll be happy to provide a written recommendation tomorrow," he added.

"Thank you, Sam," she called after us as we left the office together.

The door shut and I faced my unknown advocate. He was startling-looking, tall and stocky, with a wild halo-cumulus of dark curly hair, which he casually referred to as a "Jewfro."

"The least you can do," he said, cranking up what I came to think of as his Artful Dodger smile, "is tell me your name and have a drink with me." I looked closer at his expression—a sketch for my notebook: at once haughty and accessible.

"Who are you?" he repeated.

"*I'm nobody,*" I quoted, "*who are you?*"

He smiled again. "Right. Got it: Emily Dickinson. So you're a poet—the worst kind of trouble."

"*I* have never been through anything like this. I don't know how to describe it!" wailed Vicky Renslauer in a terrible stricken voice—and began to cry. A large white bandage rode across the bridge of her nose (her glasses perched precariously on top) and layers of flesh-colored gauze were wrapped tight around one of her wrists.

I was late again, slipping into a chair at the back of the room just as she began sobbing up in front. A few of the Bail Fund members surrounded her and tried to help her into her chair, but she pushed them away and stood apart from them, trembling.

"Is *this* why you didn't want to keep on taking bail out to the Women's House?" she shouted, and pointed across the room at me. I rose to my feet and heads cranked around.

"I have no idea what you're talking about, Vicky," I said. "What happened to you?"

"What happened?" she repeated, her voice choked and mocking. "What happened? I'll tell you what happened! Unlike you, I *waited* for one of the women I bailed out to come out."

She launched into a long digressive accusatory narrative about how she'd had a terrible time on the bus. She'd been forced to ride with pimps some of the way and two of them called out to her and threatened her and then she had had to wait an hour before finally being allowed to post the bails. All of the corrections officers were horrible to her and most would not answer her questions. She could handle all of this, Vicky said. What she couldn't handle was, after paying the bail and deciding to wait at the Reception Center to see who came out first—she was *attacked*! A woman appeared after *five* hours, dressed in hastily donned street clothes, staring wildly about. Vicky approached her and she did turn out to be one of the "names" she'd bailed out, but the woman was "deeply disturbed," Vicky said.

"When I introduced myself and attempted to provide information for her about the Bail Fund and our commitment to Mao and Marxism, she began screaming at me. She yelled that she didn't even know who I was, and kept shouting, why the fuck had I bailed her out? She thought I was from some church group taking her to a ministry, or a Phoenix House counselor dragging her to a halfway house. She kept screaming about how her same old pimp would be out there, coming after her for money she'd held out way back when— plus her 'wife' was left Inside. She kept yelling, why didn't I leave her alone? Then she said, since I'd bailed her out without asking her, she was going to find a way for me to get her back Inside."

Then Vicky described how the "deranged chick" punched her in the nose, knocking her glasses off and landing her on the floor. Vicky said that she put up her hands to cover her face and her wrists were battered. Eventually, two corrections officers came running over and the crazy woman was taken back to the Women's House. Awash in blood and tears, Vicky Renslauer had agreed to charge the person she'd just bailed out with assault.

"I may drop the charges," she added. "But at the time, I was in shock—I just wanted her to stop beating me!"

Corinna appeared beside Vicky, staring accusingly at me.

"So this is typical? Is this why you never waited?"

"No," I said. "I didn't wait because I never had time to hang around that long. Anyway, how do we know who we're bailing out? There are a lot of people out there who don't necessarily think the way we think."

"I know this sounds reactionary," cried Vicky. "I want you all to know that I probably won't press charges. But I never want to be mauled again by some raging six-foot bull-dyke."

"You're upset, Vicky," growled Corinna, still staring darkly at me. "But please don't speak of comrades Inside in that crypto-male-chauvinist manner. Even if you are emotionally distraught, Vicky. I mean it. Get control of yourself."

No one uttered a sound except Vicky, sniffling and blowing her nose loudly.

I nearly spoke up again to remind them that a revolution was not a dinner party, but I decided to keep that observation to myself. I was sorry about what had happened to Vicky. I wondered if I could have predicted it after all.

Vicky seemed to be calming down a little. I went into the kitchen to get her a glass of water, and while I was standing at the sink, Corinna and Martine entered.

"It's the same kind of rip-off mentality," Martine was saying. "Just like what happened with your apartment."

I turned around, the glass of water in my hand.

"What? What apartment?"

They froze in place, staring at me, and then Martine, who was quite pretty, with long lanky strands of black ironed hair like Joan Baez's, spoke up pleasantly.

"I guess this was before your time here, but Corinna's parents gave us some money and we used it to rent an apartment to be used as a transitional place to live for women we'd bailed out. There was a woman named Ronnie Bloom—she doesn't come to meetings anymore—she was the one who always went to Rikers to post bail. She would leave notes for the women, inviting them to crash in the apartment till they got going again. But that's not how it worked out."

"Right," I said. "The place got kind of trashed?"

Corinna glared at me.

"Oh yeah, like you know *everything* about women in prison."

"No," I said, "I don't. But I suppose that it might not have been wise to hand over your apartment to bailouts who might have to re-sort to living the way they used to. To survive, you know? I mean. Just a thought."

Corinna made a face and said something under her breath.

I was experiencing a powerful insight, then confidence in that in-sight. I'd never felt so certain before at a Bail Fund gathering. I was sure that I was right about what I was going to say.

"Corinna," I said, "maybe you haven't offered to go out to the Women's House with bail because you are afraid to go. Is that possi-ble? And there are some comrades here who are afraid right along with you? Because of the apartment thing and now Vicky? I mean, you want to help—just not *firsthand*. You think these women are dangerous, right?"

Corinna laughed. "I told you twenty times—my FBI file makes it impossible for me to set foot out there."

"Okay, Corinna," I said. "I'm sure that's it."

As I started to walk out past them with Vicky's glass of water, Martine put out a hand to stop me.

"The apartment had become a brothel, practically. There were pimps and johns"—she paused, a pained expression on her pretty face—"in the bedroom. There were a lot of drugs, buying and selling and shooting up in the bathrooms. We had to . . ."

She glanced at Corinna and her voice dropped: ". . . call the police."

She looked back at me and straightened her shoulders, looking resolute.

"Anyway, we're past all that. I think we should just move on and forget about what happened back there. Just forget it."

It was Mark Twain, I thought suddenly, Polly Lyle's reputed ancestor, who'd said that prison is where you put people you want to forget about—but I didn't quote him. I didn't quote anybody or anything. Instead I nodded at Martine and went back in to Vicky, handed her the glass of water, and sat through the rest of the meeting. I didn't intend to come back, but it was a good thing that I didn't sound off after all. I certainly couldn't advise anyone on the difference between what was just and what was completely naïve. Still, I couldn't help feeling just a smidgen vindicated vis-à-vis all the criticism/self-criticism. I thought of Corinna, forced to call law enforcement to throw the pimps out of her apartment, and felt a smile begin to spread across my face. I gave in to feeling amused—but if I'd consulted Polly Lyle at that moment, she might have been able to warn me: my own particular enlightenment was fast approaching.

The sun poured through the high windows of Kiehl's Pharmacy on East Thirteenth Street as Benny Mathison and I sampled scents. Benny held a small brown glass vial under my nose.

"It's called Rain," she said. "They just invented it."

I sniffed at the lip of the vial. An exalted smell of rose petals and wet pavement and silver mist wafted from the mouth of the bottle.

"They mix it up here in the pharmacy," she said. "It's one of their family secrets."

She peered at the city of glass-stoppered bottles on display on the counter in the sunshine—there was a Bonfire scent and Lime Bower and Baby Powder and Civet Cat and Fresh Apple Pie. It was intoxicating to nose through them, lift the glittering coated stoppers, inhale the brightness, and be transported via the olfactory to the Caribbean (Palm Thatch Rum) or Kentucky (River Blue Grass) or Africa (Safari Wind).

Benny was chunky, with short brown hair, glasses, and an embattled expression on her face like a young Bolshevik's. She was finishing up at N.Y.U. Law School and she did pro bono work at the Women's House. We'd befriended each other there and found that we shared frustrations and, to some degree, ideas about change. Benny was practical—I was not.

Today Benny was treating herself. She treated herself, she told me, before she went out to Rikers Island every week because she needed to store up strength.

"It's impossible to gauge how hard it is on a person," Benny noted, unscrewing the cap and dabbing a stopperful of the newly mixed scent of Rain behind her ears and on the insides of her wrists. "You need to take good care of yourself or it will get inside you. The whole situation."

She bought a bottle of Rain and so did I, and she also bought Fresh Gingerbread and New-Mown Hay. I then accompanied her west on Thirteenth to Trois Petits Cochons, where she ordered a slice of pâté campagne, a ripple of triple-crème cheese, a small sliced baguette, and six cornichons. Plus a white china mug of café presse with cream. I ordered coffee too and a little bread and Brie, but I wasn't very hungry. I felt as if Benny was eating for both of us.

Benny was on one of her favorite pissed-off subjects: Jerry Rivers, a guy who'd graduated a year ahead of her at N.Y.U. and had become Geraldo Rivera, famous TV news reporter.

"I can't get over it," she said. "This is Power to the People?"

"Why do you care?" I asked. "Why does it bother you whatever this guy calls himself?"

"Because." She stared into her coffee as if she were reading tea leaves. "He is the first wave of a depressing future that I foresee. A future of Professional Ethnics."

We sat there on the high stools in the window of Trois Petits Cochons, looking out at the sun shining on the hurrying passersby and the delivery trucks and taxis and the trees in their wrought-iron ankle bracelets. I noticed after a while that we were giving off a kind of tropical fog of scent. A man reading *The Village Voice* looked over, sniffed, and went back to his paper, then looked up and sniffed the air again. *Rain? Why do I smell rain? Or is that fresh gingerbread? Or Caribbean tree toad musk?*

I asked Benny to tell me what it meant when the women at Rikers talked about falling off the calendar.

Benny set her coffee down carefully, then pounded her chest just above her heart.

"Habeas corpus!" she cried. She pounded her heart again—with such force it frightened me.

"What they are doing out there is detaining those women illegally. They're flying in the face of habeas corpus—the law says you have to be charged with a crime in order to hold the body for any extended period of time. They're supposed to 'produce the body' before a judge! These women go to court for a hearing and sit in the bullpen all day because the system's all backed up. Then they're hauled back to Rikers, uncharged. It's scandalous. Off the calendar, they can sit uncharged for two years! You know what the ratio of sentenced to detained women is at the Women's House, right? It's one big holding cell out there!"

I asked her if she planned to launch a class action suit.

She shook her head.

"I'm in way over my head as it is."

She sat staring into space for a minute, her engines still running.

"Tell me something," I said. "Speaking of someone very much *on* the calendar, do you think Akilah Malik will get off?"

She chuckled grimly.

"Akilah Malik? Never. Her companion, Rembala Mahmud, was killed in the shoot-out. She was in the car when the New Jersey state trooper was shot, but eyewitnesses—I mean the cops—say that she fired a gun from the passenger side, and they'll have ballistics experts testifying at her trial to prove it."

She spread some pâté on her baguette and took a bite. She swallowed, then started up again.

"Akilah Malik! It doesn't matter if she turns state's evidence or cops a plea—she'll still be staring through bars the rest of her natural life."

Aliganth caught me as I was hurrying down the hall to the Social Services office. It was noon, and I was deep into my AfterCare identity. I'd never seen Aliganth in the daytime before, she always pulled the night shift. Seeing her before dusk was shocking, like glimpsing a vampire at lunchtime. She was in the institution, she told me, to sit in on an officer review. She looked furious, as usual—because she was. Her eyes flashed and she showed her large teeth and her voice rose to falsetto as she began her rant.

"How dumb you lookin' to be? Didn't we go over that you never ask the ladies what they in for?"

"We did," I admitted. I started to defend myself, but she cut in.

"Between Kohler and Keeley you got the threat of violence within the institution, and that half-sex hulk tossing her cookies all over my polish shoes. Not bad for one class meeting, Mattox. You thinkin' of continuin' teaching here?"

"I am," I said. "And I'm sorry, I just didn't think it would lead to . . ."

"You thinkin'," growled Aliganth. "There's your problem! We do the thinkin' for you when it comes to the inmates. You got it through your head that you endangered every person in that room, including me and your own self?"

I nodded and felt an uncomfortable smile crossing my face and shifted my weight from one foot to the other. I didn't know how else to respond. I knew that Aliganth had the power to get me kicked out of the Women's House.

"I got my eye on you, Mattox. One more slip like that and you'll be peddlin' your epics back on the bus outta here."

"Right." I held on to my tongue, amazingly, though my mouth was full of potential retorts.

"And another thing here. I don't know if it's wise that you got them writin' about what they done to get Inside."

"They're writing about what they know."

"Right. And what 'they know they don't know' too?"

"C.O. Aliganth," I said. "I do believe you're picking up some writing tips. Maybe you'll grace us all with a poem."

Aliganth snorted loudly. "I got poetry in me you hope not to see."

She started to turn away and I called to her.

"I know that I'm not supposed to ask about inmate charges, but since it's just the two of us here, can you tell me anything at all about Polly Lyle Clement?"

Aliganth glanced at her watch and sighed.

"I will tell you next to nothin', which is what I know. Well, only this: she headin' upstate eventually to a psych residence. She come in last month, they fished her out the river. She was actually swimmin' out there and talkin' to herself. Nobody could follow her. Maybe she got a rap sheet—can't recall. So they tranked her, but nothin' stops that mouth. Like all the goddam rest of you. I'm tellin' you this so that you be aware—and not make any more dumbass mistakes. Just let her talk—she can become agitated."

"Right. But why does she say she's speaking in Mark Twain's voice?"

"You got a half man, half woman; you got a leader of a shoot-out gang; you got a drug runner and a pimp killer; and you ask me why this one *talk* funny?"

"Jesus, C.O. Aliganth. I thought we weren't supposed to discuss charges."

"*You're* not supposed to," she said. "But I'm a corrections officer. I know better than you. When you gonna get this through that thick skull, Mattox? I know better than you."

*L*ater, back in the AfterCare office, I pulled the piece of paper, worn and crumpled, from my pocket and dialed the number printed on it.

"Hi, my name is Holly Mattox. I work in the AfterCare program at the Women's House of Detention? I'm calling on behalf of Darlene Denisky—I'm trying to reach her children, or their guardian?"

The office was quiet, everyone else was at lunch—the social workers gathered to eat from their brown paper bags on the cement benches in front of the Women's House: a little tuna salad on rye under the landing gear of a 727, droplets of jet fuel bubbling in one's Dr Pepper.

The woman who had answered the phone had not sounded unfriendly when she picked up. Now her voice turned icy.

"She has no business asking you to call about her children. They're in school now anyway."

"Listen," I said. "She has a right to—"

"She has no rights. None."

"If you'd just listen to me for a second. . . . She just wants to know that they're all healthy, okay? How they're doing in school? Don't you think you ought to be able to tell me that?"

"You can tell that monster that her children are alive—her husband sure ain't!"

I started to ask another question and she cut me off.

"Tell her that her children still remember seeing their daddy on the kitchen floor after she shot him in the head. Lying there, dying in his own blood. Will you tell her that?"

There was a choking sound.

"My brother!" she cried. "She shot him from behind! Tell that cunt never to make contact again. Do you understand me?"

How dumb are you? How dumb you lookin' to be?

*B*enny looked at her watch. She offered me a cornichon and I shook my head. I was on my third cup of coffee. She ate the pickle delicately, in two quick bites. Then she leaned forward.

"The thing to remember about women in prison is this. There are no 'middle' crimes with them. Women either are busted for the so-called victimless crimes, like prostitution, shoplifting, drugs, et cetera—or the charges leap up to big crimes of passion. No Burglary One, no Breaking and Entering, no Knocking Over the Gas Station or the Seven Eleven, no Armed Robbery. No middle crimes. But at the other end: women will kill. They'll kill the husband, the pimp, the boyfriend, even the child. You know what I mean? It's either stealing a goddam Twinkie, or Murder One."

I tried the "Where I'm From" writing exercise. Darlene was not praying so loudly anymore, just her lips moved lately as she addressed Jesus. I suggested a variation on the original assignment— I asked them each to come up with one word (two at the most!) to give the rest of us a sense of their origins.

Baby Ain't was quick: "The street."

Roxanne: "Bad timing."

Darlene: "Jesus."

Sallie: "My face."

Never: "Respectability."

Polly Lyle: "The river. I come from the river."

"Next," I said, "we're going to try writing a ballad using words like the one or two you came up with—so we can read where you're from—within a time-honored poetic form."

"I come from Switch," called out Gene/Jean. "Switch."

"So," said Sam Glass. "Here you are."

"Here I am."

We'd met for a drink at a dark little restaurant/bar on Irving Place in Gramercy Park. I'd shown up just because he'd asked me to. I wasn't sure how he got me to do things I wasn't keen to do; but somehow he managed it. Billie Holiday sang with pure tortured bliss in the background. The waitress set down our drinks: my wine, his scotch.

"I have good news all around for you," he said. "The *Sam* editorial staff has voted to take three of your new poems for publication. And there's an adjunct position in the Columbia graduate writing program for which you're being recommended. By me. I have pull there. Just in case you don't know whom to thank if they hire you. You're in line for an interview. And best of all—you get to share the afternoon with me—who knows where it will end?"

"Far out."

He stopped smiling and took a judicious sip of his drink.

"Far out? That's all you've got to say about news like this? *Far out?*"

"I'm sorry. I'm thrilled—really, I am. It's just been a very bad day. And it's a lot to take in at once."

"You are, without a doubt, among the most repressed individuals of my acquaintance. Yet you have this occasional energy and even humor. Why are you so uptight the rest of the time?"

"Why are you such a prick all of the time?"

I took a sip of white wine. Sam lit up a cigarette, and I briefly considered asking him for one. I'd been fantasizing about taking up smoking. Women poets like Edna St. Vincent Millay, maybe even Louise Bogan, smoked. Suddenly I pictured myself with a martini glass in one hand and one of those long thin cigars that Swedish models smoked in the other, lounging on purple velvet cushions in some goddam opium den with a Moroccan theme.

Sam shook his head and blew smoke skyward. "I'm a prick? I know you like me, Holly. I can tell—despite all your attempts to deflect it. It's not easy to admit this, but women love me."

"Right," I said. "Show me a man who says 'women love me'—or my other favorite, 'I really know women'—and I will show you a man who has fucked up royally with the opposite sex."

"Then you must stick to your type, Heidi—the safe guys—men women love because they always agree with everything women say."

I took another sip of wine. I was weighing what I was about to say, but couldn't figure out if it was the right moment or, more to the point, if I was being honest with myself about why I was saying it.

"Well, guess what? I have some news too. I'm married. And have been for a while. And not to someone who fits either of your stereotypes."

He didn't flinch. I watched his face. If he was shocked he covered it up with a quick cynical laugh. He exhaled a quick bark of smoke.

"Did I hear you? You've opted to become chattel? You, the diehard square-head feminist?"

He asked me about K.B. I told him about K.B.

"And no, he's not like other men," I added. "He doesn't always agree with me, but he has this thing about him that sets him apart from a lot of other guys. For example, he's capable of loving someone besides himself."

Sam laughed again and signaled to the waitress. *Another scotch, please.*

"How touching. The Little Woman: Mrs. Severn."

"I haven't changed my name. I would never do that."

"Of course not. Your groom might mistake you for a person who wishes to identify with him. But why would you keep it a secret for so long?"

"Because it was just for us," I said, unsure what I meant, even to myself.

The waitress put down his new drink and took the empty glass away. I shook my head at her. I didn't want more wine. He smiled into his drink.

"Okay," he said. "Ask me how married I think you really are."

"Ask me how uninterested I am in your answer."

"You're using this thing to hide from your own desires, I can tell you that."

Billie Holiday sang on, praising the child that's got his own.

"Like I desire . . . what exactly? Or whom? You?"

I stood up. I no longer wished to see Sam Glass in front of me.

"Leaving so soon? Do you have to cook dinner and darn his socks? And he's a doc—I was just about to ask you if he would take a look at this mole on my arm."

"I have to get away from the sight of you. Nothing personal."

"Right on, sister!" he called after me, waving. "Don't keep hubby waiting. And I'll pick this up."

I marched back and threw a couple of dollars on the table.

"I'm afraid that won't quite cover your wine."

"When women make the same hourly wage as men, I'll make up the difference."

I turned to leave, thought better of it, and tossed a twenty-dollar bill in front of him.

"And that," he said, "doesn't begin to cover the cost of my analysis of your rather staggering marital error."

"Well, then," I retorted, "how about if I buy a new poem slot in *Samizdat*? You know, the way your patroness purchases ad space? Or is that taken out in trade?"

I'd finally scored a direct hit.

"Fuck you, Holly."

"Ditto in spades, Sam."

"Call me when you need a divorce lawyer. I know a doozy!" he shouted after me. The bartender raised an eyebrow at me as I paused before the door, taking a deep breath, then another, before I opened it and went out.

God Told Me This

In church, where I go to ask help from Jesus,
God told me ten years was enough now.

He beat me every night all that time.
Every night he come home with the bottle
All over him, then he took his fists to me.
He sat in the same chair after the worst.
Black eyes, my nose smashed up.
I got a cast one time. From going down the stairs.
He sat in the same chair in the kitchen,
At the table. The kids screaming. God said to me,
In church that day, Let him beat you like he do
Then sit himself down and pass out cold as before.
When he snores, get his gun from the chifforobe.
Walk around him three times where he laid
His face on the table. Say I praise, I praise,
I praise three times unto My Spirit. Make the sign
Of the cross upon his head three times. All things
Three times and when you have spoken what I say,
I am the God of Three, put the gun unto his head
And offer him to me. Then Darlene, he said, then the trigger.

—DARLENE DENISKY, POET

five

I passed through the gates, the guard stations on the first floor, then took an elevator up to 2 Main. Some of the C.O.s knew me and nodded at me. I was on my way to see Polly Lyle Clement. I had a pass in my hand, signed by the Dep and C.O. Aliganth.

Two Main was the Loony Bin. Actually, it was Pre–Loony Bin. It was a Detention, not a Sentenced, floor, since most of the inmates were psychiatric cases waiting to be transferred to upstate mental hospitals. Others were locked in their cells after infractions and disciplinary hearings prior to being taken to PSA—the Punitive Segregation Area—solitary confinement. Also known as the Bing.

The C.O. station on 2 Main, like those on all the other floors, looked like a bubble, a spaceship cockpit from which the on-duty officer could open the cells electronically, snap the lights on and off in the cells, and speak over a two-way microphone to inmates in their dorm-room-like spaces.

I handed over my pass to the C.O. in the bubble, then walked down one of the two cellblock corridors leading from the bubble, with another C.O., named Janson, till we arrived at the place where Polly Lyle Clement lived. A few inmates penguin-walked up and down the halls, snowed—I could hear others yelling in their cells, calling for the C.O. to open their door-gates. There was radio music and the usual thundering P.A. announcements from the Watch Commander's office.

C.O. Janson stopped in front of a cell, and the C.O. in the bubble buzzed the cell door open. Polly Lyle Clement was standing there, in the center of a space with a cot, a closet, a desk and chair, a bookcase, a metal mirror embedded in the wall, a toilet, a sink. Behind her, the window–prison bars combination of the Women's House. She was smiling at me.

"I need to talk to you," I said.

"I'd invite you into my temporary abode," she said, "but, alas, there is nowhere to rest one's weary bones."

"Come on, Clement," piped up the C.O. "Let's go to the Day Room."

*B*efore I'd made arrangements to visit Polly on her floor, I'd consulted Dr. Bognal, who was the AfterCare Services psychologist. I sat in his office and asked him questions about Polly's case. On the desk in front of him was a half-eaten bologna sandwich he'd brought from home in a greasy brown paper bag. He was tearing the brown paper bag into small perfectly aligned strips as we talked. He lined the strips up carefully in a row.

"She's delusional," he said, focusing on his design. "Like the rest of them, she's around the bend. Irreversible damage, psycho. That type of thing."

He realigned the strips of paper.

He was a big man and it struck me that he must have been quite handsome. His dark, once-alert gaze was now peevish and hooded, a mean bloated squint. Today he'd softened this squint with a large pair of black-rimmed bifocals canted down the bridge of his nose. I'd noticed once, following him down a prison corridor, that he walked with a side-to-side sway, like a bear. He was like a bear in a cage, harassed, as he saw it, by disturbed caged desperate females. I'd also noticed once, sitting in his office, a very raunchy porno magazine peeking out from under a stack of intake files. He preferred passive willing fuckable fantasy women, I suspected. Instead, all day long he got something else: bigmouthed combative troubled bitches, used to making men pay hard cash on the line for each ride on the pony. If they called a man Slick or Sugar, if they put their tongues and other parts to sex-work—it was, and had always been, just a contemptuous rendering of service. What their bodies accomplished was not seen as affection or even recreation. It was cash, a dime bag, a meal, a place to live, protection. Sex was a way to keep alive.

It was clear to me that Bognal wasn't going to help much, but I nonetheless asked another question or two about Polly. His information on her was less complete than Aliganth's—and he told me that his final opinion was that she was "unsalvageable."

I stared at him, taking in that word. *Unsalvageable.* He looked up from his line of paper strips and grimaced at me. I thought of deserted ships, of sinking hope, a dark hold below deck—I thought of someone, an indistinct figure, in the hold, or outside, in the sea, drowning, reaching out for a spar. *Unsalvageable.*

"So whaddya want from me?" he asked.

We sat across from each other at a scratched-up table in the Day Room. The TV was on, low volume—the *Flintstones* theme song filled the air. *Yabba-dabba-doo.* There was only one other inmate in the Day Room, sitting at one of the other multicolored tables, and she was nodding out on Thorazine and mumbling about what she had had for lunch. "They got that corn salad with them little bitty red things in it, uummhumm . . ." There was graffiti everywhere—scratched on the walls and the table and chairs with forks or bobby pins: Death Mamba and Cola, Touch Up and Number 9. Sweet Baby, 6-Pack, Love Tunnel, Princess-You-Got-It. The stove and the refrigerator bore OUT OF ORDER signs, also touched up by graffiti.

C.O. Janson stood by for a few minutes, then got bored and went off to shoot the breeze with the C.O. on duty.

Polly sat before me with her hands folded and the same odd radiant smile on her face. I noticed that her hands shook a little, then they stopped.

"Polly, I would like to ask you some questions about yourself. I'm interested in what you said in class the other night about Mark Twain."

"You mean my great-granddaddy."

"Yes," I said. "Yes. Your great-granddaddy, Mr. Twain. Samuel Clemens."

"You know his family name used to be Clement?" she said. "Like mine. You know what you asked us to write about? Where I Come From?"

She was suddenly extremely animated.

"My people are from New Orleans, colored on my side. Samuel come to New Orleans as a riverboat pilot—on the Mississippi?—and had what we call a dalliance with my great-grandmother, who took the name Clement as hers. Since it was his, passed down. Now mine. His blood come up through me. His voice—I got that too. And I got his books and his memories stored in my head, just as sure as if they happened to me. He speaks through me. I proudly bear his name. Though my great-grandmamma was a just-freed slave when he took up with her. It was before the Civil War. She was a whore. Prettiest whore in New Orleans. She had asked her master to be free to go on ahead and set up in Louisiana. And she more regal than any queen. She didn't call herself a high-yella Nigra, as they might say down there; she called herself a woman of means. And Samuel was a dashing man, a captain, you know. Clement was the name of his ancestors in England. They were earls. So she up and become a Clement—she said they were married in a whorehouse way. Anyway, she wrote all this down, his line-age—in the Whorehouse Bible. Where she kept her thoughts. And Samuel Clement signed his name, his new American name, Samuel Langhorne Clemens, in that Bible. His name is right there for all to see."

"Do you have this Bible with you?"

"Alas. See, I come here on a raft and I couldn't risk carrying it with me."

"Where is it now?"

She winked at me. The burn on the side of her face appeared to glow.

"I stowed it safely away, where I can find it if I need to."

She smiled at me and sat up straighter.

"That Bible full of sayings she and the other whores wrote down on the edges of the pages. Like 'Blessed is Jesus who never casts the first stone.' And 'Blessed are the whores whose legs slide open like the Gates of Heaven.' "

I didn't know what to say to this, so I smiled at her encouragingly. "Tell me more."

"So my great-grandmother took up his name. And then he left— the War was coming. They'd already fired on Fort Sumter. He had to get out. They turned all the riverboats around in New Orleans and sent them back up the river. And my great-grandmother honored what he gave her—and she made him ours."

The penguin-type at the next table cried, "Get them M&M's with the peanuts in Commissary? Y'all hear me? Red 'n' yellow?"

"I see things," Polly said, speaking louder now. "And I see my great-granddaddy all the time, he watches over me. And I see . . ."

She leaned closer to me and I drew back from her involuntarily.

". . . inside things. Deep inside. Right before I get the spells."

"You mean seizures? Epileptic seizures?"

"They used to call them fits. Julius Caesar, born with a caul like me, he had spells. They called it the Royal Disease back then. And just about when I have them, everything is quiet and everything is clear and I get a rainbow sliding in, wrapping itself around my brain."

She began to tremble a little, alarmingly.

"Are you all right, Polly? Should I call the C.O.?"

"I'm all right. I ain't near that lightning now, Teacher. But I see *you,* I see inside you. Forgive me, Teacher, I can't help it."

I couldn't resist, of course.

"What do you see?"

"You not happy staying with those who love you. You don't let people love you—why is that? You say you want one thing, then you turn up wantin' another."

I stared at her shifting, altering face, the mouth moving quickly.

"Why?" I asked stupidly.

"Because," she said. "There's one thing from before still on your mind. Floatin' there. It's like the Christian Bible say—No rest for the wicked!"

I saw my mother standing in the sun, her hand fluttering nervously—her mouth moving with that quote.

"But you ain't been bad, Teacher, you ain't been bad. Anyway, like the whores say, 'No rest for the wicked, but better the Wicked than the Holier-Than-Thou!' They the ones snore righteous, then get up and sign death warrants!"

She smiled her unnerving smile again. I was getting used to it now and it seemed kinder suddenly, a more genuine smile. She was slowing down a bit.

"I see where you going," she said. "But you can't go there for your Mama. You must go your way for yourself."

She sat back in her chair, relaxed now, twirling a strand of her white hair.

"Of course there ain't no difference now a'tween him and me. He tells me what he wish to say and I say it. He just said to me this about jail: First American jailbirds was patriots. Convenient to keep 'em locked up. Now it's convenient to lock up the ones we want to forget."

She chuckled. I touched her hand, which was trembling again. How could it be that she was repeating the same quotes I'd been hearing inside my head?

I was conscious then of C.O. Janson back on the case, moving closer to see if anything material had passed between us. Pills, a nail file. *She is most likely gone crazy,* I thought. *Like Billie Dee.*

"So you memorized just about everything that he wrote? How did you manage that? It's amazing."

She looked puzzled, then smiled at me again.

"I told you. He speaks through me."

I shook my head at her.

"Polly," I said. "You don't have to say that."

She looked around suddenly, as if she were seeing the Day Room, the Women's House, for the first time, surprise on her face.

"Did I ever tell you"—she kept smiling at me as she spoke—"how much time I spent on North Brother Island? Upriver from this island here? You can travel there by raft, but you got hell to go."

When I didn't respond, she stopped smiling for a second.

"I ain't told nobody. But it's Where I Come From More Recent, and I'll give you the shadow of it, if you listen close."

"I'm listening," I said. "To every word you say."

*L*ater that day I sat down opposite Albert Cantwell, the head of the Columbia University graduate writing program. He was a kind-looking gentleman, an academic of the old gracious doomed school—in a bow tie with a Phi Beta Kappa tie clip and ruddy cheeks.

"Tell me, Miss Mattox—I've read your lovely book of poems—but let's review, where have you taught before? I believe I received a copy of your résumé, but I hope you don't mind my asking for an extra?"

I handed him a second copy of my résumé.

"I've taught at the New School and N.Y.U.," I said. "Poetry and fiction workshops. And now I teach at Rikers Island."

He looked up from the xeroxed pages.

"Rikers Island? Do you mean the prison?"

"Yes," I said. "The prison. I'm learning quite a lot teaching there. At the Women's House."

"The Women's House," he repeated. "That's a prison as well?"

"Yes, it's a prison for women—detained and sentenced," I said.

"Well," he said. "We'll have to give you extra points for bravery."

He looked at the attachments to my résumé.

"Oh yes, look here," he said. "I see you have a dazzling recommendation from Baylor Drummond. Very impressive, Miss Mattox. He rarely writes recommendations. He mentioned that his friend Samuel Glass—the editor of the journal *Samizdat*? Do you know him?—asked him to speak for you."

*S*am Glass tried to kiss me and I turned just slightly away. We were standing under the Washington Square Park arch that same day, as it turned to evening. Sam Glass wanted to kiss me, and for the first time, I began to think about kissing him back. Then shook myself awake and pulled away. I had come from my job interview at Columbia to the *Sam* offices to tell him off, to order him to stay out of my life, out of my attempt to make sense of my life. If I applied for a job, I wanted to know that I got it on my own steam. Our argument about whose business was whose (his right to do what he had a right to do, plus where was my gratitude? after all, he'd offered me a vote of confidence in my work, et cetera) had somehow ended up here. After an hour or so of shouting and intense talk at a wobbly table in the dark and smoky Cedar Tavern, we'd washed up under the historic arch in the heart of the Village.

"What," he murmured, "are we going to do about this?"

"Listen," I said, pulling away again. "I have four brothers. Men don't impress me."

"So? I have three sisters. Women don't impress me—that is, if you think there is some kind of mystery attached to secondary sex characteristics."

"Mystery. That's just it. Romance obscures what's really going on."

N.Y.U. students passed us on their way to evening classes, arm in arm, carrying books. There were the usual background scents of dope and body oils, vetiver, attar of rose, musk—and the new scent, Rain—and someone was playing a guitar on the other side of the park past the fountain, the strummed bass rose and fell, and then a clear ethereal heartbreaking Joni Mitchell–like voice sang Leonard Cohen's "Suzanne."

And you want to travel with her, and you want to travel blind . . .

"I used to talk to my mother candidly about my sexual feelings as I was growing up," said Sam.

"You talked to your mother about sex?"

"Sure—it was a very open household—everybody said what was on their minds."

I thought back to the Golds', their dinner table, their animated candor.

Sam Glass put his arm around me again.

"You don't have to overthink this, you know. And you don't have to underthink. Try to stay alert."

We stood there, swaying in place, trying to stay alert, as the wavering soprano voice sang on about the seduction of traveling blind, of boats going by on the river, of tea and oranges that came all the way from China. And trust—yes, trust between women and men. What an idea! So why did Sam Glass's arm, draped casually around my shoulders, feel light and tender and also like an eight-hundred-pound weight?

When Sam Glass was in Tangiers, he met everyone in the world. He developed a coterie. He was an uncommonly talented editor, he was a poet—and when he founded *Samizdat West,* all of his international writer friends sent work for publication.

Overnight he was a literary sensation—overnight everyone wanted to publish in his pages—and he was invited to all the parties. Besides the water-softener heiress, he acquired other devoted patrons. When other literary magazines were struggling, printed in basements with stapled binding—*Sam* was laid out on elegant paper with perfect binding and hand-set type. It was distributed by a major distributor, and it actually turned a profit.

I fancied myself a woman who was not impressed by men, but Sam Glass's chutzpah and editorial acuity impressed me. And his ready sexuality hypnotized me. Made me oddly passive. I wasn't even sure I liked Sam Glass—but I couldn't seem to shake free of him.

"I have to go," I said.

"No you don't," he said. "Stay for a while."

We lingered under the arch as lights came on in the great literary neighborhood before us: in the redbrick Washington Square town houses, in the trees, and in streetlamps marching straight up Fifth Avenue, straight up the blocks Henry James walked, and Mark Twain, and Marianne Moore—right before us, as we lingered there, almost kissing.

Somehow or other I got Aliganth to tell the workshop, very hesitantly and sketchily, about Where She Sort of Came From: about how she had worked at the old Women's House in the West Village. She'd filled us in on prison history. Prison history from her point of view.

"It was hell on stilts," she roared. "All them bitches yelling out of windows. Standing on the toilets with they big mouth out the bars, out them little bar-windows—calling to pimps, johns, hippies, tourists, lurkabouts, you got it, from up there on the floors."

It *had* been hell on stilts. I'd done my research at the Jefferson Park

Library, just around the corner from the old Women's House, another red tower on a corner, a Big Ben clock in its brow. I lived a block or two away, and on Saturday morning, before I went to Balducci's to browse among the fresh sun-ripened tomatoes and vivid green basil and parsley and the little cracked pale frescoes of pecorino and Romano (I was not exactly learning to cook, but grazing around the subject), I sat in the stacks and read some local history.

"We had ladies crowded in, near hangin' from the rafters. You all got it *good* out here on the Island! You hear me 'bout that?"

As Aliganth talked on, I envisioned the old Women's House of Detention standing at the crossroads of Village Square. Greenwich and Sixth and Eighth and Christopher all ran together there. What it must have been like! It was Village history for my notebook: the crossed streets filled with tourists and shoppers heading for the Eighth Street Bookstore or Jefferson Market or Balducci's. Ten copies of Abbie Hoffman's hot-off-the-press book (*Steal This Book!*) blazing in a window. Prosciutto in paper-thin slices and brown sexual figs in a bright red woven basket. Hippies from all over America, buying Zig-Zag rolling papers and penny candy and copies of the *Voice* to read Nat Hentoff and Jill Johnston and Alexander Cockburn. Cream and Hendrix swirling up air shafts. Gay men cruising up and down Christopher. The Village Fairy with his/her tutu and sparkling wand, six feet tall, bare hairy legs, on roller skates. Couples eating outsize ice cream cones with rainbow sprinkles. Comics. Dr. Brown's soda. Egg creams. The Village smell of restaurants and hot dog vendors and patchouli oil and the drifting blue hempy stink of joints. Power to the People.

Then Aliganth described what it was like for the inmates looking out between the peeling maroon-painted bars, looking down on all that carnival atmosphere, the smells wafting up, the music spiraling higher, the longhairs in capes and jeans and top hats. Six hundred women in a space built for four hundred. I thought about those hot

Village nights, ten P.M. and still eighty degrees, a slice of orange moon over the buildings—and those voices unwinding from the blood-colored tower, the jammed-to-the-rafters redbrick tower. What it felt like, Aliganth let everyone sense it—standing on tiptoe on a broken toilet seat while someone at ankle level tried to push you out of the way as you gulped down the quick sparkling night air, the heat—wild, caged, shouting down, hoarse, to the gawkers below, faces upturned:

"How's it hangin', Ray Dan?"

"Sherifa, you need to call my sister!"

"Who bringin' bail? You got bail? You got a dime bag?"

"Hey daddy, you need a slow hand?"

And Aliganth: "Those were the days, ladies. Y'all think hard about the roaches and rats they had *there*. You could saddle 'em and ride 'em—and loudmouths screamin' out the tower all night! You gonna tell *me* about lunatic asylums?"

Number Ten Greenwich Avenue. Later, after the workshop, I walked west and stared at the empty building, Romanesque Revival, redbrick, for a long while. I thought I could hear the ghostly voices, the screams and lengthening shouts. But the voices were gone, transferred—ferried across the Queensboro Bridge, out through the borough streets and across the water to the new holding center, where the voices, they hoped, would be silenced. It was far far away, it was not the Tombs of Manhattan or the old Women's House of D. It was modern, antiseptic, automated. It was an island. In a fast mean lit-up river. The planes flew over nonstop. But the plan had failed. *There was no way,* I thought, *they could ever silence those voices.*

For the moment, I turned to thank Aliganth, who bowed oddly, formally, to us all, then straightened up again. She nodded at me to continue teaching the workshop. She looked a little less annoyed than usual. Being listened to as a storyteller rather than a lock-and-key jockey seemed to have made her gentler.

"Polly wants to talk to us about something," I said. "She told me about her time on North Brother Island. She told me that she was there, on the island, for several weeks. She's going to tell us about it as her Where I Come From, okay?"

Aliganth settled herself at her post near the door. I looked up, but she just nodded, mildly. She was not going to give me or Polly trouble about this, I thought with relief. She was looking nostalgic, sentimental—in other words, not like C.O. Aliganth.

I smiled at Polly, who waited expectantly, nodding nervously.

"Okay, Polly is going to talk about how she lived in this place. She wants to write a poem about it, and she wants us to help her write it. Most of us don't even know where North Brother Island is—right in the middle of a busy river next to the busiest city in the world: a deserted island."

There was some mumbling and fidgeting, but overall, the response was good. Even Gene/Jean, who was back in class, looking a bit pale, a bit medicated, seemed cheerful about tuning in. Gene grinned at me, ran her index finger around her lips, made a kissy-face, then stroked her goatee, still smiling at me.

"Hold that thought, Gene," I said.

I nodded at Polly and she straightened up and folded her hands in front of her, as if she were about to recite something from memory.

"North Brother Island," she said, smiling at everyone, "lies, as the crow flies, just southwest of Hunt's Point in the East River. It don't pretend to be a big brassy island—it might be anywhere from thirteen to twenty-some acres. Modest as islands go. Now it turned into a sanctuary for birds—all kinds of birds, wading birds and herons, cormorants, and great egrets and snowy egrets. They're very, very noisy, those birds, but damn industrious."

She paused and looked around her. Everyone was listening, startled by the odd way that Polly was speaking.

"But there no humans on the island. You might say it's been deserted—maybe even by ghosts! But there are buildings there, hospitals and doctors' houses and a lighthouse and docks. All empty and falling down. All the clocks stopped around 1954. That was when the City closed the big old hospital there—the cornerstone says 1886. North Brother Island was the place where they brought the poor souls with TB and smallpox and typhoid fever and scarlet fever—to the contagious hospitals. Typhoid Mary had herself a bed there."

She glanced around again.

"You may recognize that name," she said to their uncertain faces. "She was there in the early nineteen hundreds. And you'd swear that time had stopped then. All the beds and furniture still in the hospitals—old-fashioned washstands and little old candlesticks. All left behind. Gas lamps along the cobblestones."

Roxanne looked up suddenly from doodling on her tablet.

"Why was it deserted?"

"They didn't need it anymore for TB and such. Then they put in the opium eaters and all in the nineteen fifties. But then there was no more money. They just closed it down and left. There are vines growing over everything, over the brick and cobblestones, over the old docks. And there's rats, some the size of dogs."

"How you get there, and why you stay there?" This from Sallie.

"I arrived on a raft, and I—"

"You sayin' you come over them currents in the river on a *raft*? Child, you plannin' drag us this line?"

"Let her talk," I said.

Aliganth cleared her throat.

"Then let her come to a point soon," Aliganth said.

"Okay, so you come on a raft. Now you tell me how you keep yourself alive and store up whoppers to tell on that island!" Sallie added.

"I come on a raft, yes, ma'am. The currents were awful, high wind all the way. But I hauled up on the crumbling dock and I ended up staying on. I found a way into the old lighthouse keeper's house—there used to be a tower on top with the light eight sides. The light's gone and the tower, but the house is still hospitable, in its way. All I'll say more is this: I fetched up, I made a fire, I boiled water. There were rusty pots and pans and spoons and forks. I found many eggs from all the birds. I apologized to them for takin' their offspring. But I was hungry every day. I found edible greens and I even caught a fish or two. The river was good to me."

Gene made a sound. She stared longingly at Polly.

"Would you be my wife? Or could you suck my dick?"

"Shut up, Gene," I said. "Please."

Aliganth shook her keys.

"Keeley: ease back, you hear me?"

"Jesus," whispered Darlene. "Jesus."

Polly smiled at Gene.

"You are a fine-fangled gentleman," she said. "But I'm not amorous."

Gene looked confused, a more or less typical look.

"Gene," I said again. "Think estrogen. In other words: *think.*"

"Gene," said Sallie. "Think Sallie Keller whup your ass."

"I apologize for my eruptions," Gene said, nodding to everyone, then burped softy and looked away, petulant, chastened, pulling her goatee. I glanced at Darlene to see if she was still running her prayer, and she was: silently, lips barely moving.

"I'd like to write a poem about living there on the island. About living with all the birds, under the sky—"

"Well, there's your poem," said Baby Ain't. " 'Living on the island, living with the birds under the sky'—it soundin' good! Just like a song there."

"Write it down," I said. "You're making this poem together."

"Eatin' birds," Gene contributed.

"She didn't say she eatin' *birds,*" shouted Sallie. "She say she eatin' birds' *eggs*. After the sky part, you could put in about eatin' the eggs."

"And rats big as dogs," added Never, shuddering. Darlene, praying silently, shuddered too.

"Honey, you ain't seen the rats *here* yet? Where you been? They so big they eat *you*," Baby Ain't laughed.

Roxanne laughed too and added, sotto voce, "Yeah, and they all wear uniforms."

Aliganth stuck her ear in then, trying to hear better, but to no avail—as the class began rustling industriously, pulling out tablets, writing down the first lines.

"This a weird poem," said Sallie. "But I'm goin' to say how she set there all alone, makin' up stories."

"Me too," cried Gene. "I'm getting' in about her eatin' rats."

Never moved her chair away from Gene and looked at Polly.

"What else do you want to say?"

"I want to say that you can get there. Any of you can get there. From here, from Rikers Island. That's all."

"Sharks eat you up," Billie Dee said.

Sallie laughed. "Ain't no sharks in the East River. But you got such bad pull—you put your toe in, it *bent backwards*."

"But it can be done," said Polly Lyle. " 'Cause I done it—I rode that river and I'm here to tell."

Aliganth jangled her keys. Then I noticed that Akilah, who had said nothing and had been staring at Polly, had opened her eyes wide.

"You could put that in too," she said. "About getting there. How you got there, and survived."

"I got a question for you, girl." It was Sallie again. "Where you come from? In the first place?"

Polly's hands began trembling again, ever so slightly, I noticed.

"I come from the river. My people are all from New Orleans, so

I'm upriver North just a strong wind from my home, I know. I travel where my great-granddaddy went before. Like he said, I reckon I got to light out for the territory ahead of the rest. Like the Whorehouse Bible say, 'Blessed are those who come quick and leave faster.' "

Baby Ain't looked up and laughed out loud, but Darlene popped awake and sat up suddenly, furious, squinting, and shook her finger at Polly.

"If you speak of whores and the Holy Book in the same breath, you blaspheming against God himself—and against Our Precious Lord!"

Then she bowed her head quickly and started up the Jesus prayer again—building her familiar wall.

"Wait."

Polly touched Darlene's hand and then reached out and lifted her chin. Darlene twisted away from her, but her expression was startled up: even more awake. Then she looked frightened. I sensed Aliganth straightening up too.

"Wait," I heard myself echoing Polly. "Forget trying to solve this argument, okay?"

I glanced sideways at Aliganth. How had the class slid again so quickly into anarchy? I called to Polly again but she ignored me and continued speaking to Darlene directly, still trying to look into her eyes.

"Well, everybody know Jesus took a shine to easy-natured ladies—and saved a Fallen Woman from stoning by the horde of Holy and Righteous, but what about further back even: the story of Ruth and Naomi? When Ruth's husband died and she traveled to a new country—her two daughters-in-law, also widows, came with her, re-member? And one of them was Naomi, who said to Ruth, 'Whither thou goest I will go.' Now everybody think some woman deep in love said that to a man—but no. That was said by a daughter to a mother. So when they arrived in a strange country and they had barely a place to live—what did Ruth say to Naomi? She say, 'Hey, you know Boaz, who works down on the floor where they thresh the wheat?—he's got some years on him, but he's a fine man. Why don't you just drop down there, dressed up, after hours, and lay yourself down on the bed where he sleeps after work. Wear your good dress and also your pretty shawl.' Naomi did what Ruth told her—and when Boaz went to bed, he found a beautiful young woman there holding out her shawl, saying: 'Fill me up.' "

Darlene crossed herself and held up her hands.

"You saying now that Naomi and Ruth were whores?"

"I'm saying that Boaz fell in love with a woman so bold as to show up in his bed—and, in fact, he was the one who said, 'Hold out your shawl: I will fill it with wheat.' "

Baby Ain't chortled: "Hold wide, hot-pants—I got some Wheaties for you! *Sugar-coat.*"

"Listen," said Polly. "There ain't no blasphemy to say that Naomi fell in love and opened her—shawl—to a man who could love her right."

A strange look crossed her face.

"And you married a bastard jackass—a man so fearing of love as to beat you senseless."

Aliganth, standing now just behind my chair: "Clement. We all heard enough now of your preachin'. You listenin', Clement?"

Polly shook her head. "Just one more thing. You love Jesus, then you know a way to live—he said whoever give someone thirsty a cup of cold water in my name, that's the way. A little water in a cup. That's all."

Darlene pointed a finger again at Polly.

"Who are you? Say who you are! I believe you come from Satan!"

"Truth is, I'm a seer," said Polly mildly. "I get fits, and I can look into the Now and the To-Come. I can see into you, one by one. See what is past and what to be."

She smiled at the circle of faces, all rapt except for Darlene, who had started repeating her Jesus prayer again. I noted particularly Akilah's face. She was staring at Polly, startled and amazed, as if Polly had unfurled the wide wings of an earth-hopping angel, then soared aloft.

"And I seen many river accidents in my dreams, and real ones too, so I would like the river to do some good. Real good. So I say: Blessed are those who ride the current what would ride them. Blessed are those who ride hard against the pull. That's what I say."

North Brother Island

I lived under the sky
With the birds but I didn't eat them.
I lived wild with ten rats! Gene, I ate
Eggs from my wing-friends. Fly me!
Fly me! I'm Billie Dee! No people left,
Empty hospitals and ambulances and the wreck
Lighthouse. I caught a fish because I figured how.
Why do you make up lies? Ask Old Man God—
he tells some real whoppers! No, no, God is good.
Listen now to Jesus. Here comes Jesus and the Jesus Police!
Step in that river it play you for a fool. Typhoid Mary
Killed folks by cooking for them. Always boil water
And wear a hat. I never killed no one. I built the raft, set it
in the water and when the waves got worse, I dreamed him
at the wheel of the riverboat. Harbor captains sailed
in the Bay of the Brothers for one hundred years.
The river will swallow you if you don't watch your ass.
If you alive you got a smell. Gene/Jean look & smell like a goat.
This goat turn you into hot poontang and baa like a sheep!
There was a terrible crash on the island. Fly me, I'm Billie Dee!
I lived on North Brother Island so long I thought I'd never sail
back like a chime, into the stop-clock, still run by Time.
I never killed no one. Jesus already said that. Just ask our Lord!
No, Marx said it first. Child, the Whorehouse Bible say it best. You
Ride, ride the stop-clock, ride the River whenever you please.

—POLLY LYLE CLEMENT, POET

(IN COLLABORATION WITH THE WORKSHOP POETS)

six

I was at home with K.B. on a sunny-bright Saturday morning, looking up some street phrases and drug terms for an upcoming AfterCare meeting on counseling, and checking a New York City Department of Correctional Services guide just to keep myself current on what rules I might be breaking. K.B. was on the phone with a nervous intern, talking him through an E.R. complication, looking at his watch as he talked. He too was due at a meeting— at the hospital. He opened and shut the living room window blinds on bright sun as he talked, so that his profile was lit then shadowed, lit then shadowed.

The Glossary of Drug Users' Slang had its own pharmaceutical and social poetry, twinning in my mind with K.B.'s instructions to the intern on administering blood thinners (heparin IV, stat) and how to "keep the patient comfortable. He was close to V-fibbing last night."

I turned the pages of the Glossary:

BLUE HEAVENS: sodium amytal tablets
BLUE VELVET: paregoric and pyribenzamine
BOMBITAS: Desoxyn, methamphetamines (Little Bombers)
BOOT: An autoerotic masturbatory experience: feeding blood back and forth into the works once the heroin is partially injected into the vein, to obtain a more lasting effect
CHIP: a small habit, using drugs only on weekends

CRACK A CRIB: burglarize a home
CRACK A SHORT: burglarize a car
MACKMAN: pimp

I heard K.B. hang up the phone, then open the hall closet door, looking for his jacket.

"It's in the bedroom closet," I called out, and he laughed distract-edly and thanked me. He found the jacket, picked up his bag, kissed me on the lips, and was halfway out the door when I spoke again.

"I love you," I shouted, and I heard him pause in the doorway. He turned and came back inside, then put his bag down and knelt at my side as I sat at my makeshift desk in the living room. I had made a de-cision. I wasn't going to play with fire, Sam Glass fire, anymore. I loved K.B. and I didn't want to hurt him. I felt powerful guilt about the little tango I'd been dancing with Sam Glass so far.

"I love you too," he said. Sirens and car horns sang out suddenly from Sixth Avenue. "Don't forget that, okay?"

We kissed again and then he was gone. I turned back to the New York City Correctional Institution for Women's Guide for Inmates.

"I love you, Kenny," I repeated, whispering, and I meant it. I loved him with all my conflicted heart. I loved him, but deep inside I knew that I did not want to be a wife. It was as if I'd married a friend—we were friends, the two of us. I was content to think we'd be together al-ways: in my mind at the time this made sense. Two friends—or brother and sister. Not a wife. The day before our wedding in Min-nesota, I had been sick with doubt, sleepless. I'd gone to K.B. and told him I didn't think I could go through with the wedding. I told him that the marriage idea had been too impulsive—or maybe not so impulsive. I'd had the idea before, I admitted, but I hadn't concen-trated on the contract: a signed document that bound us legally. He held both my hands in his. *It's just nerves,* he said. Nerves. *And nerves are my specialty,* he said. *We'll go through with it—it will be just for us. Nobody else.* I agreed at the time. But thinking back, I wasn't sure to what each of us thought we were agreeing. I put my head in my hands. Nothing in my life made sense to me, so I turned back to the rules of a strictly ordered society:

LINEN–Your allotment is: 1 mattress, 1 pillow, 1 pillowcase, 2 sheets, 2 blankets, 1 gown, 1 bath towel, 1 washcloth, 1 floor mat, 1 bedspread. EXCESS LINEN IS CONTRABAND. Once weekly you must clean your bed, mattress, and pillow. Linen will be collected from your room, laundered, and returned—CHECK IT. It should have machine sewn hems, no holes, burn marks, or embroidery. Report any irregularity to the officer BEFORE YOU USE IT. Do not tear linen or use it as floor coverings or cleaning cloths.

Or, I thought, with sudden melancholy foreboding, *as a noose.* I flipped the page, then turned from the inmate guide and the street drug glossary to notes for a poem I'd been working on.

I'd written:

River, East River. Sixteen miles of saltwater ring. Silver estu-ary flooding the famous page: Opening lines of Moby-Dick—or Walt Whitman singing, crossing Brooklyn Ferry. River of Houdini unchaining himself underwater. River of mob infor-mants dropped straight down in cement booties. Stretching from the Upper Bay to the Sound and through to the open sea south of Long Island. Atlantic tides shuddering round the is-lands. River of the Brothers: North and South. River of Randalls Island, Wards Island (where the mad were kept), Governors Island (haunted by ghosts), Hart Island (where the dead poor, those with no money to pay for a space for their bod-ies to lie, are buried). River of Rikers Island, Cellblock Isle— and just past it—the floating miraculous city. River of the Island of Manhattan, its illuminated script of skyline there in

the Passage, *its waves of burning Bright. River of the Twain,*
as the twain is marked: two fathoms—twelve feet, twelve feet
down.

Twin Cities, I wrote, *I come from Twin Cities*—and just like that
(the way a poem happens!) I leaped from the East River to the Mississippi.

I come from Twin Cities, where
the river between, surging, stands.

And that was as far as I could get. I tried again:

I believed once that what I called desire

What is desire? I wondered. *"I believed once that what I called desire"*—longing for someone, something fulfilling? What was desire and what did it have to do with the river which, surging, stood? *Flowed in that confluence,* I thought, of two things—two souls, two opposite beings who are nevertheless twinned. *Flowed in that confluence between . . . twins.* I jotted this down, then dropped my pen. Ambivalence, ambivalence: nothing certain—except departure and return, like waves.

I opened the inmate guide again and consulted their glossary of in-house lingo:

boosting: shoplifting, stealing
bulldagger: homosexual woman, butch
dragging, playing drag: conning, getting over
flatback: prostitute
jostling: picking pockets
juggling paper: writing bad checks
rap sheet: history of arrests and parole violations

I wrote:

> capitol and columned future. I come from
> twin cities: Dark and Light. But the river . . .

Then leaped again—to yet another water passage—the Red River, which flooded, unexpectedly, the page.

> *My mother and father came from the Red River Valley, the legendary Red River Valley—where the river flows, perversely (against geographic expectation) straight north, where the soil is loam and clay, sixty feet down. Where farmers and cowboys lived as neighbors, but far away from each other, isolated by the great distances of the plains, by the great grieving winds, the open distances of the reservation lands of the Chippewa and Sioux. The tunes of the cowboys, the prairie dog banjo notes and the soulful cornball yodeling, flowed into the music of the farmers— Swedish, Norwegian, Czech, or German—oompah polkas, the flatulence of brass. Danube waltzes and schottisches, the high-pitched fiddles, and finally, simple-as-breath singing—pure laments, the bitter twang of defeat and lonesomeness: "Hard times, come Ye again no more" and "We do not live, we only stay / We are too poor to get away." And the cowboy chorus about someone who did get away: "Come and sit by my side ere you leave me / Do not hasten to bid me adieu / But remember the Red River Valley / And the cowboy who loved you so true." Muted sound of Native American voices, the chants and drums on the wind near the Dakota borders. All of this sung history was passed down to me—plus what adults sang in groups, around pianos: "Beautiful beautiful brown eyes / Beautiful beautiful brown eyes / I'll never love blue eyes again!" Church choirs, prairie gospel . . . "The Soul Never Dies!" in tandem with church Latin, the sweet warbling Panis Angelicus and the*

off-key Bach, Gregorian chants: O Salutaris Hostia, Tantum
Ergo, and the minor-chord echoing Dies Irae, a song about
Judgment Day, sung at funerals. A thin-faced nun conduct-
ing the children, rehearsing the funeral liturgy, her round sil-
ver pitch pipe grasped tightly, flashing in sudden bolts of
garish colored light shot through the stained glass windows of
the sacristy.

I remember the nun silencing the warbled refrains with a
downward sweep of her hand as she asked me to sing a pas-
sage. I stood up and set the pattern of dark minor-key punctu-
ation of plainchant in my mind, breathed deeply and opened
my mouth.

Dies irae, dies illa, I sang. Day of Wrath, Day of Ire. Day of
Judgment, Day of Fire. Our souls will be burned by an angry
God, in judgment, in hell. I sang on till her bony hand swept
down again, cutting off my voice. Behind me, my pal Signe
Skoglund sang in a small froggy rebellious counterpoint: "Ten
thousand Svedes ran through the veeds / Chased by one Norve-
gian!" and someone (Wendell Moosbacher?) further back be-
hind her offered a series of tubalike farting noises.

I paused and stared into space for a few minutes. Was I writing a
long poem or the story of my life?

For my parents' generation, the most ridiculed state was ig-
norance. The worst thing, to be dumb—there were dumb im-
migrants and dumb Swedes, dumb oafs and dumb farmers.
Dumb was slack-jawed, dull-eyed, slow-to-speech. Smart was
learning, smart was erudition, but not pretentious, self-
congratulatory, "showy" learning—rather passionate love of
books and the well-turned phrase. The prairie love of pure elo-
quence. And humor—humor was smart: sly and surprising. For
example, there was my uncle Gene Klostermann—an unlikely

wit and bon vivant, yet there he was. He lived just outside the little town of Wyndmere, where my mother had been born—on a dairy farm with his family.

I remember visiting their farm when I was around twelve. Sipping lemonade, prodded by my mother, I asked him politely how things were in Wyndmere. He grinned at me. He was very fair, but the back of his grizzled neck was sunburned scarlet.

"Well, see here, that's the thing, Holly Ann. Things have been goin' so well in Wyndmere that they had to go and shoot somebody to start a graveyard!"

He tipped his hat at me and winked. Aunt Marie chuckled and stirred more sugar into the lemonade. Earlier, I'd downed a glass of milk straight from the stanchioned rows of swollen udders, milk tasting of green green grass. I looked at my mother, alarmed, but she put her index finger to her temple and smiled.

"He's kidding, Holly Ann," she said. "The whole family's either dumb as fence-posts or they're smart alecks."

Uncle Gene winked again. "Now, you got a distant cousin, Ole—so dumb he once pulled over to the side of the road in his jalopy because he said he'd been driving with a busted cloud over his head."

"Trying to say it was about to rain," my mother added.

"He sounds like a poet to me," I offered, trying to ally myself with the smart-aleck branch of the family. "I mean: the busted cloud. That's poetic."

They all stared at me.

"No," said Uncle Gene. "Wish that was true. Poor Ole was just dumb-ox dumb and had a rear end five axe-handles across."

I understood why he needed to be funny out there in Wyndmere, out there on the plains. Somehow the obsessions of people with the internal workings of their John Deere tractors, with

*their grain silos, milkers, and Grange feed stores, led to danger-
ous humorless nonstop obsession with the Government or God.
Obsession with the Government's attempt to stanch the eco-
nomic bloodbath on the plains, welfare payments to those who
would take them, called The Dole. ("Eating out of the public
trough!" my father snarled in cold contempt.) The question was
asked often and straight-faced, in my family: "How dumb are
you?"*

*It was not meant to be a rhetorical question, necessarily. I
wanted not to be dumb, I wanted to be smart the way it was
understood by my family: quick-witted and eloquent. I never
thought once about what it meant to be wise.*

I stopped writing and pondered the plight of my students behind
bars: locked up for copping a tube of lipstick, for snagging a bottle of
Rain. (*If I'd slipped a glass bottle into my pocket that day at Kiehl's—
would I be locked up?*) Women behind bars for loitering. Behind bars
for palming a nickel bag, for lifting a handful of potato chips for a
two-year-old, for blowing a pimp's head off.

I would not be locked up. I was white and educated and middle-
class. Society would provide me with all the answers. Unlike my
imagination, which asked all the questions. What I had written
would not interest society, I thought. I wasn't sure it would interest
anyone, even me.

I went back to work on my poem.

I come from twin cities: Dark and Light.

Two hours later, K.B. came in. He put his bag down, shrugged out
of his jacket, and waved. His collar and tie were pulled askew and he
sported the beginnings of a beard, red-brown five o'clock shadow.

"Have you been writing?" he asked.

"I'm dragging," I said. "Dragging the muse. Cellblock slang."

"I'm starving," he said. "Let's get dressed and go out."

"A penny for your thoughts, Holly," K.B. repeated. He laughed. "Or a cool million for the entire syntactical map."

We were dining at a French bistro in the neighborhood. I loved to go out to dinner—I loved candlelight and flowers—a glass of wine, tête-à-tête conversation. I admitted this to almost no one (*How bourgeois was I?*), but K.B. of course knew. So on his nights off, we sometimes indulged. He put on his dark brown corduroy jacket and a tie and I wore a granny dress and boots. I always thought that the waiters assumed we were brother and sister, with our long blond hair and twin nervous gestures. Brother and sister, sometimes holding hands, wrapped in intense conversation, faces candlelit.

I put down my menu. "It's just the usual," I said. "I don't know where I'm supposed to go with this class. What good is it to teach people how to write poetry or write about their lives when they're either locked up for stealing penny-ante stuff or facing life in prison? Or in the madhouse?"

"I would say that's exactly the reason to do it."

"But you *help* people—I mean, you help them in practical ways. They end up healthier, they get knowledge about medical care. You find a wheelchair for somebody, free X-rays. I try to help them find a way to express themselves—but every poem sounds like a cry for help and I can't do a damn thing."

K.B. looked tired, as always: dark circles under his eyes. He'd been up late all of the preceding week. He brushed his hair back from his eyes and nodded to the waiter. He had such quiet acuity, such grace in restraint and authority in that restraint—his family had Quaker roots. He had an uncle, a pacifist, who had stood on street corners in Sacramento in the fifties wearing PEACE and BAN THE BOMB signs, a teacher who lost his job because of his quiet protest.

When K.B. and I were married in Minnesota, this uncle, Gordon, had sent us a silver hurricane lamp and a poem by Rabindranath Tagore.

"Language," K.B. said, "words, the power to express consciousness: that's monumental in terms of the brain. And then poetry, the power to express consciousness perfectly: beyond our ability to describe neurologically. Some combination of the limbic and pure lateralization? No wonder it's considered the highest art. And in terms of the brain, a mystery."

The waiter arrived. We ordered, wine was poured.

"Here's the thing," said K.B. "I have a patient who has aphasia—you know, aphasia?" He looked inquiringly at me, over a pair of invisible spectacles.

"Post-stroke? Where the patient loses speech?" I struggled to remember what he'd told me, what he'd read to me at random from his clinical texts.

"Or ability to communicate through writing or any sign. It can be ataxic, which means motor, or sensory—or both."

"I'm not sure I remember the difference."

"In motor aphasia, patients know what they want to say but can't manage to get it out. They just can't coordinate the muscles controlling speech. With sensory, if the auditory center is involved, the patient is unable to grasp spoken words. If the visual word center is affected, we have simple visual aphasia: the patient cannot see the written word, a.k.a. word blindness."

"Word blindness," I repeated.

"And then there's a version called fluent, where the words are easily spoken by the patient but those words are incorrect and may be unrelated to the import of other words articulated. It sounds like nonsense, but with structure. Then there's optic aphasia, where a patient can recognize a thing but cannot name it—the patient has to have sound, touch, and taste all involved in order to identify anything."

The waiter brought plates of food. We barely noticed him as he set them down in front of us.

"I have a patient, a woman, who has fluent aphasia—she sounds inspired, till you really listen to what she has to say. Today she said to me something like: 'Doctor, why are the windows crying? I want to talk to you about the wings, the colors I've been waiting to break here on my shoulders.' I memorized it, because it was so wild."

"But that's poetry. She was speaking poetry."

"That is language pathology, a neurological deficit. She cannot communicate what she thinks she is actually saying."

"But maybe it's not a deficit. Maybe the stroke bumps language to a poetic plane? Maybe she is communicating perfectly—it's the rest of the world that is limited in understanding. If evolution has given us language—and if poetry is its highest expression—then as far as poetry can go represents the far edge of consciousness. A refinement through pathology—is that possible?"

"Holly—she was trying to ask for her knitted shawl, because she was cold."

K.B. smiled at me across the table, then touched me lightly under the chin with his fingertips.

"Let's eat, Holl," he said. "This is going to get cold. Speaking of cold."

"Meaning," I said, "is just something we all shake hands on. I mean static meaning, imposed meaning. Look at my mom. I can track her syntactical leaps—is she a linguistic blender, or an evolving alternative form of consciousness?"

"Holly," he said. "That's a filét of sole in front of you. There's also rice and a couple spears of asparagus. And a glass of pretty good wine. Drink up."

"Okay, K.B." I said. "Why are the windows crying?"

"Holly." He gazed into my eyes, smiling. "She's still freezing cold, she still needs that shawl. Are you going to praise her poetical aberration—or are you going to translate, and get the poor woman what she needs?"

I began to wonder if I myself were suffering from a form of aphasia—a word loss, a word disconnection or twisted desire that made me unable to confront K.B. in language, talk to him about what I was feeling. What was there in my past that made me unable to articulate what I most wanted to say?

I thought of my father—a man who spoke directly, but as a salesman, a businessman. He believed in self-reliance and industry. His looks reinforced his views. Six foot three and blue-eyed, his thick black hair turned white at thirty. He towered like a snowcapped peak.

His mother, my grandmother, looked like a mountain as well. She was untouchable, not one to hug—tall, strong-boned, with a graduate degree in education: lone teacher in a one-room Dakota schoolhouse. An angelic presence gone hard, her red-gold hair pulled back severely, her pale freckles. *"Uff da,"* said my grandmother, taking me aside in the parlor of their farmhouse and opening her family Bible to show me the frontispiece—the list running down the page. "My parents, my sisters," she noted proudly. I looked at the column of names, writ in a delicate spidery hand, then out fell a sepia photograph. She pointed to a blurred figure.

"Caroline, my mother's sister, in our town, outside of Oslo," she said. "Before the family came here.

"She wrote poems," she added, and glanced down at me. "It made her excitable. She ran outside in the dead of winter to look at the night sky—with her long hair soaking wet from her bath. She did not dry herself properly, Caroline, she ran outside! And listen here, Holly, she died of pneumonia, her little poem in her hand. *Yah, yah,* think of such a thing!"

She clucked disapprovingly, her pale brow a kind of insurmountable statement, composed. I thought of her suddenly as Plato, Plato in a housedress and apron, throwing all the poets out of the Republic for being irresponsible, for making it seem somehow intoxicating to run outdoors in glacial cold, half toweled off, wild wet hair blowing, to recite poems willy-nilly to the sky.

I stared again at the shadowed figure in the snapshot.

She's mine, I remembered thinking, secretly thrilled about the poems, the wet hair, the White Night sky. *My ancestor.*

Maybe that was it, I thought. Maybe I'd acquired the gene for *dérangement,* as in the image of the Poète Maudit. Yet somehow the decadent passions of Baudelaire or Rimbaud simmering in the DNA of my Norwegian ancestors seemed less likely than a legacy of stolidness: I was just another stiff inhibited leaf of the family tree.

But perhaps I was more an Ibsen character—a woman struggling to free herself from repression, the bonds of misogynist convention? I began to warm to this idea—perhaps this was the explanation for what seemed wrong with me. Maybe having been a misfit as a little girl was truly the basis for enlightened feminism, not a clumsy resistance to self-expression. (I hadn't noticed that I'd come full circle in my thinking.) Then I thought of my tribe of brothers and jotted down a memory:

> *"She's like a mad dog," my older brother said to my mother, looking over his shoulder scornfully yet fearfully at me. "She gets punched and kicked, but she won't let go. She gets you by the ankle and hangs on with her teeth."*
>
> *My mother set down a mixing bowl and sighed. It was a hot July day and my other brother had recently demonstrated to her that he could burp the entire alphabet in the key of G and she was not tremendously interested in this new yet familiar sibling information.*
>
> *"You let your sister play—whatever the game is," she said. " 'She has a heart too soon made glad'—so you let her play."*

She went into the pantry for more flour and I grinned horribly at my brother and held my nose. I was ten years old, skinny, with bedraggled pigtails.

"Hey, Einstein," my brother sang out, "how does it feel to be ugly beyond all human comprehension?"

"Hey, you tell me first how it feels to combine the intelligence of a concrete slab with the energy of a whippet!"

We traded quick brutal blows, silent and deadly. He grabbed my upper arm and twisted it in an Indian burn, slow and steady. I kept pummeling him with my free fist, and I did not cry out though my arm hurt a lot. I was more or less indifferent to the pain inflicted by my four brothers. I was spectacularly unpopular with the male sex, mainly because I tagged along, the lone girl, to events to which I was not invited. I was used to hockey sticks tripping me up on the skating rink, beanballs, bloody noses, my head held underwater for long counts, a long string of drool suspended above my face as I was held down, then the drool cheerfully sucked up at the last minute: I would never cry out or give up, ever.

My mother came back with the flour and my brother quickly released my arm with a final pinch and banged out through the screen door. The truth was, despite the fact that I thought my older brother was the funniest person I'd ever known—in my terrible proud heart I believed that I was smarter than my brothers, that I was stronger and braver, and I would not accept evidence to the contrary. Death was preferable, I thought, to conceding defeat.

My mother looked at me as I balanced on one foot, twirling a little, mindlessly, rubbing my arm.

"Holly Ann," my mother said, "I see a difficult life ahead for you, especially when it comes to men. You have a mouth that could stop a twenty-ton truck and a heart full of pride."

She strode to my side and took my arm—still sore, though I didn't wince—and looked into my eyes.

"*There are actually young women who think about pleasing men—who dress nicely and flatter these men and try to get along with them. If you persist in your willful stubborn and unattractive behavior—not only will men run screaming from you—if they somehow get stuck with you at some point, they may try to push you out the window, you know?*"

I looked into her wide face like mine, her light eyes like mine, and smiled.

"*Bring them on,*" *I said.*

"*Pride goeth before destruction, and an haughty spirit before a fall,*" *she quoted.* "*You know that.*"

I knew that, but I was that terrible combination, martyr and arrogant troublemaker. I had read, with the encouragement of nuns, about the virgin martyrs. For example, Saint Maria Goretti, a young Roman girl, whose fevered face floated before a kind of banner: DEATH BUT NOT SIN. I wasn't clear on what the sin was supposed to be, but I liked Maria Goretti's all-or-nothing style. I thrived on extremity. Maria had been stabbed for refusing to commit whatever sin it was. I had made her approach my own, though my motto was slightly altered: Death but Never Concede.

"*Though it's true,*" *my mother added as an afterthought (it was her afterthoughts that drove me crazy—the coda that usually contradicted what came before),* "*that I was named salutatorian at graduation. I should have been valedictorian. But that honor always went to a boy. Is that unfair? Yes. 'Wail, for the world's wrong!' And, Holly? It's men who keep it that way.*"

I found myself more confused than ever. K.B.'s shawl for the aphasic woman wasn't enough, I thought sadly, or Naomi's shawl, held out for wheat or sex, *sugar-coat*. Surely great kindness and passionate love both deserved words beyond the gesture itself. And how could I determine what anyone in the workshop needed beyond lessons in how to write a poem? Each one of my students' faces appeared before me. I found myself staring as I thought of Roxanne's megawatt smile. Just the week before, Roxanne had stopped me at the classroom door and confided in me. She'd been busted with a very famous counterculture celebrity. She'd been his date and hadn't really known what was up, she said. They'd been smoking dope, then doing lines of coke. They ended up at a party at the Chelsea Hotel, where she suddenly grasped that a major coke deal was going down. "I had no idea," she kept repeating. "I had no idea that he was carrying all that blow." The celebrity attempted to sell several grams of pure pharmaceutical cocaine to what turned out to be narcotics agents. She and the celebrity were arrested and taken away. They were both released on their own recognizance. The next thing she knew, he'd skipped town.

"He disappeared," she said, her Liza eyes wide. "Nobody knows where the fuck he is." In the wake of his disappearance, she was taken into custody again and held without bail.

"So you're the fall guy," I said, recalling a screaming newsstand headline in the *Post*.

"No," she said. "If they'd'a got him, they'd'a thrown the book at him. They were gloatin'."

"So now they're going to throw it at you?"

"Here's the thing," she whispered. "I just don't want anyone in the workshop to know who I am. He's so famous, you know? And the case has been all over the papers. My name's kind of been in the background and I want it to stay there. Plus I want to protect him, you dig? My pal X?"

"Sure," I said, without really understanding. "I won't say anything. Don't worry."

She smiled at me. "It wasn't even great blow," she said. "It was overcut with Menit, a French baby laxative. You know what I mean? Inferior shit. Must've kept those narcs fuckin' regular for a month."

She laughed for a while at her own joke. It was only after I'd left the prison that day that I realized she was probably going to turn state's evidence against her pal X, the counterculture celebrity, in order to save her own ass. And who, knowing the score, would ever fault her?

"I wrote something different than everybody else's so far," she said in the workshop. She passed out copies of her poem that she'd somehow gotten made, probably in the Social Services office.

"I wrote about astrology," she said. "The stars, you know?"

"The wilderness of stars," said Polly, sitting back and closing her eyes. "You can set sail in them stars."

"A good place to start," I said. "The wilderness of stars."

Roxanne's poem was funny. The workshop was laughing together for once, and it made me happy, even in my uncertain mood. I looked around the table at the faces—Never, Sallie, Polly, Akilah, Darlene, Gene/Jean, Baby Ain't, Billie Dee, and Roxanne—and I thought, *I'm so lucky. I thank my lucky stars that I'm here in the company of these women.* Even Akilah was laughing—I'd never even seen her whole-heartedly smile before, and now she was throwing her head back and wiping her eyes. I glanced at Aliganth, and she was smiling too.

*I*t was good that we had that moment, because the Future was preparing a little something for all of us. Those ink-black eyes staring out of the unknown (not Where We Come From but Where We Are Headed), those eyes staring back into the self as the dead stared back at those gathered around the bed weeping—in long-ago days, when pennies were placed on the eyelids of the gone. Back when a mirror was held up to the dying mouth, the hand holding the mirror trembling, the heart hopeful for a little cloud of breath on the clear surface. We also stared, and laughed, as if prison were a kind of hypnotic state and we were all just waking up from a trance. The Future could be imagined even in this stopped time, this detour around life: prison. I was not a prisoner, but I felt it too. What kept the mind hypnotized was the idea of Someday. Someday we'll walk free, Someday step out of jail—Someday saunter out of confinement, smiling out of the new self, moving forward. But it wasn't going to happen like that, on that day or any other day. Not for any of us. We were going to pay for the pennies to close our eyes, for the splinter of mirror to confirm our stopped breath. Pay for our elbow room in the morgue. You had to be able to afford Hope. It belonged, like Justice, to those who could handle the bills. We were all moving toward that future, one Polly Lyle Clement knew about. Polly Lyle, who had the gift of Sight, looked into each of us and knew what was to come. These were women who had come up against the law, and the law was not going to be any kinder to women in the future. I believe that that's what she was thinking then, though she said nothing at the time; she only smiled, and when Baby Ain't winked at her, winked back.

In the meantime, in the poetry workshop, the matter at hand was to find (as it always is in poetry) not just a way to hint at expression, but rather a way to find the right words for it all, as we live. The right words for confusion and desire, for rats as big as dogs, for the wilderness of stars, the pennies and the mirror, the Red River Valley, a name in a Bible, for Twin Cities, for Switch, for the man/woman, for the shawl and the gun, for the gift of Sight. As Polly's great-granddaddy said, "The difference between the almost-right word & the right word is really a large matter—it's the difference between the lightning-bug & the lightning."

My Horoscope

So my horoscope said today
I'd voyage to exotic isles: I'd
Meet up with a snazzy Romeo,
Sip cocktails under the stars.

From this exotic isle, I've traveled
from prison to court and back. My
pay has rocketed from zip to a
few red cents per hour.

Weird freaks have tried to sell me
rolls of toilet paper, weird freaks
try to make out with me in the showerstalls.
Weird stars, stay away. Strange days

under strange stars. Where is the tall dashing Romeo,
You weird freaks?
Where is the cocktail on the balmy isle?
Weird Jupiter: what's the rising sign in this house?

—ROXANNE LATTNER, POET

"Your mother called," K.B. said. He was at the hospital, I could hear doctors being paged in the background and harried voices outside his office in the hall.

"Thanks," I said. "I'll call her back."

"What's the matter?"

"Nothing."

"It's not nothing. I can tell by your voice."

"What the hell can you tell by my voice?"

"Holly. What's wrong?"

"I don't know," I said.

I didn't know. I didn't know. But something was wrong in the vague enormous way the poet Shelley (and my mother) had it: "Wail, for the world's wrong!" I'd thought more about Sam Glass. I was still attracted to him and I couldn't seem to separate my feelings for him from my feelings for poetry, the world of poetry. I'd stopped trying to write, as I felt guilty about K.B. every time I jotted something down. It was as if using my imagination was a betrayal. I loved K.B.—what terrible poem of my life was I writing?

And then there was the Bail Fund. I had definitely decided not to go back there, but I took no satisfaction from having made that decision. I had gained no insights from the time I'd spent bailing women out of jail. Freeing women from prison had had about as much rehabilitative effect as AfterCare Services, which appeared to have almost none. Nobody seemed to want to hire ex-offenders—and conversely, what argument could be made to an ex-inmate to join the workforce at Ma Bell for peanuts when a night's dirty work could produce a bankroll? ("We all sittin' on our money-makers," Baby Ain't was fond of saying, her sweet bright face shrewd. "We all sittin' on our *livin'*.")

I felt a little sorry for myself then, sitting there on my money-maker at my desk in the AfterCare office, reading the falsely hearty House of D newsletter with my money-loser. And I felt sorry for the women who cranked out the fake news. The newsletter was ostensibly produced by inmates, but it was more or less an administration mouthpiece. Boosterish articles about how well the prison was running, with sudden dark undercurrents of melancholy, dissatisfaction.

> The women who work in the kitchen—inmates as well as the staff—are no doubt the most underrated group of workers in this institution to say the least.
>
> The kitchen workers' day begins at 5 AM and runs till 9 PM. The kitchen workers must serve the entire population, as well as the staff. There are three feedings. Then every eating utensil must be washed and inspected.

The Laudatory Reporter, Stellene J. Mattson, bustled about interviewing other inmates at their jobs:

> I visited the institutional laundry and I was quite impressed to see the women working in such a harmonious attitude.
>
> While there I interviewed Juletta Ponder, and I asked her this: "Approximately how many garments do you press per day?" Her answer was "Ninety Sentenced women's dresses per day."

One had only to watch her professional performance to know that she was an experienced presser.

Juletta said she would work on the outside as a presser, but only if she were paid union scale wages.

Well, good for you, Juletta; and how many days can you stand to keep folding, catching, and popping in a laundry basket the repetitive tedium of your hopeless life—this job of pressing life into garments—knowing that, by the way, you are certain to be denied union wages in the future?

Ninety garments stacked, then:

Elizabeth nimbly catches, folds and deftly places each item in a laundry basket, as it comes off the mangle.

And shouldn't she be given a union contract? A woman who could turn out ninety uniforms a day and not slow her pace? A nimble wonder at the mangle?

I glanced at the file numbers in the Rolodex. I had made calls to the union offices. I had heard what they had to say. No one who had served time, no one convicted of a crime or misdemeanor. *Great,* I thought. *Jimmy Hoffa needs to consult on this.*

Just as I was about to pick up the phone (someone at the local to explain union policy again), an inmate entered. I thought (surprising myself), *Here's what's wrong, walkin' in the door.*

"Hi," I said. "You're not supposed to be here. It's lunchtime."

"You the poetry lady?" she asked.

She was tiny, with a baby face and an arresting head full of elaborately set plaits, strands of dyed-blond and blond-brown hair woven into her own. Her eyes were bruised-looking. A sidelong pickerel smile, as a famous poet once said about a student of his who had died tragically. She held out her hand. She was wearing a too-big detention uniform blouse, but I could see a familiar sight—scars on her arms. Probably drug tracks.

"I'm Lily Baye."

I shook her hand, wondering what was coming.

"I want you to help me," she said. "I just want to go to my baby's funeral. That's all I ask."

"When did your baby die?" I asked Lily Baye.

"My baby die yesterday."

On closer inspection, I saw that her eyes were bloodshot, bright red from crying, not bruised. She looked so small and frail and waif-like, it was all I could do not to hug her.

"I wrote a poem," she said, blinking back tears. "I brought it to you so that you could read about how my baby die."

"How come you're not in the poetry class?"

"I just got here. I been brought in on an Aiding and Abetting, and while I here the first night, last night, I was told about Lil Bit. It the cops' fault she dead. They took me out my house when she was still calling for me, and hurt. You want to hear this poem?"

She didn't wait for my response and began to half read, half recite, swaying in place:

My baby girl lyin' in a cold steel drawer, dead.
She fell down through a rotted hole.

Slumlord wouldn't fix it,
'Cause I'm a whore.

Two years old, like her mama small.
She had the gift to sing. Call me wrong,

Why she in a crib of cold steel?
My baby girl could sing.

She could sing, Lil Bit.
Now I can't touch her, I still hear her cry.

They lock me up—and why?
I don't know where my baby gone.

My baby could sing.
I hear her voice,

I hear her singin' to me
Under the ground, singin'

Tell how I shoot my way to her—
One for the warden, two for the dep!

Find my way to her over the dead bodies,
Over the screw blood that oppresses our people.

But I'll be kneelin' at your grave, Lil Bit.
They can't stop your sweet voice singin' to me.

"Do you like it?" she asked, and looked ready to cry again. She wiped her eyes and I saw that she wore a thin gold wedding ring on her left hand, a pattern of intertwined hearts.

"It's pretty powerful," I said. "Are you saying that your little girl died because she fell through the floor?"

"I am sayin' so. And when the cops came to arrest me and my baby father—they took us and left her there, callin' for me—they just left her there to die. Old auntie I had takin' care of her run off when the cops come."

She began to sob, terrible wrenching sobs, and I finally hugged her. Her small body shook in my arms.

"How can she be dead?" she cried. "How can she be dead and her mama not with her? How?"

She opened her mouth then sobbed without sound, like a small animal panting.

"I need a furlough," she said. "I need forty-eight hours or seventy-two hours—just so I can see my baby one last time, before they lay her in the ground. To hold her in my arms like she still alive."

I let her go and she wiped her eyes.

"You a mama?"

"No," I said. "I don't have any children."

"I thought only a woman bear a child understand this. But you look like you can see what I'm tellin' you."

It was true. I kept seeing the baby trapped alone and crying out, dying as her mother was taken away from her forever.

"Where is the funeral?"

"At the Baptist church, the ladies there seein' to it. But it set for three days from now. So I need to hear fast."

"I don't know," I said. I tried to think clearly. I doubted if the warden would agree to let her go on furlough. Plus I knew nothing about her.

"I just read in the newsletter that last November they did initiate a furlough program: seventy-two hours. But it's for sentenced inmates who've already served some of their time. So I'm not sure. I should make a file on you here in Social Services and we can figure out a strategy."

She began to cry again, the same terrible sobs.

"It's okay," I said. "Don't worry. I'll go see the warden. She's out today—but I'll try to meet with her as soon as I can. I'll see if I can find your intake file before I talk to her."

She smiled at me through her tears.

"And my poem," she said. "You say you like it, then? You believe I should let the sisters here Inside hear it?"

"Why not?" I said. "You wrote it to be heard, right?"

· · ·

*L*ater, still sitting in my office, I read over the ballads the work-shop poets had written and I found that I could not stop think-ing about Lily Baye and her lost baby. Darlene had written:

I once was a mother,
Now I walk alone.
I once held my children by the hand.
Now I walk alone.

Alone is how I walk
Down a path made of footsteps.
Now I walk alone.

Later that day I stopped by the *Sam* offices, still thinking about Lily Baye and her baby, though I didn't mention her to Sam Glass, who was in a contemplative mood.

"I think what fascinates you about it all," he said, "is the language. You know, it's like a code they speak. They say, you know, 'Sally Go Round the Roses' and that's supposed to mean something else: roses are protection or drugs or something. Or 'C. C. Rider'—the white guys who recorded that song didn't know that—"

"A c. c. rider is a pimp," I interjected, finishing his thought. "The guys who recorded that song were a fifties college band—I read this somewhere. They knew one black guy named Rider and they wrote the song for him. Without knowing."

"You see a lot of riders out there on the Island?"

"Yeah, I do."

"It's fascinating how they get women to do what they do. Espe-cially since you know what the sexists say, don't you? 'Men don't pay prostitutes to come, they pay them to leave'?"

"Typical male respect for women," I said, "for that ever-so-holy state of matrimony. But hey, these women know how to even the score! Out at the Women's House they say they're sittin' on their money-makers."

Sam Glass did an ironic double take as if he were shocked. We were in the *Sam* office after hours, reading through submissions.

"Say what?"

"You heard me. In some ways it's a horror, in other ways it's a kind of skewed feminism."

Sam Glass touched my cheek.

"You can't," he said, "have it both ways."

But he was wrong. A woman could have it both ways. Baby Ain't, for example, proved it. She was a flatback and a pleasure boat but also a businesswoman.

"I got a little sugar bowl made by my own sugar bowl—put away," she told me once, "where ain't nobody find it but me."

Sam Glass smiled at me and opened an anthology: a test. He would read lines of great poems to see if I could guess the authors. He loved quizzing his friends and fellow writers. Because he prided himself on having read almost everything, as he said, he had to set himself up as a kind of human quiz show of poetry, the Groucho Marx of literary reference.

The first poem excerpt floated an image of a white bed in a white room with sun pouring in through translucent white curtains. And lit by sun on a polished bureau-top: a key.

. . . and the immaculate white bed

I knew that bed, that room, that key. I suddenly realized that it was a rented room and the key seemed to hint at an illicit affair. I'd never understood the poem that way before.

"It's 'Nantucket,' " I said. "William Carlos Williams. I always thought I'd like to find that room and never leave. Hide out. Die there."

"Here's another," he said, and moved closer and read "Queen-Anne's-Lace," a poem by Williams that lifted off the page, describing a white flower with a "purple mole" at its center. ("Wherever/ his hand has lain there is / a tiny purple blemish.") A poem about sexual desire, in its close-up of the flower and its broader image of the field of white nodding blossoms, rooted as wild carrot, delicate as nerve endings. It was also a poem about stubbornness, I realized, about refusing to give in, even as pure humming instinct took over the field. When had I learned that Queen Anne's lace, also known as wild carrot, had been ground up and brewed as a morning-after tea for centuries, counseled by midwives? That women imbibed it when their monthly bleeding was late? It had estrogenic properties, Queen Anne's lace, it was an abortifacient. To the doctor-poet it was a dream of wildflowers nodding in the drowsy summer field, a dream of bowing-down blossoms, acres of bride-white stitchery, tumescent as clitoral flesh. To the woman exhausted by and fearing birth, it was a midnight solution, bitter distillate drunk down in swift gulps—an escape from Nature through nature: an urgent detour out of time, out of the prison of the body—through the tunnel-passage backward, back out past the wet reddened lips, past the ambivalent heart of the flower, past the entrance through desire

until the whole field is a
white desire, empty, a single stem

"Try another one," I said to Sam Glass. "I know Williams better than my own poems."

O ur previous workshop meeting had featured a poem by Never Delgado as well as Roxanne. Never stood up to read her poem and made a loud trumpeting noise to get everyone's attention.

"Da-da-ta-*da*!"

"Never Delgado has no guilt," she began. "We can start right there."

Polly grinned at her.

"Guilty or innocent," she mused. "The Whorehouse Bible say you only as guilty as the person who lay down with you."

"Forget your Whorehouse Bible!" cried Never, stung. "I'm only talkin' about how a young girl could get sucked into some scheme without knowin'—being asked to carry a suitcase back and forth on a plane to and from Bogotá. How could she know what was inside?"

"I hear you carried a chunk of H in your pussy." Gene/Jean winked at her. "About the size of Newark."

"How much more I'm expected to put up with this horny sow-pig?" Never pointed at Gene, appealing to Aliganth. "Everybody know I am a lady!"

"Can it, Keeley! You lookin' at an infraction. Miss Delgado? You set to read what you wrote?"

Then she glanced away, distracted, and left briefly to talk to an officer in the hall.

"Drug runner," murmured Akilah under her breath, apparently referring to Never—and we locked eyes. Next to her, Gene/Jean abruptly laid her head on her arms on the table and was instantly asleep, breathing loudly through her mouth. Darlene was chewing on Jesus. *A typical workshop session,* I thought.

"My poem is not about, anyway, what I did or did not do."

"Just read the damn thing," said Sallie.

Never read it slowly, in her lovely low voice with its delicate, soft, barely-there Puerto Rican accent.

When she was finished, and after a few suggestions for revision, Polly sat up straighter and said: "I don't see *you* in your poem—where are you?"

Never considered this, then looked back at her poem, chewing her lip.

"I just need to find another word for 'screwed up.'"

"You got the same pelican lawyer I got, Never? That guy Kaplan?" asked Baby Ain't.

"Pelican?" I envisioned lawyers in conservative black-winged suits and ties flying overhead, their large scooplike beaks dripping torts.

They all looked at me.

"Oh wait, I get it," I said. "Appellate lawyer. Pelican. Right."

Polly looked thoughtful.

"I believe that our Heavenly Father invented man because he was disappointed in the monkey. Probably he got it backwards."

Then she looked sweetly at Never.

"Couldn't you say, instead of 'screwed up,' 'discombobulated'?"

Akilah, incredibly, glanced kindly at Polly.

"You are filled with some pretty astonishing words, Polly," she said.

"There's a poem by Emily Dickinson," I interrupted, "that I think you'd like, Akilah. It's the poem I brought in to talk about today."

I was taking a chance, but the poem seemed perfect for her. I opened my notebook.

"Here's a part of it: 'The soul has moments of Escape— / When bursting all the doors— / She dances like a Bomb, abroad, / And swings upon the Hours . . .'" I stopped, unsure.

Akilah looked at me, light eyes level: a sphinx.

Polly said, "'The soul has moments of Escape'—it's true, isn't it?"

"Yes, it is," I said. "Each soul has moments of escape—even trapped as it is, within the body."

"Yes," said Polly Lyle. "I agree. In the Whorehouse Bible, they say: Blessed are the humpbacks and the clubfoots. Blessed are the twisted-in-the-brain and the brain-shakers like me—for we will all be straightened out by the Golden Hand."

"Sure," I said. "The Golden Hand."

Sallie cranked around in her chair to look hard at Polly. "I got a question. How your hair turn so white, girl?"

Polly Lyle nodded at her.

"You'll know when the Golden Hand tell my soul to tell you."

"I think you all should know," I interrupted—jumping in à la Baby Ain't and changing the subject to relieve tension in the room— "that I've been using the library to look up things and borrow books. Reading? It's called creative reading, and it's as important as creative writing. Read every book you can get your hands on."

Even as I exhorted them to read and made my soapbox stand, I pictured C.O. Hardringer, the corpulent brassy-haired officer who ran the Women's House library, standing in the doorway of the little book room with its woefully understocked shelves behind her—its *Reader's Digest* condensed volumes, its *Dictionary of Facts,* and its three or four legal tomes. I was standing before her, nervous. I'd just managed to persuade a famous poet or two to talk their publishers into donating poetry, fiction, and nonfiction—anything interesting from the publishing house catalogue—to the Women's House. Box after box would be arriving soon. After close inspection and some "borrowing" by C.O.s along the way, the books would be delivered here to the prison library for shelving.

"It will be terrific," I quacked at C.O. Hardringer. "Nothing will stand in the way of the women here at the library—they'll be free to read!"

Hardringer snorted. "*My* library," she cried, "this is *my* library, this is my assigned post—and they come at the hours I say, or—"

She paused. I picked up.

"You're saying they'll be stopped if they try to enter and read?"

"They'll be stopped by my body in the doorway if it ain't a time when I allow people in. I got my schedule. I got my lunchtime and my breaks, I got hall duty. They come when I say they *can* come. This library run the way the institution run, you payin' attention?"

I *was* paying attention, that was the problem. The women always figured out a way *not* to pay attention and still solve the problem. For now, C.O. Hardringer owned the library, and shipments of books were about to arrive.

"It's all right," Baby Ain't said to me later. "We can boost anything. She too fat to chase us far."

In Court

I go to Important Court, special section—
Where I see the words In God We Trust
Up above the Judge's big chair in letters of gold.

I must trust that there is a God and that this God
is Just. They call my name and the female officer
says, When you walk by the Bullpen, keep
your dignity, Lady. Don't let them take that
away from you, Lady.

Those mouths shout at me, but
I keep walking. I end up in the
Chamber of Justice, past that

screwed-up (discombobbed) baying.
Leather seats. The Court Clerk & the Judge
and the Pelican. I look up and see

In God We Trust. I pray hard to this
God. Why don't these people look in my eyes?

—MISS NEVER DELGADO, POET

eight

*T*win cities: *Dark and Light. But the river was dammed....*
I was on the bus to Rikers Island. I was writing the poem in
my head at the same time as I was making my plan to see the
warden about Lily Baye's furlough—I'd ask to see her as soon as I arrived and checked in at the Social Services office. On the bus, I
thought about the women's discussion of whether an escaped soul
could swim against the tidal rips of the river—whether one could
swim from Rikers Island to another island in the river, to freedom.
Billie Dee piping up about sharks in the river made me think of Vir-
ginia Woolf likening the impulse to write to being harnessed to a
shark. Then I thought of Polly Lyle's exhortation: Ride what's trying
to ride you! That was it—that was writing itself: *Ride the current
that's riding you.*

*T*he inmates were in a line that snaked out of the auditorium into
the chapel area. It was ten in the morning and I was headed up to
the Social Services office when I saw Baby Ain't and Never in the
line, gesturing to me.

"Wow," I said. "They must be giving away three-day passes in
there."

"You close," said Baby Ain't. "Near just as fine. They got the Miss
Candy Craydon Charm School giving beauty lessons inside."

"And how to walk like a model," added Never, sucking in her cheeks and mincing back and forth. Then she crossed her eyes and walked pigeon-toed.

I laughed.

"Hey," Baby Ain't said. "You talked to that new flatback—what's her name? Baye? About her poem?"

"Lily Baye? That little girl who just came in?"

"That's right. She in the Bing."

The line began to move forward more quickly and I trotted along beside the two of them to keep up.

"What the hell is she in the Bing for?"

"She in for her poem she wrote."

I stopped, stock-still, not sure I'd heard correctly. I felt a charge of excitement suddenly in my veins—because of a poem?—as the line chugged along toward the auditorium door. There were two C.O.s stationed at the doors, checking for contraband, stolen medication, pocketed food. I caught up to the two of them again.

"What do you mean, she's in the Bing for her poem?"

They were almost to the auditorium doors and moving fast. Baby Ain't turned around to call back to me. She jumped up and yelled over the shoulders of the crowd. One of the C.O.s glanced at her.

"She put it on the drum and it went all out Inside—the Cap got heard of it and she went to Disciplinary—then they lock her in PSA."

"When we come back out we be so charming!" cried Never over her shoulder as the crowd pushed them through the doors. "You won't know us, girl!"

They were swept inside the auditorium. I turned away, charged up, then saw Polly Lyle coming along in line, watching me. I waved to her and she waved back. Then she called to me.

"Don't do what you thinking of doing, Miss Teacher!" she shouted. "That child been in the hands of hell."

"What are you talking about?" I shouted back. "What are you saying to me?"

"What I already said—don't do what you up to do."

"You lost me," I cried. "I'm not doing anything."

I waved again, impatiently, as if I were waving her away—and turned my back on her blazing solicitous face, shadowed as she was absorbed back into the line.

But I *was* doing something. I was doing something I'd never done before at the Women's House. I went straight to the superintendent's office, without an appointment, to see the warden. On my way there, a line from W. H. Auden's famous elegy for W. B. Yeats, "Poetry makes nothing happen," kept repeating in my head. "Yet it does make something happen," I murmured aloud to myself as I strode down the halls, deserted now because of charm school. Poetry brings down the walls—for poetry we are taken to jail, for poetry we die. But with the words that keep us human on our lips as we wait on the gallows. I tried to remember anything about the poem that would have made it threatening to the administration—the fact that I could not neither encouraged nor deterred me—all my earlier anxiety fell away as I hurried toward the office of the oppressor.

Poetry and politics—at last, I thought, *they've come together, here at the Women's House.* All the smuggled-in radical newspapers, the cryptic messages from Inside, the fight to be heard, the pens and paper—finally connect to the battered seething consciousness of the women themselves. Above my head an invisible banner unfurled: LIBERTÉ, EGALITÉ, SORORITÉ—I envisioned the goddess standing, spotlit, on the ramparts, Justice: her long hair blowing, her fierce blind gaze implacable as she lifted the dazzling sword. Lily Baye, in solitary confinement, had spoken the words that had called her into being.

Distracted, hurrying along, I sensed something strange about my own reaction. I was, on one hand, appalled that Lily had been locked up in solitary—and on the other, I had begun to feel weirdly thrilled, perhaps because of the unexpected power of poetry to threaten the status quo, the uniforms.

Shades of the wild mad girl, the Maid of Orleans, born in Dom-rémy, born in Lorraine. Burnt for heresy, burnt for witchcraft, burnt for sorcery—the Warrior Saint, Joan of Arc. Out of the flames, her proclamation of independence and war. Righteousness, under whose accelerating demands History bends, Law bends. (*Watch your mouth, Holly Ann*—I heard my mother's voice suddenly—*watch that mouth,* but why would I listen? *Pride goeth before a fall, Holly.*) Nor did I re-member till later what Shaw had said in his preface to his great play, *Saint Joan*—how there were two opinions of her heroic martyrdom. One that she, the upstart dreamer, was miraculous; the other that she was perfectly unbearable.

Superintendent Ross, the warden, looked up as I marched into her office. I was suddenly aware of two C.O.s trailing me. Ross looked beyond me at them, nodded once, and waved them away.

I stood in front of her, my hands clasped, realizing that I hadn't prepared anything to say.

"Where is Lily Baye?"

The warden smiled. She was a slim woman in her fifties, military-pretty, with light skin and straightened copper-colored hair. Little about her suggested a medium-security keeper—she looked more like a flight attendant in her slim navy uniform.

"Lily Baye is in Punitive Segregration."

"I demand to see her."

I was ready to list my reasons, I was ready to launch into a full-scale impassioned argument on Lily's behalf. But the feeling in the room was so strange that I stopped for a second, stepped back.

Superintendent Ross paused, looking me up and down. Then she sat back in her chair, looking a little bored. To my utter amaze-ment, she reached over and touched an intercom button on her desk.

"Josie," she said. "Could you check to see if Captain Amarillo is in the Watch Commander's office? Tell her I'd like her to accompany Miss Mattox here up to the Bing to see Lily Baye, the inmate from 4 Upper who is in lock."

For a heartbeat, I was terrified. Not once had I been afraid within the prison walls. Now, for one panicked second, I suspected that they were taking me away too—they would lock me up in solitary, I would die there. It was a smooth dropping sensation, absolute terror—then it vanished as fast as it had surfaced.

"And I'd like to request," I said, "some time with you after I visit Lily."

She nodded at me, still smiling.

"I'm not planning to go anywhere, Miss Mattox. I'll be waiting."

The Bing was an architectural migraine: a long straight corridor, bulb-lit, with steel doors on either side. Each door had an eye-level opening the size and shape of a mail slot. As the captain and I passed, the doors on either side shook with resounding blows and kicks, the hall rang with garbled shouts and accusations.

Captain Amarillo stopped at a door midway down the corridor, shook out the waterfall of keys hung next to the nightstick on her belt, and opened it.

The cell was so small there was barely room to enter. A bald overhead bulb in its claw-socket burned with all-day-all-night energy. Lily lay on her back on a thin mattress, her arms and legs thrown out casually, like a sun-worshipper on a floating raft. She pulled herself up to a sitting position. Her hair was wild, the cornrows half unraveled and sticking straight up. She didn't appear to recognize me. I glanced around: a sink, a lidless toilet, the mattress.

"Baye," said the captain. "The poetry teacher is here to see you."

Lily looked idly at Amarillo, then spat at her. Captain Amarillo glanced down at the string of saliva which swayed, lengthening, from her skirt, then fell. I watched her face grow very calm. She moved to the door and stood there.

"That's one count, Baye. One more time and you got an infraction on your hands. And then you got a cell extraction."

Benny Mathison had told me what a cell extraction was. At the failure of what they called IPC (Interpersonal Communications), Bing officers performed cell extractions by entering the cell, forcing the prisoner facedown on the floor, handcuffing her behind her back, then hauling her out. Injuries often were incurred. OC (oleoresin capsicum), or pepper spray, was often used. Benny said the pepper spray was the least of it. There were broken bones, fractured skulls, multiple contusions—all in the process of performing an extraction. And in the process of beating the shit out of the extractee once extracted.

Without asking permission, I sat down on the edge of the mattress and touched Lily's hand.

"Do you remember me, Lily? Have they hurt you?"

"Hurt me? 'Course I remember you! And 'course they hurt me! I'm in here, right?"

"What happened with the poem you wrote?"

"You told me to put it on the drum—you told me everybody should hear it. Then they jump me on it, take it all away. Stuff I write down there they don't like to hear! They had to fight me though, girl. I best near iced two screw bitches."

She laughed, then glared up at Captain Amarillo, and Amarillo glared back.

I felt momentarily confused. Had I actually told her to put the poem "on the drum"? This meant making copies, passing them hand to hand, floor to floor, or reciting the poem aloud, then, as others learned it by heart, letting it circulate throughout the institution. Had I told her to do that?

I decided not to ask her.

"Tell me what you need. I'm going to help you."

"I need a furlough by tomorrow—to hold my baby one last time? You forget what I told you? And I don't see I'm gonna get it! Look what's been done to me!"

She cried out and then laid her head on my shoulder like an ill, exhausted child.

I followed her gaze to the wall. Graffiti was scratched on the cement—how? Hairpins, a bent spoon, bones? There were the names—the universal graffiti names—Sweet Duchess and Cola, Death Mamba, La Reina de Dolorosa, Cruise Top, Shudder Honey, a cobweb of names. Fresh scratches below: Lil Bit, Lil Bit.

Lily drew an audible breath.

"I need something to write with. I need a pen. I need paper. I bleedin' poems."

"Captain Amarillo," I said. "Could you please see that Lily has some pencils and paper?"

"You just go on ahead and take that matter up with the superintendent, Miss Mattox."

"Captain—what are you afraid of?"

"Time's way up."

"The truth?" I asked.

I pulled gently away from Lily and faced Captain Amarillo. She offered me an "Are you for real?" look and stepped a fraction of an inch closer.

"I like to tell you, Miss Mattox, that I'm not afraid of anything in this here area," she said. She put her hand on her hip, just above the belt with the nightstick, and waited.

I stood up.

"I'm on my way to Ross. I'm going to make them let you go, Lily."

Lily's smile turned to a grimace. She grasped my hand as I stood up and I bowed awkwardly to her, my arm pulled out in a kind of downward salute.

Lily looked at me at last.

"I'm gonna write a book, Holly. I want to write all this down for the whole world to see."

The warden looked up as I walked in. She indicated a chair in front of her desk and I sat down. I began shaking suddenly—I tried to control my hands by folding them in my lap. I'd never seen human beings in locked boxes before, never smelled the stench of solitary confinement: dead air, terror-sweat, the sour pitch rebreathed fetid smell of animal rage. I knew that most of the women in solitary were there because of bad behavior in the larger boxes in which they'd been stored. There, too, the soul knew no moments of escape. I looked at my hands and willed them to stop shaking.

"I'm not sure where to start," I said. "But I will begin by asking you what the reason is for Lily Baye's confinement in the Bing and then I want to know what has to be done to get her released. And home for her daughter's funeral. In the meantime, I'm requesting that she be given writing materials."

The warden laughed.

"So that she can write more poems?"

"Perhaps."

I stood up, then sat back down again. I took a deep breath to calm myself.

"Why did you lock her up like that—for writing a poem? Even if First Amendment rights under the Constitution cannot apply here, there are laws against censorship—"

"You know," she interrupted, sitting back, smiling again, "you really are quite the thinker, aren't you? When you first came up with the idea of a poetry workshop, I wasn't inclined to approve."

She leaned forward a little, emphasizing each word.

"A cree-*ay*-tive *wri*-ting class? For these women?"

She leaned her hand protectively on a framed photograph as a jet roared over. I started to speak, but she went on, oblivious to me.

"I decided it was a way to let off steam, harmless: sob stories, poems, Dear Diaries. And this do-gooder college girl sorting them all out, providing a kind of—well, I guess you could say—cozy therapy. Harmless."

I felt the anger flickering in my brain, a constellation of quick licking white flames, spreading fast, lighting up branch after branch of a furious nerve tree. I opened my mouth. I was no longer shaking. I had some things to say.

The warden held up her hand to silence me.

"I'm aware that you think poetry is so important. I also know that you think the ladies are victims of an unfair system. Isn't that how you might put it? 'Victims of an unfair system'?"

I sat very still, my anger banking, waiting. A series of muffled announcements came over the P.A. system.

"I know that you bring in serious books of poetry. But besides being a poet and a teacher of poetry, you seem to see yourself as some sort of self-appointed liberation force."

She smiled at me again.

"I am aware, for example, that you bring in that newsletter, *On the Barricade,* and Hershey bars, and cookies. You bring in other contraband, like spiral notebooks and pens. Controversial political books, like *Soul on Ice* and *Prairie Fire.* Anything you can slip into their hands when the C.O. steps away for one minute. You seem to think that our security regulations do not apply to you. You store some of these books and candies up in the Social Services office where you work, isn't that right? In the file cabinets, in your poetry folders, isn't that right?"

I said nothing.

"I suppose, on one level, it seems innocent enough. A little bit of nonconformity, a little illegal sugar every now and then, and they think they're getting away with something. It makes them feel better, I suppose, that's how the thinking would go. But you see . . ." Another smile, a terrible smile. "That's not the way it is."

She lifted a little glass bell shaped like an angel from her desktop and shook it. There was a barely audible *clink.* She set it down again carefully.

"Christmas here at the Women's House—can you imagine what it's like? You haven't had the opportunity to be here at that time.

Ladies ready to break out, ladies ready to stick their heads in the toilet after a cheery visit from children who can't remember them anymore. It's a free-for-all. And all the big companies send holiday guilt donations: clothes, teddy bears, fruit, candies, games. One year some cosmetic company decided to send a little care package: a black satin pouch stuffed with cologne and powder and lipstick. We checked fanatically for possible contraband uses: took out all the metal nail files and the nonshatterproof bottles and the plastic bags. We worked overtime on Christmas Eve and then, finally, Santa Claus was sent off to all the floors to deliver the gifts. We waited. All was calm, and then . . ."

She touched the glass bell again.

"Clink, crack, clink! All over the institution we heard the sound of glass breaking."

My mind was churning, but I kept listening. A part of me was fascinated.

"The cosmetics company had tucked a deodorant with a little glass rollerball into the lip of the pouch and we hadn't caught it. Within five minutes of distribution, they were armed with glass, had cut their wrists with glass, had swallowed glass."

She snapped her fingers. "*That* fast.

"Still, your kind of contraband is not so clear-cut, if you'll excuse the pun. Nobody in their right mind would ever take *On the Barricade* seriously. We pick it up all the time on raids. The inmates throw it away—we read it at coffee break for laughs."

She laughed again, as if to capture the mood of these high-spirited lit crit coffee breaks. Another plane shook the building. I wondered why I heard the planes again, sitting here, when in the poetry workshop they vanished from earshot. I suddenly heard everything acutely—since she'd described the breaking glass, the auditory world seemed turned way up.

"Do you think," she asked, "that I don't know what's going on? I did find out, eventually, that you were actually teaching the women something about the subject. How to write. And Aliganth has stood up for you—she says you work hard as a teacher. Of course, I also have a pair of 'eyes and ears' in that class—or hadn't you guessed?"

Of all the things she might have said, this I was not prepared for. A spy? An informer? "Eyes and ears" for the warden in our midst? But who? I saw each face: Baby Ain't, Gene/Jean, Darlene, Akilah, Sallie, Polly Lyle, Billie Dee, Roxanne, Never . . . But I could not imagine—rather, it hurt too much to imagine—who it might be. The compliment from Aliganth vanished in the wake of this revelation.

I noticed her smiling at what must have been an indescribable expression on my face as I went down the list. There was a soft knock at the door and a C.O. from the Watch Commander's office entered, carrying a stainless steel coffeepot with a white china mug next to it on a tray. She set the tray down in front of the warden and then exited, with a quick sidewise glance at me.

"Coffee?" The warden poured and drank.

"No," I said. "No thanks." I was still running through the names and faces.

"But it's not your class that went so very wrong," she continued, setting the coffee mug primly on the tray. "It was this decision on your part to advise Lily Baye—not a student of yours and not a Social Services client—to violate security, to defy authority. To incite other inmates to do the same."

"I did not advise anyone to—"

"You told Lily Baye to make sure everyone heard her poem—is that not true?"

I tried to remember what I'd said.

"Yes," I said. "I guess that's true. But whatever she shared with the other women was hardly insurrectionary. I remember that the poem was about her daughter, her daughter's death."

"And quite a few other things. Miss Mattox, here we have an inmate who writes down on paper that she intends to murder the superintendent and the deputy warden in order to break out of prison.

She receives praise for this from a teacher in our institution class-rooms. The teacher further encourages her to copy these threats of violence and spread them throughout the facility."

"But I didn't do that. What I said was—"

"What you've done is tantamount, in some ways, to inciting a riot. In a sense, you're guiltier than she is, since you were in a position of responsibility."

I started to argue with her, then stopped myself.

"They were dancing in the halls to it. 'One for the warden, two for the dep!'—like that."

I pictured the inmates jiving up and down the corridors, snapping their fingers. I had to suppress a nearly hysterical laugh. I coughed into my hand.

The warden rolled back in her chair suddenly and pulled open a desk drawer, fished something out, then slammed it shut.

"You feel so sorry for Lily, don't you? I mean, seeing her up there in the Bing, crying? And you want to help her, I know."

She slid a manila folder across the desk to me and flipped it open. I glimpsed her second finger, left hand: a stiff tan prosthetic digit with a clear-polished nail. There was a story that circulated about this finger—that years earlier a very young C.O. Ross, on duty in the kitchen, had tried to show an inmate how to chop marrow bones for stew. She'd gone so far as to graciously offer her own finger as an example.

Then I looked at the contents of the folder: an 8×10 black-and-white photograph of a dead two-year-old girl. Her tiny naked body was a storm of bruises and welts, from the great blood rip of the scalp sheared away from her small cornrowed skull to her battered legs, bird-thin. At the top of the photo was stamped in red indelible ink MANHATTAN COUNTY CORONER'S OFFICE. I recognized the child's expression, a miniature of Lily Baye's, the lips upturned in a smile that was in fact a grimace of disbelief. I turned my head away.

"Why are you showing me this? I know how Lily's daughter died. She told me."

"Like you, I'm aware of Baye's testimony. Please look here."

She pulled a second photograph from beneath the first, this one taken of the child's body lying on its face. Tiny bruised buttocks and spine, the arms and legs, like Lily's in the Bing, thrown out to the sides.

"See this large discolored area? The coroner told the D.A., who tells me, that this is a contusion caused by a blow, or a series of blows, to the head and neck. I asked for these at the time of Lily Baye's request for a furlough. The coroner, the medical examiner, you see, examined this discoloration and the others here at the child's autopsy. He maintains that they could not have been caused by a fall, even through a floor. He thinks that they are the result of blows from a blunt instrument, a heavy boot heel, or, say, a walking stick."

She made her hand into a battering wedge and struck a rounded glass paperweight.

"Crunch," she said. "Crunch, crunch!"

I looked at her, shocked, but she was not laughing.

"Are you telling me," I said, "that the old woman that Lily left her baby with did *this*?"

She shook her head.

"The D.A. feels that this evidence indicates that the child received this treatment from an adult who had some strength—a man."

She indicated the photos again.

"Look."

A magnifying glass blazed in her hand. It glided across the first photograph, and the frail arms and legs leaped wildly as the lens slid over them. Then a patch of skin stood proffered, like the enlarged surface of a jewel. I could see the faintest brushing of hairs on the forearm, then three circular puckered wounds.

The warden held the glass over one of the wounds.

"Blisters? Or cigarette burns? What do you think, Miss Mattox?"

"Oh God."

I pushed the lens violently aside. They were cigarette burns, clearly recognizable, undeniable. The lens slid upward, magnifying the child's open left eye, which stared back, huge and expectant.

I sat there for a while. Then I recovered my powers of speech.

"An adult male with strength—who lived in Lily's house? So you mean her husband?"

The warden lowered her head, then peered up at me and shook it to and fro.

"*Pimp*, Miss Mattox. Lily's pimp. She's been with him for years. He went out the back door that night. Do you suppose that he'd be eager to be caught with a dying kid—and child molestation, years of it, already on his record?"

She held the magnifying glass up to the light, waving it back and forth as if drying it, then put it away in a drawer.

"Lily is refusing to turn state's evidence against him, though the D.A.'s office has been leaning on her. These whores are very, very attached to their pimps, did you know that, Miss Mattox? Can't wait to get back to them and go on being mistreated. You've seen those roosters out there waiting on the bridge?"

"Yes," I said, "I have."

I heard, far away, another plane. It seemed to hover overhead, drowning out the sound of the warden's words, though another part of my mind still heard her talking.

"The D.A.'s office feels that it would have been hard for someone of Lily's size to . . . break through the floor. *Somebody* jammed the baby down through the broken boards to make it look like an accident."

At last the plane disappeared and another sound took its place— the sound of a barely distinguishable voice, a child's voice, crying out from under the surface, under the substructure of a house.

"Then why," I asked, "would Lily want to go to her baby's funeral?"

"Funeral? I called the church and they are not holding a service. They will just say a few words over the body of this unfortunate child—over the little coffin—and then into the ground she goes. People want to forget these things, don't they? You want to know what I think about Lily? I think that Lily had in mind to *walk*. She and this pimp go way back. She is more loyal to him than to her baby. She is more loyal to him than to herself. You didn't pick up on that, did you, Miss Mattox?"

"But why couldn't . . . Could it be that she wants to get out in order to kill him? The pimp? For what he . . . what he has done?"

"Ten years the same pimp. She wears a ring he gave her on her left hand. He keeps her in heroin. Did you see the tracks on her arms? What do you think the answer might be? You have to look closely at the arms. See how many years of collapsed veins, punched veins—all there in the tracks. There's the love story. In the tracks."

She pulled the folder of photos back to her. She seemed relaxed suddenly. She held her false finger daintily aside, a teacup effect, the thumb and third finger held pincerlike.

A deep female voice thundered over the P.A.

"Count unverified. C.O.s, check your populations."

Superintendent Ross nodded at me over her coffee cup.

"The count's off. We know what that means, don't we? You and I are prisoners now too. Can't go home till we find out who's missing."

I nodded back. I had nothing to say.

"Let me ask you something, Miss Mattox," she said. "Whom do you believe now?"

Years later, far in the future, I would recollect that look: grave, keen, but somehow invested in my reaction. As if she wanted me to cry, wanted me to break down in front of her and grieve. There was the death of the baby, impossible to find language for—and then (*"Wail, for the world's wrong!"*) the death of each woman who (in fear or ignorance or desperate poverty) let a pimp turn her out, break her spirit, break her will, take away her human integrity, making her into a craven liar, street-life, piece of ass, punching bag, a pimp-wife. A pimp-wife's child would suffer, the child of a beaten-down whore would be destroyed. The woman whose man held her by the hair and beat her as she asked for more, and the woman who held her baby fiercely to her heart, were opposed in their blood, alien to each other—yet one by nature. And the one-by-nature part made me sick to my soul. If it were true. Naïve as they come—but that wasn't it. I would never, could never, find a way to accept that this too was part of what women were.

I felt like someone who'd been arrested while high—who did not entirely understand the charge, the crime, but who was guilty, entirely guilty. Like a thumbprint, a mug shot, I was on record. I was a whore too. And all this, I saw now, for an idea of Justice, sold to whoever bid. Her name used like a public urinal by every ready opportunist and cynic, in and out of court, in government chambers—Justice in the judge's chambers, in the back alley, Justice invoked by torturers and hustlers. Invoked by me.

There was a loud blast of static, followed by an announcement:

"Report 104 sentenced, 256 detention, 23 adolescent. Count verified."

Superintendent Ross smiled at me again, but her smile had hardened. Her desk intercom buzzed. She sighed and stood up. The shift was changing, she was expected to hold inspection of the officers who'd just come on duty for the graveyard shift.

I stood up too. I gripped the desk in front of me, dizzy. I felt I had to say something now.

"Lily is locked up because of me, and I'd like to take responsibility, however I can, so that she can be released."

"Miss Mattox. You are irrelevant at this point. Lily Baye will be released from lock when the Board determines that she is no longer a threat to internal security."

She paused. "Soon. I can tell you that. And now I'm going to give you a punishment. I'm going to let you keep teaching here at the Women's House."

She glanced ruefully at me, then turned to go.

"I'd like to quit," I said.

"Nevertheless," she said. "I think you'll continue here with us."

She was at the door. I followed her and touched her arm, tentatively.

"Eyes and ears," I said.

She stared at me.

"You said that you have someone who is your eyes and ears in the poetry workshop. I was just wondering if you would tell me who it is."

Superintendent Ross started to brush past me, then turned around almost coquettishly, touching her false finger to her lips.

"No, I'm afraid that you'll have to figure that out for yourself. You'll have to use your own powers of observation. Eyes and ears wouldn't hurt a poet, would they, Miss Mattox?"

That evening I waited a long time for the bus back to Manhattan. I sat on a bench outside the Reception Center and counted the planes: fifteen went over while I sat. I thought about the passengers seated in the airborne cylinders, the stewardesses already moving up and down the carpeted aisles, the jingling drink cart rolling out high above me. Then, later, a movie screen enlarging with light, a roaring lion's head, a spotlit colossus.

There was one pimp left, standing in a shadowy corner of the building, chain-smoking, though there were no more whores left to pick up. He was like the last sentinel, I thought, of an occupying army. He was here to stay, he'd be back—they'd all be back, standing watch on the bridge, the next day, and the next.

The pimp and I boarded the empty bus together and sat far apart. He got off across the bridge and I rode back alone through Queens and into Manhattan. No one else got on, no one else witnessed it: the huge lit-up famous skyline I so loved—(F. Scott Fitzgerald wrote that "the city seen from the Queensboro Bridge is always the city seen for the first time, in its first wild promise of all the mystery and beauty in the world"—unfurling like a banner as the bus crossed the Fifty-ninth Street Bridge.

At that moment, I felt the need to write something down. I reached into my pocket for the pen I'd hidden there earlier. It was gone. I remembered then holding Lily in the Bing, holding her close. I thought about it for the first time—a writing instrument and a weapon in one. It had been a ballpoint, and contraband.

PART II

"Look at it this way," one of my students said. "We agree that all dualities are man-made. Maybe it's just me—but this poem seems to keep enacting differences that present larger psychic reversals. Where Saint George bites the dragon back—good literally consuming evil? Especially, I might add, there in the fourth line. Is that inversion intentionally ironic?"

I glanced out the tall windows of the classroom. I could see part of the campus, Low Library, and imagined the pillar gates of Columbia, upper Broadway. It was sunny. Students, teachers, and panhandlers popped in and out of the subway stop at 116th, where one caught the Number 1 and Number 9, up- and downtown IRT. For a moment, I wished that I were on the subway, or sitting in the West End bar—anywhere but here, among the inquiring minds of my near-peers. I was honored to be teaching at Columbia, but I was troubled by all the aesthetic confusion.

"But the dualities here seem imposed. The poem lacks internal focus. And it lacks, you might say, passion." I tried to speak with authority, as if I'd inhabited the dualities in my innermost consciousness.

Ten graduate students looked back at me, not sure how to react. I wasn't that much older than they were and I was seriously opinionated, if confused—a possible recipe for insurrection later in the semester. I had been hired as a junior faculty member among hugely intimidating colleagues. I was now on faculty with, for example, the exiled Russian poet Joseph Kyrilikov, who insisted that his students memorize pages of poetry. He'd asked this once of himself—in order to teach himself English and English poetry during his months and months of hard labor in prison camp near Archangel. He had been sent away as a "social parasite," and the word "poet" had actually been used to convict him at his trial. "Who enrolled you in the ranks of the poets?" the judge had asked. "Who enrolled me in the human race?" Kyrilikov answered. The transcript of his trial had eventually been smuggled out (samizdat!) to the international media and he had become, in an instant, the literary hero of the world. The Soviet Union, shamed, yanked him out of the labor camp and sent him to the West. After some time in Europe, he'd chosen to live out his exile in Manhattan while teaching in the graduate writing program at Columbia. He was, in historical reality, living proof of the great shining cause I'd tried to beam on Lily Baye: Kyrilikov had actually been imprisoned for the "crime" of being a poet. Years later he would win the Nobel Prize, then die of a heart attack—he'd paid for his love of poetry back in the hard labor camp, with a (as he put it, pointing to his chest) "bad teeker." He had dark red thinning hair and bright green eyes. Once he'd shown me, kneeling down on a campus path, a *nezzabutke*—a flowering forget-me-not.

Also on faculty was Devereux Waldron, genius poet of the Caribbean, who would later be a Nobel laureate as well. And there was the wild poet and playwright Amiri X, né Lester James, who frightened everyone. Whereas Joseph Kyrilikov annoyed his students by demanding that hundreds of lines of poetry be put to heart and recited in class, Amiri X challenged his students to make their poems "relevant." He suggested, deadpan, that they go down to 116th and Broadway and read their poems to people on the street: *See how many of them will connect to your imagery, you dig? Cool.*

His students were outraged, but a few actually trooped down to the intersection and planted themselves, cawing out lines like

I sit alone, within my shadow, exhort the demons
Of solitude to release me into pale moon trauma,
into the flotsam of desire.

These brave, sometimes beautiful word-vessels were launched onto the great sea of traffic racket, subway roar, newsstand conversation, dope solicitation, shouts and murmurs of passersby. Once in a while a transient soul would stop and listen, then cry out: "What you say, pale? Shut the fuck up about your goddam flotsam of desire, Mary Alice! Get your flotsam-of-desire ass out of here, man!"

It was not a hospitable milieu for the cultivation of Rilkean rhetorical flourish—or for winning converts to the public ode.

I myself was a fan of Rilke, like every other poet I knew, but secretly harbored resentment against him. Why did he have to weep, as they said, every time a goddam leaf fell from a tree? Plus he'd abandoned his wife and child. Plus advised one of two strong artistic women who loved him to return to her husband and the pregnancy that killed her. She was a talented painter, Paula Modersohn-Becker, whose last words as she died in childbed were *"Wie schade!"*—"What a shame!" I resolved to have a T-shirt made up with John Berryman's dissenting vote printed on the front: RILKE WAS A JERK. Still, all the crisscross energy was undeniable: we were living in a time of poetic turmoil, antiwar poems elbowing their way onto the stage of the Spanish surrealists (rendered dramatically in Bly's translations), a scene lit by flashes of Deep Image, swept up in the drift and cumulus of James Wright's lyric epiphanies, Muriel Rukeyser's fierce and tender statements. There were the pyrotechnics of Sylvia Plath, the catapult into the red eye, the vertiginous poems of *Ariel.* And Adrienne Rich's uncompromising feminism—her unforgettable line about Marie Curie, which ran through my head night and day: "Her wounds came from the same source as her power."

I had a lot of time to think, taking the subway up from the Village to Columbia. Sometimes the crazy Poet of the D Train would turn up on the uptown IRT, rocking, staggering a little through the hissing pneumatic doors in his Ray Charles sunglasses and army jacket and knit cap, smacking his white cane back and forth and against the floor and sides of the car, belting out "My Funny Valentine" in an eerie off-key baritone. Most passengers ignored him as he stood before them (even as he prodded them with his cane) reciting his strange poems—a few people clapped a little when he was finished and dropped coins or bills into his proffered cup. I always listened carefully to his poems because they were familiar: like the ones I heard at Rikers Island.

A rainbow is a bridge to Coney Island knife in the heart—
Keep your chicken feet off my many-colored bridge!

He shouted out his lines, and his tin cup rattled with change. If you paid a dollar for a poem, he gave you a copy, handwritten, signed "The Poet of the D Train." How did he write out the poems, I wondered, when he was blind? Did he have an amanuensis, like Milton?

I read manuscripts at *Samizdat West* in its tiny midtown office with Sam Glass. I sat with the editors and staff members, hunched over black coffee and piled ashtrays, reading hundreds and hundreds of submissions. Stacks and stacks of ambitious and derivative and occasionally insane poems, short stories, dreams, sent with self-addressed stamped envelopes for safe return. ("Dear editors: Here are my latest poems: 'Signs of Crisis While Composting,' 'Scherzo of the Snowflakes,' 'Erotic Mailbox,' 'My Friend's Llama Speaks of Fate'—If you do not publish these poems, please note why in space provided below.") And then, out of nowhere: the occasional good poem, the brilliant poem by the well-known writer, or (miracle of miracles) a jewel written by an unknown writer—the story, the poem that leaped up, full-blown, syntactically fascinating, from the page.

Sam Glass hovered about, talking on the phone, shouting at the printer (who shouted back), grousing to himself. Occasionally he would sit down across from me and glare owlishly.

"I don't agree with you about this piece," he'd say. "Convince me. Tell me why we should publish it."

"It has a certain quiet tumultuousness," I said.

"Not good enough," he said.

"It's bold," I said, "and it makes its argument so skillfully you don't even noticed you're persuaded."

"Maybe," he said. "Maybe."

I took the bus to Rikers Island. I hadn't missed a workshop, but I moved carefully now—I'd stopped bringing in contraband and I asked no questions about charges or trial dates, though I'd heard from Baby Ain't that Lily Baye had been taken to Bellevue for psychiatric testing. There was a part of me that wanted to know, badly, who the spy was in the workshop—but another part of me wanted to know nothing, wanted to think only about poems and the writing of poems, wanted nothing but the pure act of the imagination, nothing more.

Never had brought her poem back to the workshop, revised, and there was further haggling over word choice.

"Neither word, neither 'screwed-up' nor 'discombobulated,' works," I said. "Never, what did the shouts from the male bullpen sound like when you walked past? Not screwed up, not discombobulated—what?"

"Like 'woo-woo,' " she said. "Like: *Ooh mama!* and *I wanna do you!*—you know, all that pussy coo. And some fuck and cunt too."

"Well, that's not bad," I said. "Listen to all the vowel sounds. Can you find a word that has that *ooo* sound?"

"Don't write down pussy coo," shouted Sallie.

Billie Dee cried, "Coo you, Flat!" and slapped Sallie's hand.

"It's a cruel sound," said Never. "You feel like a piece of meat that they might tear apart."

"Then what about 'cruel'? That's *ooo*," I said. "You might say 'I got past the cruel baying.' Like that?"

Never sighed, crossed out a word on the page.

" 'I got past the cruel blue pussy-baying of the male bullpen.' How's that?"

"That," I said, "is perfect."

"I wrote me a new poem," said Baby Ain't. "But I'll wait my next. It about fresh meat on the block. A new hooker she call herself Turnpike: you pay to get on and you pay to get off. You all dig?"

She slapped her knee twice and cackled. Darlene smiled at her, a Jesus-to-the-whores smile, and Roxanne looked bored, chipping bloodred polish from her long nails.

Sallie was staring at Polly Lyle Clement.

"I keep sayin' this, girl. I like to know why your hair so white like that."

Polly Lyle Clement had entered the workshop in what seemed a good mood. She had been laughing with Gene/Jean about something or other—Gene/Jean had a sense of humor all her own—and when Polly sat down, Akilah sat up and watched her closely.

"Sallie." Polly left her place and sat down in the empty chair next to Sallie and turned to her to speak. "Did you ever notice that dead people are once and for all *who they are*? People ought to start out dead, and then they would be honest so much earlier."

"What the hell you talkin' about, girl? You sayin' I ain't honest? Or you sayin' I should be dead?"

Everyone was listening now. Darlene was praying as usual, but quietly. I noticed that Akilah, who had seemed very protective of Polly of late, had fixed a steady angry gaze on Sallie. Aliganth was out of the room—she'd been paged by the Dep and had been gone for ten minutes.

"Honest? Sallie, we're both dead, though I can't even tell you in what certain way we ain't alive a-tall. I'll tell you—I'll tell you all now about how my hair got white—but you have to make me a promise first."

"What you want?"

"I want you to promise that you'll tell us all how your face got cut in two. I know—and it's time for you to tell."

Sallie started to laugh, then stopped and kept her split-level eyes on Polly. There was a very long silence. Then Sallie laughed again, but it wasn't exactly a pleasant laugh.

"It just so happen, Sight, just what you say—I got my poem about what been done to my face to read here today. I don't have to talk about it, it's all there on the paper. So after everybody hear you, they can hear me. Then they know two secrets, right?"

"When you're dead," said Polly, "you can talk about anything. There ain't no lies for the dead."

"There ain't no lies for me dead or alive," said Sallie, and she and Polly stared at each other, calmly, resolutely, I thought. But I couldn't really tell what was going on between them, and I resisted knowing.

Polly sighed, then I watched energy pour into her from some hyperactive astral plane. She was quoting the Whorehouse Bible one minute (*Blessed are the sodomites, they stand at the back door of Heaven, Blessed are the debauched, for they rise again in the morning. . . . Consider the hookers in the field, they neither bake nor sweep*), then staring back at Akilah the other. She shook her head at Akilah and pointed to her temple.

"I know you. I see who you are."

"You crazy?" murmured Akilah—she sat back in her chair, caught completely off guard.

"No. Wrong. You think you got this world all figured out. But the world figures you out as fast as you can think back. The world ain't on the receiving end of you figuring—you are."

Akilah started to speak, but Polly went on.

"And you didn't shoot that gun. I see you in the car with all the police lights on you. You held a weapon but your hand was shakin' so bad. That gun shakin' and you close to droppin' it before you could find a trigger. You had no heart in you to shoot. You talk so bitter, but you ain't no killer, not near."

Akilah shook her head, stunned. Her face flooded suddenly with what looked like gratitude or relief, a light came into her eyes. It was then, I think, I began to believe that Akilah Malik was innocent.

"Well," I said. "Are we sure we want to handle all this in one work-shop meeting?"

I wished that Aliganth were there—it was unclear to me where we were headed. Since my experience with Lily Baye, the strongest sense I had in the workshop was uncertainty: how to proceed, what to say—and finally, the power and danger of each woman's fear, the magnitude of each woman's longing, and the enormity of the consequent ever-present unpredictability. I was not afraid. It was just that I had, for the first time in my life, grasped what it meant to act according to circumstance.

"I won't be long," Polly said to me in a strange voice. I looked at her. Now she seemed half in and half out of herself, as if she were slipping into a trance. Her gold-flecked eyes glowed. She looked around at everyone, then seemed to drift away. She put one hand over her shadowed cheek, and the Southern accent, the deeper voice, came back.

"I'm up to tell this as it stands. If there's anyone can't hear this old story like it needs to be told—it might be best to step away now from where we're shoving off."

No one moved. No one said a word. Then I waved my hand toward the door.

"Listen, Polly," I said. "C.O. Aliganth will be back. Do you want to wait to tell your story when she's here?"

She just smiled at me.

"My hair turned white on North Brother Island. And because of what happened there, I'm now lookin' to set the river right again. I had been living fine on the island, as I told you before. I had enough to eat and I had made a lean-to inside the old lighthouse where the roof had gave in. I slept there—I found an old mattress and a horse blanket and pillows from the hospital. I had a fire I kept stoked and I'd lit a rusty lantern I found. And I slept easy—though I was lying awake looking at the stars when I first heard it."

The women had pulled their chairs in closer without even being aware of it, I thought. As with the beginning of each story since the beginning of stories, the thrill was slightly ominous, but something still kept drawing the listeners together as one.

"I heard a kind of faraway singing or sighing—and it kept on growing like it was coming up nearer, then would muffle a little as the wind shifted. It sounded to me like a choir of angels, crooning at me from who know's heaven, across the water. I got up, put on a jacket, and picked up the lantern. I climbed out over the rocks toward the shore where I heard it on the wind. There was the sound of the waves lappin', a'course, and a bird cry here and there, but there was this other sound, getting higher-pitched as the air carried it to me."

Everyone was so quiet that it must have spooked Aliganth as she came back into the classroom. But she didn't say a word—I looked over at her as she stood, eyes narrowed, at the door, listening too.

"And the birds got up flapping their wings and screeching, hundreds of birds, up in the night sky—and then all at once I saw it, rounding a bend, plowing through the water toward me—big as a city on fire." Polly closed her eyes and I noticed that her hands had begun to shake. "I heard that sound of blood screaming, louder and louder, drowning out everything. Coming at me were a boatload of people burning alive. I saw it speeding fast through the waves toward me—

three stories high, a ferryboat all ablaze, lit up like a sky-high torch. All the island birds kept on flying up and above the flames, over the burning decks—the foredeck shooting flames and people running on the texas with their hair and bodies on fire, waving their burning arms, and some leaping over into the merciless currents. I saw the name of the boat lit up like gold on the side: the *General Slocum*. I could see the captain in the pilothouse—his cap was flaming like a birthday cake as he turned the wheel. I could see that man's face. They were about twenty-five feet off North Brother when she stove on in. He ran her right on the beach, bow on, in about twenty feet of water. There were many folks aft, where the fire sprang up highest. They jumped in not knowing how deep and fast the water was and were swept right away. I heard them calling in German: *Hilfe, Hilfe!* I could see the lifeboats were on fire, showering sparks, as they tried to lower them. They were no good. Then . . ."

Her whole body shook now; the chair legs rattled beneath her. I glanced at Aliganth, wondering if she would let this go on, and I saw that she would.

"I heard the other sound. The contagious hospitals had come alive—there were patients in them, the castaways, the ones with scarlet fever and TB—and they were all beating on the hospital windows, beating and beating on the glass, crying out soundless at what they saw happening. I was looking at the island alive again—I tried to remember what year it was, that wreck. I set my lantern on a rock and I waded out. The *General Slocum* was still pure fire at the waterline and then I watched it swept by the current for another thousand yards until it crashed hard around Hunt's Point. There were people floating, on fire, in the water, and there were people shouting to each other, swimming out to help them. There were other boats gathering, picking up the still living and the dying, and they were towing the dead bodies behind them. A few of the contagious-hospital patients broke free and flung themselves into the water to help. And I saw the inmates from Rikers Island who swam the currents. That's how I know what I know. They swam all the way from this island to North Brother—and they were heroes. One was called Lewis and the other Mandy. One Irish and one Mulatto. They had asked the officer if they could risk the currents and were told no, but broke free and dived in right out here. I watched them working alongside the others, pulling in bodies, swimming out to drag the burning living in to shore. The water was cold, iron-cold. Floating by me was a girl, my age, my size, it was like looking in a mirror—bobbing on the water, half burned to death, flickering flames where her hair should have been, and I reached out for her. That's when I understood that what I saw was not there."

"What you mean—not there?" This was Baby Ain't.

"I mean that when I reached for her and grasped her—nothing. She was made of air. I could see her right in front of me, floating, gasping, her mouth wide open, little points of flame inside, her eyes rolled back—but she wasn't there. *Mutter,* she kept crying, *Mutter!* German for 'mother.' But see, when I grasped her, she seemed to come apart in my hands—dissolve, like. And all of it: the *General Slocum,* which had started rolling over on her side, the burned hull and the lit-up bodies in the waves—it was all not there, but *there.* I know what a dream is, what a Sight-fit is. But I was full awake. I seen clear what had happened right there on North Brother Island, because the island had never stopped seeing it. North Brother don't know how to make its peace with what happened there right on its shores. I spent that whole night trying to save people in the water—calling for help, trying to drag bodies onto the rocks—but all of it was air. My great-granddaddy the riverboat captain—he told me to keep trying to save them if I could. That it would matter to Time Undone. He said this here was Shattered Time on North Brother.

"He lost his own brother Henry in a steamboat accident. Boiler blew up and Henry was blasted up in the air and inhaled scalding steam that cooked his lungs. All the people steamed alive and the great paddle wheel sunk down, under water, spinning, in flames. My great-granddaddy had just missed being on that boat. He'd started out on it, then transferred to pilot another one 'cause of an argument—but see, Henry stayed on and died. A part of my great-granddaddy died on that boat. He never let it go. And you know, he was a seer too: he told me he'd seen his brother Henry dead, lying in a coffin laid on two chairs, with roses, all white and one red, placed on his chest—just as he found him in the makeshift morgue near the river and the nurses coming by to put those same roses he Seen, over Henry's heart. He had to make up stories about Henry's death so that he could go on living with himself. So he made Henry a hero, said he was killed going back to the boat to save lives. So when he spoke he said, *Keep swimming, Polly Lyle—your eyes will make sense of it!* Finally it was dawn and those drowning souls began to disappear as it got light. I waded back to shore and I crawled up on the rocks. I'd swallowed a whale's worth of water and I was bloody with cuts and bruises. I crawled back blind to the lighthouse and I tried to warm myself and clean myself. When I passed a little broken piece of mirror still nailed up on the wall, I saw that my hair had turned all white. And I thought this might be what my great-granddaddy meant about it makin' sense somehow—but it still don't get all the way up to an explanation for me. I couldn't find my way to sense. A lot of my brain went white then too—dead white after that night, in the places where the images press on, like fingerprints left on the spaces where you think. If you see what I'm talkin' about."

There was quiet so deep I suddenly heard the planes again, then nothing.

Then Akilah reached over and touched Polly's arm.

"What happened, Polly," she asked, in a ragged voice unlike her usual voice, a voice shaking with emotion, "to Lewis and Mandy?"

A day or two later, I ran up the Forty-second Street Library steps, past the sphinxlike lions, and found a seat in the great Reference Room, one of my favorite places on earth—and I looked up the *General Slocum* disaster. The *General Slocum* was an excursion ferry built in 1891, and it was huge—it could fit in three thousand passengers. On June 15, 1904, the ferry, chartered by Kleindeutschland—Little Germany, the German immigrant community on the Lower East Side of Manhattan—sailed off with just over a thousand members of its church group for its yearly picnic. Most of those aboard were women and children. The boat took off from the pier at Third Street and the East River with flags flying and an oompah band playing on the deck. They were headed for Locust Point, on the Sound. The captain was sixty-some years old, with a perfect safety record. As the boat was passing Randalls Island in Hell Gate—just about where the Triborough Bridge spans the river today—there were cries of "Fire!" on deck. A young boy named Freddy saw the flames early (in the straw in the boiler room) and ran shouting to warn the captain, who thought he was joking and threw him out of the pilothouse. Little Freddy had run up and down the decks, warning people who wouldn't listen to him. What merciful, ignored, heartbroken, god had sent him?

The fire swirled up from below, and in no time at all the entire forward part of the boat was a moving wall of flame. *The New York Times* reported that the passengers ran throughout the three decks trying to escape the conflagration. The skipper maintained full speed ahead (later ruled to be a mistake of judgment tantamount to a crime, for which he stood trial), trying to find a place to dock that would not result in more damage, and the flames shot up, fanned by the wind, as the women and babies crowded astern. At last he stuck his head out of the pilothouse and said he saw the most powerful blaze he'd ever seen.

I started to head for 134th Street, but was warned off by the captain of a tugboat, who shouted to me that the boat would set fire to the lumberyards and oil tanks there. Besides I knew that the shore was lined with rocks and the boat would founder if I put in there. I then fixed upon North Brother Island.

The rest was as Polly had described it. Exactly as she had described it. One thousand twenty-one of the original thirteen hundred people who boarded the ferry that day lost their lives in the flames or in the currents off North Brother Island. The *Times* reported on the patients of the contagious hospitals pounding on the windows as they witnessed the terrible scene before them. And the hero-prisoners from Rikers Island were mentioned in a brief footnote. I read the accounts again, then I closed the book of clippings. I looked out over the great imposing room of learning, the long tables with the dark green shaded lamps, the readers bent over their stacks of books. *Sanctuary,* I thought. Then: *Hilfe,* I repeated to myself. *Mutter.*

Polly had looked closely at each face in our circle. "I was granted to see a disaster on the river, on that island—and so now I need to see the river bless someone. Bless that island. There's got to be a blessing. Why else would I see these things?"

*T*hat night I called my mother. When she picked up the phone, I began talking quickly before she could launch into the rhythms of her inspiration.

"I'm unsure all the time," I said. "I don't know what I'm doing anymore as a teacher. And, Mom? I'm not even sure about my marriage to K.B."

"Oh, Holly," she said. "Marriage is for life. Even if I want to kill your father, do you notice me shooting him in the keester? Every woman eventually wants to push her husband out the window, whether she admits it or not. But we go on. To swear is human, to forgive divine."

"*Err,* Mom," I said. "It's 'To *err* is human.' "

"Swear, err, what's the difference, Holly? You got my point, didn't you?"

"Well," said Sallie. "It look to be hard to top that tale there. Hard to top a boat on fire and see-through bodies in the river. And now we know about that head of white hair. So I ain't up to talkin' in a new way about what happened to me, what happened here to my face. Except to say that I don't feel a tit sorry for anything I done. And I ain't askin' anybody to shed tears for me neither, like you some done over the fire on the ferryboat and the drowned ghosts. I just set to read my poem and that's it. That's all. Nobody can ever say Sallie Keller don't go full tilt shove. I said I'd tell my poem like it is, and here it go."

My Face

You ask how I got this face
and I say I got this face
by having a mind to stand up

to the bloodsucker took my
body—took my arms & legs, tits,
ass & cunt & tongue, my pretty hair.
Sold them all to bad 10 years and cheat

me straight up. And when I took my
own body back from him and all he stole—
He come lookin' for me and when he show
up & find me, he bend a hanger straight,

heat the wire white. Tie me up in front of
my baby son—so he could get-see how
my face open up by that wire.
He slice all ways. Rip side, rip back,

rip-slash over my nose-bone and up.
So he say: You never look good to no
man again. And so right—I look no good
to him that other day when I shot him once

then got the gun up under his chin.
Slick? I say—Better smile one last for me.
'Cause now you get to have a new Face too.

                         —SALLIE KELLER, POET

ten

Joseph Kyrilikov nodded at me across the dim sum table in the tiny dark restaurant in Chinatown.

"Eat, please," he cried, and pushed a steaming dish toward me. I looked, aghast, at a pale puffy clawed foot rising from the partially covered china bowl.

"I will not eat chicken feet," I said. "I'm sorry, Joseph. Dumplings, yes. Chicken feet—no."

"You must try. He insists." He pushed the bowl closer to me. "Is excellent. He knows this food."

I poked the foot with a chopstick. I found his habit of referring to himself in the third person unnerving. The chicken claw unnerved me even more.

He lifted the claw with chopsticks onto my plate. I brought it to my mouth and bit off just a tiny bit of flesh, then put it back down. Its texture was consistent with the way it looked: rubbery, with wrinkles and ridges. It had no discernible taste. I felt as if I'd just chewed off and swallowed a smidgen of someone's offered hand.

"There," I said. "I had some. It's awful."

"No," he said. "This is great delicacy. He knows this food."

He talked for a while about food. I wondered whether, when he was in prison, he'd had to eat a lot of chicken feet or goat necks, maybe scraps from the slaughterhouse floor. Or maybe he'd had so little food he'd fantasized about eating anything, anything that the earth could provide.

A line by Czeslaw Milosz popped into my head about how there were "nothing but gifts" on the poor Earth.

I was about to ask him about food in the gulag, but thought better of it. He sat before me, eating with gusto from the gleaming bowls—chicken feet, birds' heads, bird brains, dumplings—and chattering on about Thomas Hardy.

"But wait, wait—he needs to think."

He put down his chopsticks and stared into the distance. He looked both darkly contemplative and impish to me. He reminded me of Fernando Botero's painting *Mona Lisa, Age Twelve,* an adolescent anarchical smile, but transposed onto the face of a thirty-some-year-old Russian intellectual with thinning ginger hair and an imposing brow.

"A word, he is missing a word in English."

He fixed me with his piercing green gaze.

"Try to describe it, maybe I can help."

"No," he said. "He will think of it himself. He will think of it."

We sat in silence for a few minutes while he thought. I ate some rice and vegetables. I thought about the first poetry reading he'd given in the United States, just after he arrived in New York. It was an amazing literary event, 1972—I'd gone with Sam Glass. The reading was at the New School—Kyrilikov was introduced by some dignitary, then appeared onstage to wild applause, striking an elocutionary pose. Like my mother, standing up to recite her poems in the North Dakota schoolhouse or holding forth at the kitchen stove, he appeared in the grip of a divine enthusiasm. Resounding Russian syllables rolled from his lips as he stood straight, down front at the footlights, one foot forward like a colt—his right hand proffered, palm extended, declaiming, bardic. The audience rose to its feet. Most of us understood nothing of the Russian, but we recognized the sound of linguistic passion, of syntactical power. Then the distinguished academic, the professor who had been appointed Kyrilikov's official translator, stepped up to the podium. He read careful parsed phrases, with careful pauses in between—diffident, utterly removed from the cataract of musical thundering Russian we'd just heard. I watched Kyrilikov listening to the sounds of the restrained discrete phrases in English. He looked surprised. His eyes shot back and forth between the audience and the figure at the podium. What had happened to his poems?

Nobody loves poetry like a Russian, Sam Glass had remarked in the cab on the way to the reading. In Russia, he said, poetry fills football stadiums—thousands come to readings and memorize what they hear. In the prisons and underground, through samizdat, they copy the poems and pass them hand to hand. Poetry is at the center of the Russian soul. The night of Kyrilikov's first reading, I saw that he was going to have to acquire excellent English, and very soon, in order to translate his own work. I saw that he could not bear it otherwise.

He stood up suddenly.

"He will call his friend to retrieve this word!"

"Just give me a hint. Maybe I can help you."

"This friend, a Russian, he is ready, at the phone, any time of night or day, to certainly assist Joseph."

He bowed to me, then headed toward the restroom/pay phone area, nearly knocking over the tiny waitress who came bustling around a corner bearing more bowls of food.

He reappeared a few minutes later, a beatific expression of relief on his face. He sat down, replaced his napkin on his lap, and grinned at me.

"It is 'reed'," he said. "You know, water reed? This is precise word he wishes to say."

Joseph Kyrilikov, much to my own relief, then switched to the first person.

"I am nervous man," he said, "but I am also observant man."

I wasn't sure exactly what he meant, but he was contentedly sip-

ping a glass of heavily sugared tea and puffing on unfiltered cigarettes, so it seemed enough that it made sense to him. It occurred to
me, belatedly, that he habitually presented himself in the third person
because he felt, as an exile, like a separate being in the West, cut off
from his past, from Mother Russia—a completely invented identity.
He'd become, I'd heard, somewhat resignedly debauched—devout
drinking and smoking, a famous bachelor-about-town. I thought of
his great mentor, Anna Akhmatova. My favorite poem title of hers:
"Poem Without a Hero."

He spoke at length about the genius modernist poet Marina Tsvetayeva, how she could never be translated into English—she was too
complicated, he said, her rhymes were too complex and there were
the triple-layer plays on words that could never come across. As he
spoke, I considered the boldness of meter in Russian, and the great
tradition of writerly suffering out of which he came. Nikolai Gumilev,
shot to death by a firing squad while holding a copy of Homer over
his heart (maybe he thought it would stop a bullet?); Osip Mandel-
stam, taken away for penning a satiric poem about Stalin, starved in
the camps; Marina Tsvetayeva, whose praises Kyrilikov had just been
singing, who hanged herself after returning from exile, a tiny notebook of her own poems in her apron pocket. And Pasternak and
Akhmatova, who wrote unforgettably of the Terror, whose poems
were stained with blood. Anna Akhmatova stood outside the gates of
Leningrad Prison in the searing cold, in the endless line of petitioners waiting for word of their incarcerated loved ones. When a woman
in the line cried out, doubting that even a poet could find a way to articulate the horror and despair before them—"Poet, can you find
words to describe this?"—Akhmatova answered the woman, "I can."

Kyrilikov had spent eight years in Russian prison camps—and in
an asylum for the insane, where he was tortured. He had inherited a
heroic literary tradition—but in the wrong country. In this new
country, he improved his English, he continued to write, powerfully,
eccentrically—he learned to translate his own work. But he also

found himself teaching hypercritical middle-class American kids how to memorize great poems. These were the children of a super-power republic, brought up on television and committed to antiwar antibourgeois rebellion. He did not identify with their rebellion. Or their poems. He identified still with Russia, with the great literary ghosts who had led him to greatness—though he never went back. Though he refused to go back even years later, when the walls fell. He drank his vodka and smoked, touching the shirt over his bad heart every so often like a terrible charm.

He mentioned that there was a party later—a glitzy benefit for an arts advocacy society. I was surprised.

"You want to go to that?" I asked.

He smiled at me, a complex expression on his face.

"He is whore," he noted cheerfully, and touched his heart, smiling.

I found some time to write. K.B. was working late at the hospital and I sat down at my desk with my notebook. I wrote again about the river being dammed,

managed for miles above the locks:
even at the source—

I left the poem and thought about the word "source." Then I picked up a copy of a book of poems by Hart Crane and there it was—a source, a revelation. A sudden linking of poetry and politics in the lines "Thou steeled Cognizance whose leap commits / The agile precincts of the lark's return." There it was—Ho Chi Minh's "mind turned to steel." So it could be Vicky Renslauer was right after all, a mind could be steeled, according to Hart Crane. The steel trap, but leaping—because poetry is always leaping. The steeled intellect choreographing in memory the flight and return patterns of the lark. This was not the steel fist of cognition punching through a wall of oppression—or not only that. This was the same mind, hardened, tempered in the fire, but in love with beauty and compassionate—the power of the lyric was beyond proof. *A poem must leap and the heart leap with it,* I thought. *Steel made of silk.*

Sam Glass and I were at dinner at a famous writer's floor-through brownstone. We'd been served fish quenelles and béchamel sauce and had been more or less ignored by the older, established writers at the table. I was bored and wanted to go home. Then suddenly our host, a famous Southern writer transplanted to Manhattan, began talking about North Dakota, the prairie state where my mother and father had grown up. He told a story about how his father had bravely ventured out there—"into the hinterlands"—as a young man working for the Roosevelt administration. He mentioned that his father had been sent to an unknown town called Wyndmere, near Wahpeton (he pronounced it "Wa-*pay*-ton"), to calm down the "natives," who were suspicious of federal policies.

I happened to know why those natives were restless—the government was there to support the banks taking away their land, foreclosing on their farms after the great drought and the Depression, when the ruined farmers could no longer meet their mortgage payments. My own grandfather had narrowly escaped losing his farm. When it rained just a little—after months of dry blowing soil—my grandfather would stand out on the farmhouse porch, my mother said, and sing to the rain. He would make up a poem of thanks, a hymn, and let it fill his lungs—his hat off, his face, wet with rain and tears, lifted up to the dark rolling prairie sky.

"And the rain," he would sing, "the good Lord sends down rain."

I smiled up the table at the famous author—"Wyndmere? That's where my parents are from!"

The author had been relating how his out-of-place father, fresh from Harvard, had reacted to the Dakota wilds, impatient with the local hayseeds, the lack of manners and sophistication, the dull food and crude accommodations. He looked down the table at me, unsmiling.

"Fascinating," he said. Then turned back to his friends.

"His daddy was lucky he didn't end up with a rear end full of buckshot," I confided sotto voce to Sam Glass. "The farmers loathed the government types who hung around their land. They warned them off their property with sawed-off shotguns."

Sam Glass looked at me, an unreadable glance, then swallowed a spoonful of raspberry fool.

"Sort of reminds me of your own attempts at diplomacy," he said.

"We disagree about almost everything," I said to Sam Glass later. We were exiting the dinner party, where we had been disagreeing about the world, disagreeing about poetry and politics, disagreeing about what we liked to eat. "So what's the point of whatever this is?"

"I give you something you need," he said, and put his arms around me and brushed his lips against my ear. I stood still, waiting, barely breathing but feeling his breath, steady and warm inside my head.

"I annoy you," he whispered, "with a deep recurring annoyance. I get under your skin, I get under your opinions, I'm like an irritant in an oyster—but the result is something shining and tumescent, pearl-bright."

"Shut the fuck up, Glass," I said. "Pearl-bright?"

"I won't shut up," he said. "I'm under your skin. You don't know how to get rid of me. And I'm not stopping. You have to choose, here—between your pale savior and me. I'm trouble, but the kind of trouble you need."

But the fact was, I didn't need Sam Glass or his kind of trouble— I knew better than to listen. Why then was I standing there, mesmerized by his honey-warm poison in my ear? O steeled Cognizance! Why wasn't I in flight? Because—was it true?—a part of me I didn't want to recognize hovered above that honey and pearl-bright, contemplating it?

*T*he next day I worked on my poem again, but I could not add a single word. Outside a rainstorm blew up, thunder spoke under the rising sound of car horns. I sat for a while chewing on my pen, and then I got up and went to the front closet, where I'd placed our (very slim) wedding album (actually just some photo prints in a manila folder) and an album my mother had sent me. She'd typed out her reminiscences in a very organized fashion and pasted in old photographs and the silhouettes of long-ago pressed flowers. I opened it at random to a description of the house and surroundings in which she grew up:

> *On the west side of the house was a huge grove of cottonwood trees and next to that the biggest vegetable garden: everything grew, from potatoes to peas. On the east side was the apple and plum orchard. The crab apples were my favorite. There was a huge cottonwood tree close to the farmhouse with a bag swing that I loved. I had a playhouse in the grove of trees where I made mud pies.*

There was a black-and-white snapshot of my mother at about nine years old in sunlight, in her mother's flower garden—wearing a middy blouse, her blond bangs cut Buster Brown style above her level light eyes. I'd done a double take when I'd first glanced at the photo—I'd thought it was a picture of me.

> *The fall of 1921 was a great time for me, as I would be entering first grade in Earl School in Wyndmere. The school was*

just a half mile from our farmhouse and we could walk through
the meadow on the way. I loved school from the very first day
and was always sad when I heard the four o'clock bell.

There were other photographs: my mother feeding a wobbly-
legged colt, my mother and her siblings seated in a step-by-step
ascending row on the mastodon-like back of a threshing machine,
my mother and her friends in white dresses in a schoolyard holding
the flower-bedecked ribbons of a maypole. My mother as home-
coming queen with her attendants, my mother in a mortarboard:
salutatorian.

Followed soon enough, like a dust cloud forming on the horizon,
by the terrible drought and her mother's death when she was sixteen.
I couldn't bear to read once more about my grandmother's death, so
I read about the drought:

> *The dust storms continued, but the worst year for me was*
> *1934, the year I graduated from high school. That year has*
> *gone down in history as the driest year in North Dakota. Not a*
> *drop of rain fell all year. The farm turned dry as ash. The schol-*
> *arships I had won were useless—there was no money left, not*
> *even for a bus ride to St. Paul—and my dreams of college ended.*

Her hopes: dry as ash, blowing. The farm turned to straw and kin-
dling. The plum orchard and the cottonwoods and the potatoes and
peas and the poor horses:

> *Some days it would be so bad the horses would become blinded*
> *and frightened by the blowing dust and break away from their*
> *halters and run around the farm dragging their harnesses, com-*
> *pletely lost. Some days, during the dust storms, it would be com-*
> *pletely dark by three o'clock in the afternoon. The sun was blotted*
> *out by the swirling dark dust.*

I felt that dust settling around me, the sun disappearing. Outside, though, in the present, in New York City, it thundered, and rain fell, ironically, as if it would never stop. The phone rang and I answered it, expecting it to be K.B. It was Kyrilikov.

I told Kyrilikov about my grandmother, who had died when my mother was sixteen. The nurse who'd tended my grandmother (and who had come back with the body on the train from Minneapolis to Wyndmere after a botched operation took her life) stood at my mother's side at the open grave. On my mother's other side stood her high school English teacher, Miss Byers. She'd put an arm around my mother and recited poems, one after the other, a kind of endless kaddish, so that my mother would have these poems to remember, so that she would never forget how the words adorned the grave, like the wreath of irises she'd placed there, her mother's favorite flower:

> *I hang my harp upon a tree,*
> *A weeping willow in a lake;*
> *I hang my silenced harp there . . .*
> *For a dream's sake.*
>
> *Lie still, lie still, my breaking heart;*
> *My silent heart, lie still and break:*
> *Life, and the world, and mine own self, are changed*
> *For a dream's sake.*

"You know," said Kyrilikov, "all this you are telling me is in your eyes. Also the poems, there too. Your eyes will never grow old. I can see this."

He reached out and gently touched my brow as if he were blessing me, then withdrew his hand. Then he bit the filter off another Camel and lit up, waving out the match. We'd met at a coffeeshop and were having soup and tea. We'd both gotten pretty soaked in the rainstorm. Kyrilikov pulled a blue-flowered silk scarf from around his neck, shook drops from it onto the floor, and winked at me.

"Well, then," he said, "I will take vodka with my tea. This I need to restore my blood. Today he is feeling a little weak."

I smiled at him and tried to change the subject. I had been reading (in translation) the Russian poet Marina Tsvetayeva, and I was full of questions about her. I had come to revere her—a woman within whose life poetry and politics had collided. Tsvetayeva—like Rilke, whom she adored—was a poet's poet. Her poems were intensely lyrical, intensely complicated. She was moody, bisexual, willful, dreaming constantly of a male muse (*great: a* male *muse!* I thought), constantly distracted, but always lyrical. After a halcyon period of poet-adolescence in Moscow literary circles, she was catapulted into the Terror, still hanging on to her poetic purity. She was thrown into unimaginable loss and deprivation and fear about who would be taken next by the secret police. Marina watched family and friends arrested—and finally her husband (the White Russian spy) spirited away and shot against a wall. Then her daughter imprisoned, her son in jeopardy. Every person she knew under suspicion, under indictment—what could that be like? Still, she refused to accept the amnesiac narrative that ideological politics weaves: another roof garden over the slaughterhouse. Her poems veered away from the steel trap. Kyrilikov ordered more hot tea (sipping a little vodka on the side from a flask) and talked about her, then talked about his elderly parents in Moscow, whom he did not expect to see again. Then I tried to tell him about the women in prison on Rikers Island, but he would not listen and would not spare them a second of sympathy.

"You cannot see in the same light real poets—who embody the enduring aesthetic, who have stood up to death and prison for this aesthetic—and these criminals who manage to scribble one line or two behind bars."

I argued with him, but he was unrelenting, steeled in his mind.

"Try to imagine," he said, "a country that has been taken over by believers, you know? Et cetera, et cetera?" He often dropped "et ceteras" into his conversation as he searched for words. "And if, in this sad country, all the words coming out of the mouths of its citizens are the lies of this . . . belief, this invention, if lying is a near-sacred civic duty, then Poetry, et cetera, et cetera, becomes a moral act."

After a while, the rain stopped. Kyrilikov and I were walking back to my building on Twelfth. We walked down Eleventh Street, past a boarded-up town house that had been blown up one warm spring night a year or so earlier. A group of young ideologues, members of the Weather Underground, had been assembling a bomb in the basement of the town house. The house belonged to the wealthy and distinguished poet James Merrill, who had grown up there. I told Kyrilikov that I'd heard that the bomb-makers (who had planned to detonate the explosive at a military base in New Jersey) had gotten into the house through a family connection. He remarked bitterly that they had gotten out again by mis-setting the bomb timer.

"I know this poem," he said, gazing up at the collapsed roof, puffing on yet another cigarette.

"Perhaps could be called 'Revolution,' true? Perhaps these young True Believers thought they would add to poems of Mr. Merrill— a few quatrains of their own? What do you think?"

"I think your English is improving, Joseph," I said.

*F*riday night. Aliganth stood just outside the classroom door as usual, accepting passes, checking everyone in.

"Same old trouble on the way," she said to each arriving student. "You takin' your time there, trouble. Billie Dee, you slower comin' than Judgment Day."

Billie Dee was penguin-walking, which meant that she had been given an extra jolt of Thorazine. There was dried spittle around her lips. She looked at me, one eye rolling, the other unfocused, then glanced away, distracted. She began singing, in that power-quaver, "(You Make Me Feel Like) A Natural Woman."

Polly Lyle and Akilah had shown up early and were deep in conversation as I came in, with Sallie trotting just behind me. I'd watched Akilah during the previous class as Polly had told the story of the island and her white hair. Akilah's usually stoic cynical look had dropped away. She'd looked intensely involved, she'd appeared moved as she listened to Polly talk. Now she sat head to head with Polly, asking questions. Polly Lyle shook her head, then nodded slowly, then began sketching something in her Rainbow tablet.

Akilah looked up and saw me, and her face went through a series of split-second changes—from deep concentration to surprise to a hidden fearful look. I saw her reach out, about to tear the page from the tablet, but Polly Lyle ripped it away, crumpled it, put it in her mouth, and began to chew it. I heard Sallie make a sound behind me.

"All right, then, I'll *go* to hell!" Polly called out, the words a little garbled as she chewed and swallowed. She grinned at me, because she knew that I would recognize the quote. It was one of the most famous moments in literature—when Huck Finn tears up the reward notice for a runaway slave and decides to stay loyal to Jim, decides to help him escape.

"Teacher, sometimes we do what we do no matter what we're told. Even if it be told to us as Law."

"So does that make us all outlaws here?" I asked. I wasn't sure, yet again, where Polly was headed.

"Who you sayin' all of us an outlaw?" Sallie growled. I felt her swift deliberating presence, felt her struggle to grasp what she had seen.

"Do you know," Polly said, still holding my gaze, "that there are names carved into the trees on North Brother? And right there among 'em are the two inmates who saved people? Lewis and Mandy? There they are, big as an elephant's alphabet, all carved on a weeping willow tree. We were talking about that willow tree."

Baby Ain't, Billie Dee, and Darlene entered and sat down.

"Here I am, ladies!" Gene/Jean stood in the doorway. "And Yours Truly/Yours Truly holds in her hands here the best poem ever written in this class."

She waved a piece of tablet paper back and forth.

Baby Ain't held her nose and waved the air too.

"Where you been, Jean? You piss your poem before you get here? Or it got rank B.O., like you."

"A haiku," Gene/Jean announced. "But it ain't the size that matters. It's the way it used. It's like me: irresisting.

"Now this haiku," Gene/Jean bragged, "would be seventeen syllables—five in the first line, seven in the second, five in the third: count it out, ladies! An ace job by Gene—one cool stud."

"A half-ass job by a half-sex half-wit," murmured Sallie. Gene/Jean spun around on her heel and swung hard at her, a big roundhouse punch, nearly connecting. Aliganth intercepted the blow in a flash, straight-arming Gene, her hand on her nightstick.

"Don't tempt me, Mister and Missus," she growled. "I hit you so hard you come up a third sex."

Gene shrank back a little, looking dazed and surprised at herself. I sincerely hoped she would not throw up again.

"Yes, ma'am," she said. "I apologize profoodly."

Aliganth glared at Sallie.

"You keep that mouth in check, girl. You start enough trouble with that lip of yours. Don't think I don't know what you up to."

The lower part of Sallie's face smiled slowly, but the upper part—the asymmetrical eyes—remained cold and watchful. Looking at her face was like staring through a camera lens at a distorted image as one turned the focus rings, trying to align the overlapping edges of the object in the landscape, but her face never came into clarity, never got properly aligned. She looked at me and winked—a strange sight since her eyes were askew, one higher than the other.

"Bombs away," she whispered. And winked at me again.

After Gene read her haiku and we talked about it, after we discussed hyperbole and its opposite, litotes (Gene/Jean seemed to combine both), Aliganth suggested we finish up—and then she left to escort poor dazed Billie Dee to a "hand-off" officer, to take her back to her floor. The other women lingered for a while before Aliganth returned—and to my enormous surprise, Akilah came over and sat next to me, not smiling, but not looking unfriendly either.

She nodded quickly, once, twice—as if she'd heard a voice in her head saying something with which she emphatically agreed.

"I was acquitted of bank robbery charges in Manhattan court yesterday," she told me.

"Great," I said. (What did one say in this situation? "Congratulations"? "Way to go"? "Guess that'll teach them!"?)

Akilah nodded again.

"I'd really like to ask you something. I've been wanting to ask you this from the beginning. You actually think you can teach poetry? I mean you in particular. Because I believe in order to teach poetry—you have to have lived."

Her beautiful eyes looked amused but also sad. I noticed that, close up, her brow was creased, and she had delicately etched worry lines around her mouth. She wore a bright paisley bandana wrapped around her quiet Afro, and the yellow-brown-blue of the fabric somehow dramatized her gaze.

"You're right. To teach poetry you have to have lived—but lived in particular through words. Words are the key. I know this: words make meaning of our lives. Does that make any sense?"

"I think words are shit. There's a smoke screen of lying words everywhere. 'Incursion' for invasion. 'Terminate with prejudice' for kill. The pigs got it wrapped up. I've watched the love of my heart bleed to death."

"The love of my heart," I said. "*That's* the resistance against 'incursion' and 'terminate with prejudice' and 'building a bridge to tomorrow' and 'Would I lie to you?' and 'in the unlikely event of a change in cabin pressure.'"

"The love of my heart is dead. Period. The love of my heart ain't goin' to come back and terminate with prejudice any fascist oppressor. The love of my heart took a bullet in his chest on the New Jersey Turnpike. And contrary to what the cops put out, he had his hands up, he had his back up against the car: he was set up and he was shot without mercy."

All of this was delivered sotto voce. I heard Baby Ain't's bright voice across the room, laughing at her joke: "Turnpike: you pay to get on, you pay to get off." Never raised her voice a little, exasperated with Gene again: *"Besseme colo!"* And a whisper: "Jesus, Jesus." I was aware of Polly Lyle silently watching us. And Sallie, Sallie watching too.

I smiled at them both, then turned back to Akilah, who was still talking.

"I wrote a poem—I've been writing them all along here. But how is writing poems supposed to help me? I gave birth to my daughter shackled to the bed, in leg irons. They let me keep her a few days, then pigs, men in uniforms, came into the room and tore her away from me. I was nursing her when they came in. They chained my arms. She screamed for me as they pulled her away from my breast. I heard her screaming down the hall as they took her away. My milk would not stop. You think that would ever happen to you? You think you would ever write about it?"

"Have you? Written about it?"

"Yes," she said. "I have."

I didn't know what to say. I was not sure I should ask to read the poem. So I said nothing.

"I noticed," she said, "that you stopped bringing along your little stash of contraband, the newspapers and notebooks. I was watching for a while there thinking that you were pretty right on for contributing those things. And what did it take for you to stop? One slap on the hand by the warden? Isn't that what happened?"

"Right," I said. "One slap."

"One slap," she said, her mouth turning down bitterly. "That's all it took—to change the way you look at your incarcerated sisters."

"No," I said. "It changed how I looked at myself in prison. I was doing more damage than good—I learned something."

"The Department of Corrections is not exactly the one you need to learn from."

"So I should learn from you?"

"I'm a smart girl, like you. I went to college. Got down with Huey and the Panthers and the Weathermen. I converted Muslim and I fell in love. I wrote some poems. But here's the difference between us. If white people join together as a political force, it's a good thing. If black people advocate for themselves, it's a cause for fear and the violence of the state—a threat. And you believe in justice."

"I believe in justice. I just can't say what it is."

"It's not this: me in a shot-up car on the turnpike, my man dead on the ground, facedown by the bumper, his blood on the street—lights in my eyes and evidence being planted on me. I could shoot a gun—Youngblood taught me—but I looked at him on the ground and I chose not to squeeze that trigger. What kind of fair trial you think I get?"

I started to answer, something glib about the jury system—but she cut me off. Her eyes were dark with fury.

"No. You tell me, what kind of fair trial, what kind of justice you think I'd be handed?"

I knew the answer.

"There's no justice for me, you see, girl. You heard the expression: people got to make their own justice."

We sat there, looking into each other's eyes.

"And poetry can try, but it can't make this world fair—now, can it?"

I didn't answer. I had no answers for her—not even my mother's voice reciting Shelley: "Wail, for the world's wrong." Or Kyrilikov's devastating view of the kind of poetry that political ideologies end up writing.

"What is it that you want me to say?" I asked. "What is it you want me to do? You've already made up your mind about everything in advance."

"No," she said. "I'm still waiting for you to teach me something *real* about poetry. Give me please just one line of a poem about the fight to stay human in prison."

I didn't quote Ho Chi Minh's poem, or Hart Crane's—but I told her about W. H. Auden, who, I'd discovered to my amazement, had written a poem in which the old Women's House of Detention in the Village showed up. It was called "First Things First." In talking about the poem in an interview, Auden said that a friend of his, the Catholic activist Dorothy Day, had been locked up there after having been arrested for participating in a protest march. She told Auden about how all the inmates were herded in line together to take showers each day and one of the women ("a whore," he'd said) was heard quoting lines from a poem of Auden's that had been published in *The New Yorker* that week. The lines were: "Hundreds have lived without love,/but none without water." I recited the lines and Akilah stared back at me. "It makes both of our points," I said. "Not words— water. My point is made by the fact that an inmate is reading poems and quoting from them—quoting Auden. And yours is made by what is actually being said by Auden in the poem—that we must have the basic elements to survive, not just words."

It wasn't till I thought later about this conversation that I realized that I'd substituted "words" for Auden's word, "love," and that Akilah Malik had been asking me to imagine a different use of words, a different kind of love. *But the making of language is love,* I thought. Later I wished that I'd simply said it: that every poem written in our workshop had been an attempt to stay human.

. . .

*J*ust a day later, I ran into Akilah in the main hallway. She was standing close to the wall, a crumpled pass in her hand. She was so quiet, half in shadow, that I almost passed her by. I'd heard that she was about to be extradited to a prison in New Jersey—the trial concerning the state trooper's death was about to begin. I'd also heard that she was going soon and going secretly. The Department of Corrections was worried that her friends on the outside, the Black Freedom Front, might try to liberate their leader.

She'd be gone in a heartbeat, and I wanted to talk to her again. I was still intrigued by the fact that she said she'd been writing poems all along and not handing them in to the workshop.

But Akilah looked nervous, and when I asked her how she was, she replied evasively, her eyes searching the corridor as if she was expecting someone. She looked at me as if she wanted me to go away. Just as I turned away from her, Polly Lyle appeared, half running, waving a pass.

Akilah looked at her, then indicated me with a turn of her head.

"Wait," she said. "Wait."

Polly laughed.

"This is our time, this is the only time we can get and the only place to do this."

I realized that the pass Polly had been waving was in fact a piece of folded paper, which she now opened and held before us. Akilah reached for it, but Polly held it away.

"Teacher here is someone we can trust," she said. "She not about to sell you up the river."

I glanced at the paper.

"This is a poem of navigation," said Polly. "A poem with a use, you could say.

"It's all right," Polly reassured Akilah. "Miss Mattox ain't going to stop this from happening. I know that for true."

"On the other hand, I'd sure like to know what's going on here," I said.

Akilah looked away, frightened, nervous. I'd never seen her like this.

"Like I said," Polly explained, her strange gold glittery eyes alight, her manner animated, "I'm handin' Akilah Malik a poem."

Polly kept her eyes on mine, slowly opening the paper in her hand, and I saw what appeared to be handwritten lines of a poem. I glimpsed phrases like "south-facing" and "starboard turn." Below the poem there was a sketch—a map? (North Brother Island?)—with what looked like lines of latitude and longitude and skulls and cross-bones where perhaps there were rocks or the currents were most powerful. I thought I saw a path charted with arrows from Rikers to North Brother, with more arrows pointing to an open area at one end of the island: a bird in flight had been drawn in, descending hawklike over that strip of land.

When C.O. Janson came up to the three of us, she looked distracted, shouting at others in the hall over her shoulder. The poem-map had disappeared into Akilah's sleeve. Janson first asked for passes, which Polly and Akilah produced. She glanced at the passes, then turned to me.

"I need to ask you, Ms. Mattox, why you are all gathered here in the corridor. You know, now, that civilians are not supposed to fraternize with inmates anywhere in the institution, including in the halls. I need to know why you all here right now."

There was a long pause. Both Polly and Akilah stared at me. Then Polly smiled her unforgettable smile.

"Right," I said. "We were discussing poetry, going over a poem for class. An upcoming assignment."

C.O. Janson nodded once, twice—then touched my shoulder. She was a shortish woman with brilliantined hair and a sweet rabbity overbite.

"I understand," she said. "But you can't stand here in the hall and talk about poetry this or poetry that all day. You need to do that in the classroom, you follow?"

"I do," I said. "We all follow. Thank you for reminding me."

"Ladies!" Janson called out, turning away suddenly as a trio of inmates hurried past us. "Stop right there! Where are your passes, ladies?"

I nodded to Polly and Akilah.

"Good luck with the poem," I said. "Exceptional imagery."

They both murmured something as I moved away. I think it was "Thank you," but I've never been sure that's what I heard. Polly saluted, a sailor's salute—and Akilah turned to look at me with her steady assessing stare, a look I'll never forget.

"*I*t's my fault," I said, "all my fault."

I began to cry. "I love you, but sometimes I think that I don't want to be married. Maybe I just want to write. Maybe I'm a woman who needs to be alone. There are things bothering me, things on my mind. But I love you, Kenny. You know that."

I took a breath. "Look," I said. "I haven't been honest with you."

K.B. lifted his head from his hands. We were sitting in the kitchen drinking Red Zinger tea and smoking a joint I had rolled, badly. It was two A.M.

"It's that Sam Glass, isn't it?"

He took a hit of the joint and held it in, then slowly exhaled.

I stopped crying and waved away smoke.

"No, it's not about him. Entirely. Just partially. I admit that I see him occasionally, but these questions about marriage I have are completely separate from him."

"You see him all the time."

"I see him because I work at *Samizdat* and because we go to the same literary parties. Could we not talk about Sam Glass?"

"We never talk," he said. He took another hit and handed the joint to me.

"We do talk," I said.

"Then we never talk about what really matters."

"What really matters?" I put my mouth around the joint and drew out its blue acrid plant smoke as tears wobbled down my face. He didn't answer.

"I just need some time," I said. "Some time away."

"I think I know you," he said. "And then you change before my eyes. I thought this was a marriage. I thought this was forever."

"Forever," I repeated, and laughed bitterly, then began to cry again. "Forever. I cannot get my mind around that word."

"Yes," he said, "I've come to understand that. But it doesn't mean I can accept it."

We sat there weeping and smoking the joint in its rusty roach clip for a long time. We went to bed just as the sky grew light.

*H*er memories had become my memories. And her wildness my wildness. It was true, I did not want to settle down. I did not want a husband, a family. I feared pregnancy. She had been trapped— her scholarship turned to dust, her hopes for college swept away with the rolling thunder and the cracked blowing soil. The chance to be a writer—the chance to be a poet—all she had ever wanted: swirling away in the wind. She had married, had children, but there was always something about her that seemed caged and eager to break free. Why had I given up my own independence so readily? Love, yes. But love—love was a prison too. I knew if I walked away from K.B., it would be because I feared that prison.

I tried to write again. But the poems she always quoted circled the air around me.

I'll tell you how the sun rose,—
A ribbon at a time.

I'll tell you how the sun rose. Over Manhattan, over the West Village and the East River and over Rikers Island. Just as Dickinson said: a ribbon at a time. I was watching from the roof. I'd climbed up the fire escape, fearless, clumsy, teetering, still high, not caring if I fell. I stood on the tarred cracked surface, the bitter aftertaste of grass in my mouth. I stood among the ghostly vents and chimney pipes and looked out over the City. The streaked sky, the East, blood-colored and beautiful: streamers of red and then the stacked tinderbox blowing up in slow motion over the skyscrapers into the burning succession of lit hours. As Pound said about literature: *News that stays news.* A ribbon at a time.

and what we call belief thundered down in
every synonym. Two mirrored cities:

their symmetry invented as my own present,
twinned to a past

Twinned to a past, I thought ruefully, *that's what I'm crippled by, my past.* But then I realized it: I'd made the present I lived in.

I put my pen away, I let the tears come.

Gene/Jean's Haiku

Cherry blossoms fall.
I got a big dick. Plus tits.
What you lookin' at?

—GENE/JEAN KEELEY, POET

eleven

The day after my conversation with K.B., I slept with Sam Glass. My indiscretion was connected to K.B. only in the sense that our conversation had seemed to signal the end of something between us. I'd left our apartment and was staying temporarily with Benny Mathison, and I was desperately sad.

Sam Glass asked me to go out to dinner. At the restaurant, I drank some wine, and then I drank some brandy, but I was cold sober when I got into his bed. And I remained sober, even though I felt, that night, very briefly, as if I had a body, perhaps a beautiful body, loved by an ambitious lover. There was a candle by the bed glowing with a kind of devotional light, I remember that. And Sam Glass reaching across my naked body to pick up a glass of wine on the bedside table after we made love. I remember the shadows from the candlelight leaping on the walls and how he quoted a Salinger story in which a character says that his girlfriend's body is so lovely that when he touches it, he feels that he should "balance" things by putting his other hand in fire. Something like that.

"I should put my hand in fire," he said, and I smiled, flattered, though I knew that for me, there was no balance, no dipping of the hand into the fire of suffering to equal ecstasy. Still, I knew that I was fortunate in some way to feel sexual desire, to be afforded hope. To be alive in a different way. I had broken through to that. I thought of Polly's fiery being, like Blake's. I thought she'd broken through ecstasy to a state that I would never understand—perhaps where the body burns up in the conflagration of the mind's sight. Then I looked down at my own body, and Sam Glass's, and thought: *I'm free now, I'm fucking free.*

So I was a liar, an adulteress, an outlaw, a whore. *No rest for the wicked, buddy, but I'd rather be wicked than holier-than-thou. Heaven for climate, hell for company.* Of course it was an excuse, but it was mine, and I'd go to trial, I'd be burned up in Salem on it. A human bonfire. *So judge me.* At least that's what I told myself. *So judge me.* As I judged myself.

In this defiant, miserable mood I went off to teach my Columbia workshop. I felt hollow and bleak, and a certain go-to-hell reckless-ness entered my lecture.

"Wallace Stevens thinks like a French symbolist," I said. "But of course you all know that."

My ten graduate students nodded. Someone to my left at the large round seminar table made a muted snoring noise.

"It may seem obvious," I said, and held my head. I had a slight hangover. "But when you read the entire work, it's eerie to note how he is quintessentially American, yet he thinks in a poem like a recon-stituted Laforgue. And here, in maybe his most beautiful poem—'The Final Soliloquy of the Interior Paramour'—he seems to compare God with the imagination."

What a poem it was—and I wanted them to love it as I did.

"I want you to love this poem!" I shouted, and they all sat up straighter for a second, shocked. I read aloud:

> *Light the first light of evening, as in a room*
> *In which we rest and, for small reason, think*
> *The world imagined is the ultimate good.*

" 'For *small* reason,' " I said. "Obviously there isn't much upon which to base our images of the ideal. But—he also means that it is the small thing, the particular image, that embodies and grounds enormity or Big Thinking. Like Blake's particulars."

> *This is, therefore, the intensest rendezvous.*
> *It is in that thought that we collect ourselves,*
> *Out of all the indifferences, into one thing;*

" 'The intensest rendezvous'—the most charged and alive meeting—which most of us believe in, despite all the indifferences. Notice that plural—perfect!—there are so *many* ways to be indifferent! But the imagination, the imagination brings us together."

> *Within a single thing, a single shawl*
> *Wrapped tightly round us, since we are poor, a warmth,*
> *A light, a power, the miraculous influence.*

"Suddenly he wraps us in a *shawl:* out of nowhere—a shawl, ordinary, the commonplace wrap, wound tightly around us as if we're *swaddled,* like an infant in a mother's arms, or like the beloved in a lover's arms. This is what we needed, because we are poor, deprived of this attention."

I felt their minds following along, but I didn't feel they were really attending. "Listen," I said. "You know what? The other day I was teaching in the prison—out at Rikers Island? At the Women's House? And here is a poem that one of the students wrote."

I read Darlene's poem about shooting her husband.

"Well, what do you think?"

They were absolutely silent.

"Well? Is this a poem or not?"

> *I am the God of Three, put the gun unto his head*
> *And offer him to me. Then Darlene, he said, then the trigger.*

"It's sensationalistic," a student said. "It's written just for the shock value, which cheapens the overall effect."

"Probably," I said, "it was not written for the shock value. It was written down just as it happened, as the writer recalled it."

"What was her reason for writing it, then?"

"To tell," I said, "where she came from."

No one spoke.

"I don't know if it is a poem," I said, "but I think it should be honored somehow."

A few nervous coughs.

"You admire Wallace Stevens," I said. "So do I. But I also admire what Darlene Denisky has done here. Stevens's poetry, stylistically and structurally, is of the highest aesthetic order, but what he is writing *about* is empathy. What Darlene is asking for. That is the question I keep asking myself: How can we be poets without empathy? How can we perceive Beauty isolate, without feeling? Didn't Freud say that beauty has no use, nor is there a cultural necessity for it—but that civilization could not do without it?"

They nodded carefully, uncertainly. One of the very brightest, Randall Patter, looked upward at the ceiling as if Sigmund's bibliography was printed up there, and murmured, "*Civilization and Its Discontents,* chapter two, the standard edition"—just to remind me that grad students read and know everything.

"And look over here," I said, pulling a second thin volume of poems from my bag. "Amiri Baraka has written a poem asking for, get ready, poems that murder, assassin poems. Poems shooting like guns."

A few of them laughed.

"An ugly idea—not beautiful, not empathetic at all. And yet, in its ugliness, asking that the poem be a real object, like a gun. That words retain the power of things, of actions. This is what Darlene Denisky's poem is also about. The poem is the gun. Just as Stevens's poem is the shawl, the swaddling of regard, the 'intensest rendezvous.' The heightened perception of beauty or its opposite—and the response of the soul to either extremity: empathy.

"There are so many ways to be indifferent—but if what we can imagine is a kind of god—then our darkness is lit by a candle held high."

Within its vital boundary, in the mind.
We say God and the imagination are one . . .
How high that highest candle lights the dark.

" 'We make a dwelling in the evening air'—and our gathering together is enough, he says. This could be belief, religion even, by itself—except for the fact of that shawl. It brings all thinking down to the physical, the body—the holy body. This could be a hymn to the orgasm, to love, love itself." Sam Glass flashed through my mind, then K.B., then nothing. *Love itself.*

Out of this same light, out of the central mind,
We make a dwelling in the evening air,
In which being there together is enough.

"But what if we don't feel that togetherness? Baraka writes of poems as guns—but in writing about them, he concurs with Stevens. In Stevens's imaginary rendezvous, we collect ourselves out of all indifference to become one thing. What we can imagine brings us together. Even imagining a gun, a gun held to a head.

"And listen," I said. "Here's Baraka, on the subject of his ugly poems, asking us what goodness or kindness, what sort of riches might he give to the world? But what he finds he can offer us is ugliness and—shadows. He keeps saying that the imperfection of this world is a heavy weight. Then he looks up into the night sky.

"I cannot link Baraka, or this prisoner's poem, to Wallace Stevens," a young woman named Rachel said, and sat back, crossing her arms emphatically.

"But listen again: here is Baraka, answering Stevens, in a way—writing about how being black affects the aesthetics of empathy. Here is his mind, he says, 'out among new stars . . . They have made this star unsafe.' "

They have made this star unsafe.

I thought about Polly Lyle—and Akilah. This star. Among the wilderness of stars. Among the wilderness of islands.

I decided not to go any further with the Denisky/Baraka/Stevens constellation. If a poem could be an object to shock us out of our indifference (Kafka's axe to shatter our frozen sea), then it could be a candle or a shawl or a gun. A cup of cold water. Someone asked about the Stevens poem being anti-Platonic, which it was—and we discussed this. It occurred to me that Kyrilikov would have objected to the poem's symbolist appropriations. He felt that if Eliot and Stevens had read Hardy instead of Laforgue, we would all still be writing in meter and rhyme—for Kyrilikov a vastly superior, even morally superior, poetic stance. That aside, there was some excitement in the room I hadn't felt before—some spark was in the air. They were not just trying to one-up each other intellectually. They were engaged with the poem—agreeing, disagreeing—living inside the poem, that intensest rendezvous.

We talked excitedly for a good while. I found myself telling them about the prison workshop and the poems that had been written by the women. There might be a future there, I thought. One or two of them might want to come out to the Island to teach the inmates. They had responded at last. As if the poem were a shawl wrapped around them—and a gun held to their heads.

. . .

*T*hat night I went to stay with Benny for a while, to think my broken thoughts about my marriage and my life—the night after I
slept with Sam Glass. That was The Night—the night that the impossible happened. Against all logic, all probability, Inmate Akilah Malik,
a.k.a. LeeAnn Kohler, managed to escape from Rikers Island and she
rocked the foundations of that island jail as if she'd set off an atomic
bomb. I wrote it down in my notebook on my way out to the prison:
Akilah Malik has escaped from Rikers Island!! I wrote it twice, then a
third time—then added exclamation points (several), then scribbled
below the repeated lines, in large capital letters: HOW??? How had
an inmate so controversial, so distrusted, so continuously observed,
lifted up and off the Island with the ease of a bird?

Aliganth sat me down and told me how in detail when I arrived on
the Island that Friday. I'd read the newspapers, but the reports were
vague, plus I was distracted, shocked at what was happening in my
own life—and I'd hardly been able to read the newsprint. The truth
was, I'd been crying and I couldn't see words or even screaming
headlines through my tears. What was the story? A missing person, a
dazzling jailbreak, a lost cause?

The Island was alive with the news: Akilah Malik had disappeared! It had happened on Thursday night. When I arrived on Friday, it took me an hour to go through the checkpoints. There were no
pimps out in front of the Reception Center, they'd been temporarily
barred from the Island. There were armed guards at the entrance to
the bridge and at the other end. Powerful new searchlights, installed
in a day, raked the water, but rayed low, out of the way of the airport
lights. The escape had created a shock wave—Akilah Malik's breakout was being interpreted as a personal insult to the security capabil-
ity of Rikers Island, which indeed it was.

When I finally made it inside the Women's House, I was frisked for the first time, just inside the electronic gate. I didn't recognize either of the female C.O.s searching me, but when I looked around, shaken, as they handed my bag and jacket back, I saw Aliganth coming out of the Dep's office. She nodded to me, then pointed with her chin toward the classroom.

When we were inside, she shut the door and told me to sit down.

"Listen to this," she said, leaning across the metal table toward me and speaking in a low urgent un-Aliganth voice—as if she thought the room was bugged. "When it happened was when she was being taken in a Corrections transport vehicle to New Jersey. She'd been acquitted of the Freedom Front bank robbery charge in Manhattan court, so this was the extradition to Newark—you know, where she set to face trial for the murder of the state trooper? All been planned carefully and went off smooth and quick."

She described how they took her out at night in the armored vehicle under heavy guard—on the assumption that the swiftness and secrecy of the transfer would prevent possible interference. They were wrong. Not far past the bridge, past the main gates of Rikers Island, the vehicle was commandeered, the tires shot out. It was boarded and Akilah Malik was spirited away. The guards were overcome and forced to lie down flat in the transport van, then they were thrown out—roughed up but uninjured.

"Don't repeat what I say, because I'm givin' you a heads-up here! We got it back that figures dressed in black, all masked up, with guns and silencers, shot out the tires, shot open the locks, overcame our C.O.s, before an exchange of fire could get going." (*In other words*, I thought, *they were significantly outnumbered*. Later I also heard a rumor that a guard who'd come aboard from the Manhattan court was an infiltrator and had held a gun on the C.O.s in the van till the others boarded.)

Aliganth was still talking low. "The vehicle was found a few blocks away, they drove it right off the road, tires flat—left it sittin' near the water."

Aliganth said it was thought at first that the fugitives had jumped into another, waiting vehicle, but no evidence had been found of such a vehicle at the scene. It looked as if Akilah Malik and her liberators had simply vanished into the river.

"This kind of thing not supposed to happen," said Aliganth. "She run amok a few yards from the Island! They going to track down anybody Inside who had anything to deal with her."

I tried to think, to make some sense of what she was saying.

"Do you suppose they'll question me—or the class?"

"What you think I'm tryin' to tell you? Listen close: if you remember anything or you overhear anything—if you even got a mild suspicion in your mind—you need to tell me now! 'Cause they gonna be lookin' to ask you a whole lot of why's and what for's. Do you follow me now?"

Of course I thought about Polly Lyle and the navigation poem with the map on it, and what I'd said to C.O. Janson. Akilah had done the impossible—unless they caught her soon, she was out of the net. She had escaped from Rikers Island—and on the river! I still couldn't seem to take in what she had managed to do. The whole world seemed unreal to me now—as if I myself were vanishing slowly. I felt as if, having left K.B., if only temporarily, I'd left myself behind, a ghost, in the apartment we'd shared. The night before, I'd sat on Benny's couch in her cluttered living room and watched her eating a snack.

"You might try some tea with a buttermilk scone or two," said Benny, chewing grimly on a twist of red licorice, "and maybe some clotted cream. The ritual of tea, you see, gets your mind off yourself."

I had laughed a little, I wasn't sure why. Nothing seemed really that funny anymore, not even Benny's clotted cream and scones, which could be thought of as mildly hilarious.

Still, I must have chuckled to myself at that point, because Aliganth jumped all over me.

"You think this is joke time, Miss Teacher—you better think again! This going to change a whole lot of what around here."

I found Akilah's poem in my files about a half hour after the prison workshop ended that same Friday night. I'd gone up to the Social Services office—I'd heard there had been a prisonwide raid the night she'd broken out. They'd turned the residence and social service and medical floors and each cell inside out, searching for any clue as to how she planned and managed her breakout. They'd ransacked the four or five folders of writings (no more contraband!) in my AfterCare office. There were papers half pulled out of files and crumpled pages and folders on the floor. But in searching for clues to Akilah Malik's disappearance, in searching out manifestos or revolutionary tracts, cryptic notes or code words—they'd overlooked the alternative language of revelation. The language she'd chosen for her goodbye poem was not the armored rhetoric of revolution. The poem, in her hand, unsigned, had been placed randomly inside one of the folders. Had she hidden it there herself? Had an accomplice Inside left it there? I looked at the sure steady handwriting; I recognized it from the workshop. Bold, simple. Disguised by its lack of disguise. I saw that the poem was not about Killing the Pig or Bringing Down the Oppressor, there was no Black Power or antiwar rhetoric leaping out from the page—so they hadn't picked the writing out as hers. Poem Without a Hero. It must have looked to them like a typically irrelevant little effusion. They hadn't read all the way to the end. It was a poem that I too wanted to read—again, carefully—but I also didn't want to be caught with it in my hand, so I slipped it into my underpants. I'd seen the inmates do it and it seemed to work like a charm—though it was undeniably a tad uncomfortable.

I looked at the cabinet that held copies of the intake files. The intake files were sketchy—they contained very little information beyond date of birth, place of birth, vital statistics, and history of medication. Occasionally employment history. I'd looked for Akilah's file before, but of course it was not kept in Social Services. I imagined that there was a special file box just for her in the Dep's office. I opened the drawer idly now—and my eye fell on Polly Lyle

Clement's file. I'd looked at it before, several times—there wasn't much. Polly had provided nothing in terms of vital stats. Her medication history since arriving at the Women's House was pretty alarming. There were numerous entries at the Infirmary and from the med cart. They'd really been trying to keep her sedated, but I pictured her "tonguing" the pills and spitting them out later. Corrections always checked the inmates' open mouths after medication, but Polly was ahead of them.

"I got a wise and thinking tongue," she'd told me.

They had worked their damage on her, the so-called health and social service professionals. Some of the medical doctors and psychiatrists spoke little English; they could not understand the inmates. Many had had trouble finding jobs elsewhere. One or two had even had their licenses revoked. Reading Polly's medication and treatment history, it appeared that the goal, if there was one, centered on wiping out her consciousness little by little. She had been allergic to Thorazine, so they'd given her something that looked like secobarbital sodium. Plus Dilantin and phenobarbital for seizures. Substantial amounts.

I heard something and looked up. Aliganth was at the door, beckoning, her expression thoughtful. We stared at each other for a second. There were extra officers everywhere in the wake of Akilah's disappearance—so I was relieved it was Aliganth herself who came for me.

"Ross want to see you, Mattox. Right away."

She was waiting for me, her face grim and set. I hoped that I wasn't walking funny—I had, after all, a poem in my underpants. Then I stopped thinking about the poem—I felt a flash of sympathy for Warden Ross. How bad was she looking these days? I wondered. To the upper administration, to the City, to the newspapers? How many of the guards riding in Akilah's transport vehicle had been from the Women's House? This time there were no shadowed implications, no bemused instructions—she went right to the point.

"Miss Mattox," she said. "Both Akilah Malik and Polly Lyle Clement were, or are, students in your poetry workshop, is that correct?"

"That's correct."

"Miss Mattox, did you ever notice any exchanges of information between Polly Clement and Akilah Malik?"

"Do you mean conversations?"

"Conversations—yes."

"If you mean conversations—they, like all the members of the workshop, talked to each other."

"Miss Mattox. I am particularly interested in any exchanges, or conversations, between Miss Clement and Miss Malik that seemed out of the ordinary to you."

"I have to remind you that I teach poetry. Almost any conversation in a poetry workshop would seem out of the ordinary to a random listener."

Ross inhaled slowly, deeply. She looked at me in a mild and courteous way that was somehow deeply intimidating.

"Miss Mattox. You were the instructor. You noticed things about your students, am I right?"

"You are."

The warden sat back in her chair, smiled, and shook her head at me.

"In keeping with this routine observation, I'd like to ask you to relate particulars about how Akilah Malik and Polly Clement interacted."

"They talked to each other—they weren't friends, exactly, but they did talk."

"Their topic of conversation?"

"I don't know," I cried in exasperation. "Poetry, the weather—who knows?"

"Would you say that they talked about possible methods or routes of escape—or perhaps about the islands around Rikers Island?"

I sat back in my chair. *She knows,* I thought, *she knows something.* Probably much more than I did. She had taught me (in the matter of Lily Baye, in the matter of the battered child, of the lied-about lost baby) about paying attention to what was in front of me—understanding the difference between what I actually saw and what I wanted to see. Understanding my own naïveté. And understanding the difficulties of maintaining order in the institution.

"I don't know," I said. "I did see Polly drawing some pictures for Akilah once. That's all."

Ross shook her head at me, then pressed a button on the intercom. "She can come in."

I knew who was going to be coming in before I saw her. I prepared myself for her face. And here she was: the eyes and ears in my workshop.

She looked different. She looked serious, subdued. There was no wiseass, smart-off aspect to her at all. She walked in slowly with her head down.

"Hi, Ms. Mattox," she said.

"Hi, Sallie."

Ross nodded at each of us.

"Miss Mattox, Sallie Keller says she saw something transpire between Malik and Clement, which you also witnessed. She says . . . What did you see?"

Sallie glanced at me, a frightened split-level glance, her only betrayal of uncertainty. What I found most eerie about her was how her diction had changed—she spoke now like a bureaucrat, a buttoned-down official witness, not like a cool street mouth: no more jailhouse bitch rap-and-swagger.

"I believe Clement was showing Akilah Malik the safest way to travel between Rikers Island and North Brother Island. I was right behind Ms. Mattox as she came in—she may have seen even more."

The warden pointed at me impatiently. "Did you witness this as well?"

"No, I only saw them drawing something on a piece of tablet paper. That's all."

Sallie smiled her Picasso smile at me.

"I know what was in front of me. There was a map being drawn for Malik by Clement. It couldn't be missed."

"What happened to that map?"

Sallie snorted, reverting in a flash to her other tongue:

"She done ate it up like a monkey."

Ross looked at me.

"I saw her put something in her mouth. Was it this map that Sallie seems certain she saw? I don't know."

I moved around a little in my chair, suddenly remembering the oddly stashed poem. Sallie apparently took this as a sign of guilty discomfort.

"Ms. Mattox may recall where the weird story that Polly Clement told the poetry class was set."

I looked back at her. She really was transformed. She looked older, more damaged somehow—her terrible uneven face looked balder, and its jagged across-the-middle cut more savagely raw.

"North Brother Island," I said. "But you've already told the warden that."

Warden Ross stared at me and then asked Sallie Keller to leave. Sallie nodded, stood up, and went out quietly. She did not look at me as she left.

When she was gone, I shifted in my chair again and tried to think what was best to do. If Akilah had in fact gone to North Brother and taken her time about it, they'd have captured her by now. I would have assumed that the currents were too deadly for her to have negotiated easily. Even with a boat, a small craft, wasn't it supposed to be extremely difficult to land on this island?

I looked into Ross's eyes and repeated these thoughts word for word. She nodded.

"It would seem so. But it appears to those investigating that

Malik did find her way to North Brother. I'm not at liberty to tell you what they found, but there was evidence that she had been there very recently."

"But she was gone when they arrived? How did she get off the island so fast?"

"I can't tell you her means of transportation onto or off of North Brother. But let's just say that she appeared to have vanished into the sky."

"How?" I asked. "A small plane? A helicopter? North Brother is totally deserted—so it would be possible, right?"

She stared at me, silent.

"So now," I said, "you're interrogating Polly because you think that she's been an accomplice somehow?"

Again, official silence. Then what I expected.

"I am not here to answer your questions about the connection between Clement and Malik. I'd prefer that you answered mine."

"The thing is," I said, "Polly Lyle is . . . a little unstable, as you know. Whatever you think she's done—I mean if you believe that she aided and abetted Akilah's escape—you would have to bear in mind that she has a kind of tenuous grip on reality."

I sat forward, crackling.

"She believes that she is, what would you say—'channeling' the voice of Mark Twain. You know, Mark Twain?"

"I know who Mark Twain is," Superintendent Ross said in an icy tone.

I crackled back in my chair, chastened. I had offended her without meaning to. She continued warily, reciting Polly's intake file.

"Polly Lyle Clement came here on a vagrancy charge. She was staggering around in the shallows here off Rikers, raving about a raft she'd hidden somewhere nearby. They picked her up in the searchlights. She was shouting at the planes overhead and she was potentially violent, so she was given tranquilizers as she was processed in. She was also given a routine medical and psychiatric workup. She is delusional, as you are inferring, plus she is epileptic—prone to violent seizures. It is after these seizures that she claims to 'see' things. Her hallucinations, as you apparently know, are powerful and convincing. It would seem that the Mark Twain delusion came from one of these hallucinations."

"I looked at this copy of the intake file we have upstairs," I said, "and I agree there's not much there."

The superintendent looked at her watch.

"There's a new shift coming on and I have to hold inspection."

"Where is Polly now? She wasn't in the workshop tonight and—"

"She is being held in PSA."

"Polly Lyle? You have her in the Bing?"

It's funny how you know these things. I'd thought about it. I knew that just about every woman in the workshop could stand up to the Bing for a little while. A little while—they could take it. Even Billie Dee. I flattered myself that I might even be able to stand it for a little while. But not Polly Lyle Clement.

I stood up. I held my hands out in appeal. I was aware that I looked silly, melodramatic—but I didn't care. *Here we go again,* I thought. *Only this time I have it right.* This time I'd figured it out.

"Please," I said. "Please don't keep her in the Bing. She will die. She will not be able to survive it. Please."

Ross stood up too and glanced at her watch again.

"You do remember how convinced you were not long ago that Lily Baye was a persecuted victim?"

"I admitted my mistake there. This is not crying wolf, this is different. Polly Lyle . . ."

"Clement attacked an officer as she was being questioned about her involvement in the Akilah Malik escape. Just this morning. She lost all control and had to be restrained. She was medicated and taken to PSA."

"Please," I said. "Let me see her."

She moved around the desk and stood before me. I stayed very still and tried not to crackle.

"I thought you would make this request. We feel that she knows more than she is telling us. She was seen talking to Malik—regularly. I will let you visit her in PSA, but the arrangement has to be that you will question her about Malik—and anything she knows about the escape and how it was put together. And where Malik is hiding out. If she cooperates, she will be released from Punitive Segregation and I have the D.A.'s word that she will not be formally charged with obstruction of justice. Do you understand?"

"Yes."

"Do we have an agreement on this?"

"Yes," I repeated. "I just need to see her as soon as possible."

"What we particularly want to know is where Malik is now."

"Yes. Okay. I understand. If I manage to find out something—will you let her go back to population?"

She stared at me a moment. Her eyes looked very tired, but her jaw was set.

"If you find out anything that the authorities can use, I will return her to population."

I held out my hand and she took it.

"Thank you," I said. "Can I have some time? I need to talk to her for a while. It's hard to follow her sometimes."

"I'll have the Assistant Dep go with you. And I'll arrange for you to have forty-five minutes maximum with Clement."

"Okay," I said. "Okay."

"And let me ask you one more time—and think carefully before you answer. What, if anything, changed hands between Clement and Malik when C.O. Janson saw you standing with them in the main corridor?"

"I think I already told you," I said. "A poem. What passed between their hands was a poem."

· · ·

*S*he was lying in the fetal position on her mattress. I came in with Assistant Deputy Superintendent Knapp, who was heavyset and mightily incurious. She stood in the corner and yawned and looked up at the ceiling. I felt a little sorry for her. She had told me as we walked down the hall together that she'd been up all night, pulling an extra shift, like many others. They were on emergency status, she said. They had to find out somehow where Akilah Malik had gotten to, she said. They'd all been made to look bad over this.

I felt a little poem-line ripple and adjusted things before sitting down. Knapp didn't notice. Neither did Polly. *The soul has moments of escape,* I thought. Thus Polly was gone, her soul traveling somewhere.

I touched her shoulder. Her yellow-orange prison uniform was soaked with sweat and her pale hair was plastered to her forehead and cheek. She stirred slightly when I touched her.

"Polly?"

She made an unintelligible sound. Then she sat straight up suddenly, so suddenly that I cried out and jumped back. Knapp looked over, then went back to contemplating the ceiling.

Polly was staring at me wildly. She looked utterly deranged. I called to Knapp.

"Listen—Polly is epileptic. Has anyone taken the precaution of having a tongue depressor handy? And some medication—Dilantin, maybe? Phenobarbital?"

Knapp looked confused.

"Hold on a minute," she said. She unlocked the heavy door and called out for the officer on duty at the end of the hall. I heard the muted shouts of the caged women up and down the corridor. I heard Knapp asking about what was on hand.

She shut the door again.

"Pierce says they got the tongue thing and the medicine."

I thanked her. Polly was staring at me, still blank and wild—but now there was a glimmer of recognition in her face.

"Sis?"

"No, Polly, it's your teacher, Holly Mattox?"

She touched my face with shaking fingers. Her touch was unbelievably cold.

"Poem," she said, and smiled. The burn on her cheek looked bright red. There was a tooth missing in the front of her mouth, lower gum—I'd never noticed that before. There was also a dark blue bruise on her forehead at the hairline.

She began to shake violently—her legs, stretched out now, kicked as if she were swimming. I looked at Knapp, who was living up to her name, nodding dreamily. I reached out and pulled Polly into my arms. Her teeth were rattling in her head and then her whole body convulsed. After a minute the convulsions eased and she gently moved out of my embrace and sat up straighter.

"Tell me how you are," I said. I couldn't think of anything else to say.

"I been on the river," she said. "Lordy, it *is* lovely to live on a raft. We had the sky, up there, all sprinkled thick with stars, and we used to lay on our backs and look up at them, and discuss about whether they was made, or only just happened—Jim allowed they was made, but I allowed they happened; I judged it would have took too long to *make* so many. Jim said the moon could have *laid* them. . . . We used to watch the falling stars, too, and see them streak down the sky and trail their sparkly tails behind them. Jim reckoned they had got spoiled and was flung out of the nest."

I brushed tears from my eyes. I couldn't help myself. Not only because she was still shaking (though less violently now) and looked as if she might have a fit at any moment; not only because she was in the Bing and alone and sick and crazy; not only because I couldn't do much of anything to help her; but because, in her extremity, in her madness, she turned to them: Huck and Jim on the raft—she turned to them, the untamable renegade boy and the gentle indomitable soul—and let her soul glide with them on the river of their words.

She put out her hand and traced a finger along my tearstained cheek.

"Don't cry," she said. "The stars that are flung out from the nest fall, but they don't die. I promise."

"Tell me," I said. "What can I do to help you?"

Do we think that the world imagined is the ultimate good? What is the intensest rendezvous? Between one soul and an-other—or between the words that help us apprehend it—what happens as it happens? What was my rendezvous—whom did I love more? The real person before me—or the words that my imagination gave me, always, to conjure that person into words? Then I woke up: I was here now—the woman was cold, she needed a shawl. The poem is alive, it is as real as a shawl, a gun, a cup of cold water.

I leaned in close and whispered in her ear.

"Listen," I said. "Polly. I haven't told them about the 'poem' you wrote for our friend. I haven't told them that I was there when you gave it to her to 'read.' You and I know what it said. I haven't told them, but if you tell them now—or tell me so that I can pass it along— they will let you out of here. And they won't pursue this further."

She began shaking again, a series of terrible convulsive shudders, which she controlled finally, then laughed a little.

"What are you asking me to do again?"

I smiled and shrugged. What *was* I asking?

"Are you asking me what they've been tryin' to get out of me now for hours?"

"I don't know," I said. "What *are* they trying to get out of you?"

"Where she is. And how she got there."

I looked around at Officer Knapp. We were whispering, but I was still worried.

She shook her head, smiling, shaking. Then she rolled over on the mattress, away from me.

"They want to catch her." Her voice was muffled.

"Polly," I said. "I don't think they'll catch her. This was all planned carefully. They may find out where she's been, but I don't think they're going to bring her back. But if you can tell me specifically what your navigation 'poem' said and where she landed—I can get you out of here."

She sat up again and touched my hair.

"Forget what the Law says," she said.

"Hold on, Polly," I whispered, "there's a poem in my underpants."

Knapp was still nodding as I moved the paper a little.

Polly stared at me.

"It's Akilah's poem," I said. "I can't explain right now. I'm smuggling it out."

I was whispering very softly and she leaned in to hear me.

Then Polly, beaten and nearly broken, looked at me as if I was crazy and began to laugh.

For My Daughter

There is a flower in a field
I won't compare you to that flower

There is a bird on a branch
I won't say that you are its song

You are the beginning, the first morning
the moment in which words open their eyes

and their mouths and speak themselves.
You are last night budding at my breast

You are this morning budding at my breast
Your face beginning to take form

out of your powerful dreaming milk-hunger—
More beautiful than the field flower

More beautiful than the bird-song
More beautiful than all comparisons to beauty—

Which mean nothing in the face of the face of love.
Flower-mouth on my nipple:

                    You are ripped away now
by men, your new ears opening on the sound of their

boot-heels, their brute shouts as they pull you,
your mouth opening, milk-filled, away from me.

Your mouth re-filling with sound, a sound of terror,
as they strike me, then tighten the irons that bind me.

This is not the world I would have made for you. You deserve
a world made by love for love—instead of this island

where I am left, chained, without you. Instead of the island
where I will always hear you calling for me—
      Karina Mahmud—where I cannot answer you.

—AKILAH MALIK, POET

twelve

I called Benny Mathison and asked her what could be done to help Polly get out of the Bing sooner rather than later.

She laughed.

"You must be kidding," she said. "They do what they want."

"What about this guy," I cried. "Geraldo? Can he help?"

"No," she said. "The last time he investigated the Women's House it was on a tip that said there was a hunger strike going on. It turned out that the 'strike' was a floorwide diet—promoted by the Candy Whatever-It-Is Charm School."

"So he won't come back?"

"Get real."

"What can you do to help?" I asked.

"I don't know," she said wearily. Then: "Okay, just tell me the facts. I was having breakfast, but I'll find a pen and write this down."

"I'm not going to say I told you so," said Sam Glass.

"You'd better not," I said. "Or you will leave this life."

We were in the *Samizdat* office. We'd just finished selecting the poems and stories for the new issue.

"It wasn't a real marriage," he said. "You have to admit it."

"What is a real marriage?" I asked. "Can you tell me that? Does anyone have a real marriage? What the fuck is a real marriage? What is an unreal marriage? Ozzie and Harriet? Roy Rogers and Dale Evans? And a real marriage is two people living together and driving each other crazy? I love K.B.—I love him. The fact that I've hurt him makes me . . ."

I covered my face with my hands, then looked at him.

"Every time I lie to him," I said, "I am killing his heart. Yet I know I love him."

"Calm down," he said.

"I don't think I'll ever be calm again," I said. "There are some things you just can't forgive yourself for. And they make you crazy and unforgivable forever."

He pulled a cigarette out of his shirt pocket and lit it. He took a drag and I held out my hand. He looked shocked but handed it to me and I took a long pull, then coughed a little and handed it back.

"Vile," I said.

"It is indeed."

I was eager to change the subject, move the conversation away from my failure as a wife, a human being, a trustworthy friend.

"Have you been reading the newspapers?" I asked. "About Aki-lah Malik's escape?"

"Oh, right," he said. "I think I read something."

"I have a poem of hers," I said. "Do you want to read it? It may be something for *Samizdat*."

He looked skeptical but took the poem and began to read.

"You'd better fucking like it," I said. "I carried it around in my underwear for the better part of a day."

Sam Glass gave me the same look that Polly had. Only he didn't laugh.

"*I* saw him," Polly said. "I saw my great-granddaddy and he spoke to me."

"Tell me what he said."

"You want to know about North Brother? You want to know what I seen in the air? His blessing, a falling star—it was his blessing, so I know nothing can hurt her. Nothing in the wilderness of stars can hurt her. She's on a raft out in them stars—you can see her out there too, can't you?"

She was still trembling, but not nearly as badly as before. She smiled at me and pushed her soaked hair back from her face.

"He hovered over and he told me that there? on North Brother? her name is carved right below the other two on the weeping willow tree. Below Lewis and Mandy. She carved it there as a sign. Falling stars and this one took. Akilah Malik—that 'k' at the end, with its sparkly tail. She stood right there long enough for them to land and take her away."

She looked over at Knapp, napping.

"You saw it, Holly. I made a drawing for her of the whole island. A place for them to dock a craft and then . . . she wanted to know if there was a wide and open space. Maybe for a landing and takeoff. I told her there was such a space. At the north end of the island, open meadow, not so marshy. I know the exact dimensions, the latitude and longitude. I gave them to her. And from there they could take her away."

We looked into each other's eyes—she was telling me what she wanted them to know. It was the truth, but maybe truth slant, just enough to send them after her, not enough for them to capture her. Or maybe it was the whole truth, whatever that is. The whole truth.

"To another island," she said. "There she was, on a deserted island in the river, and then they would lift her right up in the sky and fly her to a new beautiful island."

"Can you say which island?"

She began shaking badly again. Her teeth chattered and I reached out again to hold her.

"It's okay," I said. "Forget it now. Let's stop."

"They sent for her," she said, shaking. "The people sent for her—they were all in touch."

The shaking had gotten so bad that I turned to Knapp.

"I think we need some medication."

"No," Polly whispered, in a terrible hoarse whisper, more like a gasp. "Listen now. Listen to me. They took her to another island. You know—a hot island, sun. Sugar and cigars. Waves rolling in. An island south of the river, south of the States."

"It's okay," I said. "Let's stop now."

Finally, whose side was I on? That of the arrogant mercurial revolutionary fugitive—that is to say, the side of radical underground politics, of inevitable change itself, as I had known it on campus and beyond? Or the side of Order, the court system, the sobersided working out of the old ambiguous pursuit of Establishment entitlements? Just-Us. What we often refer to, without reflection, as the Law. I was on Polly Lyle's side, that was all I knew—and now I felt as if I too were breaking her down.

She stopped shaking. She looked spent—as if she'd just run a race. She was sweating heavily and her breathing was labored. She pointed in the air, smiling at me.

"You know what my great-granddaddy said? What do we care for the Statue of Liberty when we have the thing itself? What you want of a monument is to keep you in mind of something you haven't got—something you've lost. I like to see a monument: a willow tree with names carved on it."

"Officer Knapp," I said. "Are you awake? I think Polly needs another blanket."

There was no more out-of-the-cradle-gently-rocking America, alive in its wildest sublimity. Out in the harbor, in the moving reflections, she stood, as the vessel lights washed over her fierce face—keeping us in mind of something we no longer had.

Still, the monument: the iron torch in her raised hand. The primordial feeling of crossing water—toward something we never had. Helicopter, plane. Portals open. The soul dancing like a bomb. Remote access. Her wounds from the same source as her power.

I discovered later that C.O. Knapp *had* been awake—off and on. Her ruse of falling asleep would have allowed her to listen in unobtrusively on most of our conversation—had we felt encouraged to speak loudly. Ross verified one or two things Polly and I had said through Knapp's witnessing. But, then, I'd assumed that the Bing cells were bugged in any case. Only whispering worked. I told them only what Polly had told me, her mouth to my ear—only enough to get her out of the Bing.

S he picked up the phone after a few rings.

"Hi, Mother," I said.

"I sense you're feeling sorry for yourself, but remember his words: 'Darkling, I listen. And I am pretty much half in love with easeful death.' And think about what *he* went through. Dead at twenty-four of galloping consumption. Yet he boxed the butcher's boy, our little Johnny Keats. Barely five feet tall."

"Great, Mom. That helps."

"Keats: better than that modern hooey. I remember when I first read 'Ode on a Grecian Urn' . . . Miss Byers, my English teacher, opened our book to it once . . ."

"Mom? Am I living the life you wanted to live? I remember your life as if it were my own."

"Holly, you've always been overly dramatic. I don't know why. You were always like that—when you were a little girl, you—"

"Mom? K.B. and I are separated at the moment. Just taking a break."

"I wish I knew what you wanted," she said. "I wish I could understand what it is that makes you keep getting it wrong. Wait—is that the neighbor's dog barking again? I'm going to have to shoot that bat-faced yapper out of a cannon! He's like Cerberus—you know, Holly: the three-headed dog at the gates of hell? Do you know the dog I'm talking about? At the gates of hell? Why do you think you are never happy? What is it that you want?"

"I want what you wanted—and gave up. I want my own life."

Akilah Malik is on her way to Cuba," I said. I was almost embarrassed to report on what Polly had told me in the Bing. It sounded like a B-grade adventure movie. Then I thought suddenly of the Department of Corrections as Cerberus at the gates of hell—outwitted despite its three heads, three brains, and a triple set of teeth.

She frowned at me, her face shadowed with disbelief.

It *was* beyond belief in some ways—but in other ways it made complete sense. The Black Freedom Front had longtime ties to the 26th of July Movement and to Castro himself. Political prisoners, political exiles—some, it's true, wanted for crimes or acts of terrorism—had been given asylum in Cuba since Castro had taken over. And they had been aided in their travel to the island. Castro took delight in welcoming these exiles—especially when they came from his superpower neighbor to the north.

"Cuba," I repeated. "Though maybe the authorities already know that."

She didn't say anything. She still looked incredulous.

"I admit this information sounds surreal," I said. "But we had a deal. And Polly absolutely needs to go free. She had another episode—like the start of a seizure—while I was with her."

"She will be released tomorrow—as soon as the Disciplinary Board can meet. I'll write down all the information—and I assume that there is more—that you will give me."

"Wait a minute—you told me that if I got some information for you, you'd let her go. You made it sound like you'd let her go immediately."

She laughed, a rueful sound.

"In prison, there is no 'immediately.' I'm surprised that you haven't learned that by now, Miss Mattox."

I started to say that apparently Akilah Malik hadn't subscribed to that theory—but I wisely, for once, kept my mouth shut.

I called Benny when I got home. She didn't pick up, so I left her a frantic message.

"Help, Benny! If you can think of anything to help spring Polly from the Bing *now*, please call me. No matter how late. She's not going to last through the night in there."

But Benny didn't call—she didn't pick up her messages till morning.

I tried K.B. at home and at the hospital. He did not answer. I had hoped that he could visit the prison as a regular volunteer physician and ask to see Polly—but my efforts to reach him failed.

Sometime that same night, in despair, I slept again with Sam Glass. It happened again in his apartment, where I'd gone to break it off with him, to tell him that I didn't ever want to sleep with him again. If I had had Polly's gift to look into the future, I would have seen myself going through what I had to go through—leaving K.B., still loving him deeply, living with Sam Glass, but only as long as we could stand each other, which wasn't, as it turned out, very long. I certainly didn't fit his ideal. I was going to be unhappy in love most of my life—not all, but most of it. Mainly because I wanted to be alone, I wanted my own life, and yet couldn't face it. The soul has its moments of escape. After Sam Glass fell asleep, I sat on the edge of the bed and dialed K.B.'s number again and again and listened to the ringing. I tried his number until three A.M., but he never picked up.

. . .

*L*ater Benny acquired the transcript of the C.O.'s incident report and time log: Polly was left overnight in the Bing, where she had two seizures. About four A.M., she was medicated. At five in the morning, she was shouting, disoriented, and when they unlocked her door and set down a metal breakfast tray near her mattress, she waited till the door closed, then shoved the tray back out through the door slot—her Wheaties and milk and styrofoam cup of coffee scattered all over the PSA hall floor. The other locked inmates cheered as the C.O.s cleaned up the mess. They brought a second tray and she threw that one out too. A psychiatrist and two C.O.s then entered her cell to talk to her and she tried to talk, couldn't—shouted unintelligibly. She let them put together the medication and offer it to her to drink in a paper cup—she threw it in their faces.

At 6:02 A.M., the medical doctor on call and two IPC (Interpersonal Communications) officers entered Polly's cell and tried to calm her down by administering a syringeful of oblivion. She knocked off one's eyeglasses and pushed another. At seven A.M., masked and helmeted Bing officers with nightsticks and clubs came into the cell, forced her to lie down on her stomach, and pulled her hands behind her back, handcuffing her in order to perform a cell extraction. Pepper spray was administered when she resisted. Polly was pulled by her bound legs from the cell into the hall, where she was "forcibly restrained." At this point, it was reported that she "lost consciousness" and was returned to her PSA cell.

Benny Mathison called the ACLU for advice on how to proceed. She also called Superintendent Ross as Polly's lawyer—and Ross told her that if Polly remained "noncombative" for the following six hours, she would be released to general population. She would see that the Disciplinary Board agreed.

. . .

I tried to write my poem. "Twinned to a future, stunned / in its white eclipse," then later: "Like this single mind, forever / unable to refuse its over-statement." I suddenly remembered riding in the car with my father when I was a very little girl. We drove along together at twilight and he was singing to me: his favorite song, "The Tennessee Waltz." Then all at once a wall rose up like a gray wave before us and we drove past an immense gated fortification with guard towers like turrets at the top, rotating spotlights—I saw men with rifles looking down.

I asked him what was before us and he told me that it was a prison—Stillwater Prison, Stillwater, Minnesota. I asked him what a prison was and he explained that it was a place where people who had done bad things were taken and kept in cages. I looked back up at the towers and the searchlights and I thought about the cages and the people in them.

Then my father sang a song to me, his voice filled with beautiful sorrow, one hand on the wheel:

> *If I had the wings of an angel,*
> *Over these prison walls I would fly;*
> *I'd fly straight to the arms of my darling,*
> *And there I'd be willing to die.*

Full fathom five our grandfathers lie. The wings of an angel. Stillwater. Still water, twain deep—and the lit towers above. Twain deep. *And there I'd be willing to die.*

*T*he phone rang. It was Benny.

"Did you hear the news?" she shouted. "Malik has turned up in Cuba!"

After I hung up, the phone rang again. It was K.B.

"I'm sorry I've been out of touch," he said. "I worked extra shifts and have been staying at the hospital. I didn't answer all my pages. I'm sorry. I needed to have this time."

Before I could respond, he added, "I just heard something crazy on my car radio—something about Akilah Malik?"

I ran into Kyrilikov at Columbia on the library steps. I couldn't help myself—I asked him if he'd heard about Akilah Malik escaping to Cuba. I shouldn't have been surprised that he hadn't—he had no interest at all in Western politics. Rarely read the papers.

"This runaway—is she beautiful?" he asked.

I laughed. "Why do you ask that? Yeah, she is, actually."

He looked very serious.

"When one is young and believes in literature, one associates style with substance sometimes. Literature is not, of course, the same as politics—we learn this."

I didn't know what to say.

"She is in Cuba," I noted stupidly.

"Cuba is now Russia," he said. "And I will never go back to Russia."

Then he waved, an Italian backward wave, and took off down the stairs. He turned and retraced his steps suddenly—then he bent and kissed my hand.

"Your life will begin to be clear to you," he said. "And since mine is not, I wish the same for me."

The workshop felt completely different—without Polly or Akilah, but with Sallie present like a kind of ghost-spy, the feeling was off-kilter. Still, Baby Ain't read her new poem about the hooker named Turnpike and Billie Dee read a poem about her mother, who was dead but who showed up in Billie's dreams. There was a line: "She watch me from a big blue cloud behind the clock on the shelf."

Aliganth surprised everyone by pulling a poem out of her pocket and reading it. It was funny and everyone laughed. I wanted to cry because I was touched. But then Aliganth looked at me and said, "Don't get all sobby on me—I wrote this on a bar napkin."

Aliganth had told me that Polly Lyle had been returned to 2 Main. I asked her if I could have a pass, after the workshop, to visit her. She shook her head.

"I don't think you're going to want to see her right now. She in bad shape."

"I saw her in bad shape up in the Bing. How much worse could she be now?"

Aliganth half laughed, half coughed.

"She could be more worse than you could imagine."

It took me a while, but I persuaded her to let me have a pass. After the workshop, I sat in the empty classroom for a minute, collecting my thoughts. Then I headed up to 2 Main.

I knew the C.O. on duty in the bubble on 2 Main: Officer Macon. If I hadn't known her, I realized, she would never have let me see Polly. Because Polly was, as Aliganth had said, in far worse shape than I had seen her before.

After I argued with Macon for a bit and talked her into letting me visit Polly in her cell—after she'd walked me down and buzzed the door open—I realized, looking at the figure looking back at me, that there was no more Polly Lyle Clement.

She was sitting straight up on her bed in her yellow-orange uniform with her hands folded in her lap, as if she were waiting for a bus or sitting in church, listening to a sermon or a choir. Her body was rigid and her face was completely devoid of expression.

When I called her name, she looked up and smiled at me, a brief flicker of a smile, but she wasn't there behind it. Her right eye was blackened and there were swollen bruises on her brow and neck and along her arms and there were deep scratches on her hands. Her white hair was sticky with cuts, still bloody.

I took her hands and said her name again and she smiled again and nodded at me.

"Polly? Are you okay?"

She turned abruptly to me and a strange animation, much like the puppetlike energy I'd noticed in her early on, surfaced suddenly.

She grasped my hands so hard it hurt.

"I ain't about to ask you to pray for me," she said. "But I know if you did, I'd be saved in a flicker! I shan't ever forget you. You say what you want to, but you got more sand in you than any girl I ever see—you got grit, enough grit to turn roun' Judas if you took a hang to doin' so! It sounds like flattery, but I ain't no flatterer. I don't know if it would do good at all to pray for me, as I said, but if you took a notion to get me in your petitions, what with your grit, why I know leastways I'd get to the pearly gates, if not past 'em.

"Y'see, I knew a man fell down a well twice. He said he didn't mind the first time, but he thought the second time was once too often. That's about how I feel now. I been down that well twice over and as Providence has it, that's just about enough. I may be dazed with admiration for this old world, but I can't stand to be civilized, I can't stand to be taken up and made much of—so it looks to me to be time to light out. I got no time to chaw over a lot of gold-leaf distinctions when I see a chance to hog a watermelon. Too much soul-butter for me with these churchly types. I'd rather go back down home on a steamboat, in style. Now, that ain't no slouch of an idea, though a raft voyage suit me too. And sometimes I think these presidents and congressmen and wardens might be liars, maybe even humbugs and frauds. Y'see, you don't want any unfriendliness on a raft—for what you want, above all things, on a raft, is for everybody to be satisfied, and feel right and kind towards the others."

"Polly," I said. "Can you hear me?"

"They ask me considerable many questions, but I ain't up to answering all I'm asked. I ain't up to answering—I can bear, just bear it—but I swallow the sawdust, I break my leg in the moat, tryin' to hitch a rope-ladder to the battlements. Here a captive heart busted. Here a poor prisoner, forsook by the world and friends, fretted his sorrowful life. Here a lonely heart broke and a worn spirit went on to its rest. Oh, and a little music like the notes I hear in my head, but I ain't standin' on top of the bed, raising Cain."

"Polly."

She went on for a few minutes, then she gradually grew quiet. I sat with her in silence for a while, holding her hands. At one point she smiled beatifically at me, a beautiful ruined smile. When I got up, finally, to leave, she clasped my hand. Her gold-flecked avian eyes glittered. I sat down again.

"The angels are here," she said. "They're here now, arguin' just out the window about who up to comin' in first to ketch me a beckoning. I told them heaven for climate, hell for company, but they are an earnest lot and would druther spend hours wing-brightening. You could see through blindness with one wing-feather."

Then she seemed to grow more aware of my presence and talked to me about the end she saw coming in very particular terms. She gave me a set of instructions about what to do with her personal effects. ("What part of me be assignable," she said, quoting Dickinson.) Not much made sense to me, but I listened closely to everything she said.

I walked down the corridor, barely breathing. In the main hall downstairs, I leaned against the wall as inmates and C.O.s passed me, talking, cursing, calling out. He had come back to save her, the old man, Great Granddaddy—in his white suit and his white hair and his glittering, hot-tempered, great-hearted, profane, sentimental, run-river, sugar-hogshead style. The inimitable monument, winking. A good going-over, grace triumphant—sounding the river, her heart sounded, the heart of a child, wing-brightening.

*H*e said if you find yourself on the side of the majority, it is time to reform. He said that the trouble ain't that there is too many fools, but that the lightning ain't distributed right. He said, neverthe-less, that on a raft, what you want above all things is for everybody to be satisfied and to feel right and kind toward the others. *That's what you want, Polly Lyle,* the old man once said, *if you can get it to hap-pen.*

The Ballad of Aliganth

My name is C.O. Aliganth
I don't know how to sing
and I don't know how to danth.

But I know how to write a poem
Because I've spent all this time
when I should have been home—

Guarding the poets, guarding
the class. If you don't like this
poem you can take it fail or pass.
(or fill in your own line here!)

My name is C.O. Aliganth
and I get stuck with Gene/Jean,
neither woman nor a manth.

My name is C.O. Aliganth
And if you took the time to care
You'd know my first name: Nanth.

          —NANCE ALIGANTH, POET

thirteen

I f Superintendent Ross had suffered momentary doubts or any
dark moments of the soul relative to the loss of Akilah Malik, a
high-profile, highly controversial "political" prisoner about to
be extradited and tried on a Murder One felony charge who had
vanished—poof!—into thin air, then parachuted from a cloud down
into Havana, all on her watch, she wasn't letting on. I had hoped that
whether or not she acknowledged the scandal of Akilah Malik's departure, it could happen that she would admit that they had system-
atically brutalized Polly and that it might also be possible to find a
way to help her. But Ross sat sphinxlike before me, acknowledging
nothing. I suggested that Polly needed care—that I knew a neurolo-
gist (K.B., of course) with experience with inmate patients who
could visit her. She took his card and nodded. There was nothing
else to say.

I called Information in New Orleans. There were two Clements
listed. One number was out of service when I called it, and the other
was answered by a woman who had never heard of Polly Lyle
Clement, but asked me if I wanted to subscribe to her Save a Pet
newsletter. There was no other information.

I took out my key to our apartment on West Twelfth, but decided
to knock before entering. I'd phoned K.B. to make sure that he

was home before I'd come over. He didn't respond to knocking, so I opened the door and then stood in the doorway.

"Kenny?"

He called out, "I'm here," and I recognized the range of his voice—he was in the kitchen.

As I walked in, he was fixing himself some scrambled eggs, shaking the frying pan and adding Tabasco sauce and pepper.

It made me sad to see him there, in his scrub-tops and boxer shorts. I put my purse down and kissed him.

"I'm hungry," I said.

After we'd eaten, I presented my case.

"Maybe she's a kind of 'fluent' aphasia," I said. "She speaks readily and easily, but the content of the words, the words themselves, do not necessarily reflect what she'd like to say."

"So it's all a kind of nonsense?"

"No, it's not nonsense altogether," I said. "It's her focus, perhaps? She shifts into this free-floating alternative diction when she's kind of giving up on the reality of the present."

"Are you saying that she's suicidal?"

"I'm saying that I think that if you could visit her, if you could diagnose her—it would help get her better treatment. That's all."

He took a sip of coffee and smiled at me.

"I can request a visit as her personal physician," he said. "Is that who I am?"

I smiled back at him across the table.

"That's who you are in order to help Polly Lyle."

He put his head down, then lifted his plate and fork and stood, wearily, up.

"I'm telling you that I'm also me," he said. "K.B. I am also *me.*"

I was working alone at *Samizdat,* reading manuscripts, when K.B. called to tell me that he'd finally been allowed to see Polly

Lyle. I had been staring at a collection of stories written in the "Eastern European" style—*Dr. Floppo's Blue Sedan.*

"She's in bad shape," he said. "She's seriously bruised, possible concussion, and may have a broken rib or two—but more worrisome than that trauma is her psychological state. She's in shock from being beaten and from seizing. The epileptic incidents have depleted her, and her personality is clearly fragile. She needs to be hospitalized, and I've recommended that."

"Will they do it?"

"It helps that I'm affiliated with a hospital on the outside—they may respond to that. Or not. But my concern is that Polly is so depressed—she kept bringing up death. She's not strictly aphasic, Holly. Though you're right, she's lost in her own 'language.' "

He paused. "When I had to leave, she put her hand in mine," he said quietly. "Like a child. And she asked me to take her out of there. Like a child—she just wanted to go home."

"I know," I said. "She just wants to go home."

We both waited. I began to cry, then caught my breath.

"How soon can she be taken to the hospital?"

"If they cooperate—in one, maybe two days."

"K.B.," I said, "I don't think she'll last that long."

There was a sigh at the other end.

"You want me to go back tomorrow?"

"Or sooner," I said, and held my breath again.

I tried holding my breath in order to hold my tongue the next day at the Women's House. I was in the middle of a meeting with two newly recruited AfterCare workers—who looked like members of the Ladies' Liturgical Society—and Dr. Bognal, who was delighted to be shocking them with his highly idiosyncratic priapic view of the Psychology of the Inmate Patient. He sat back in his sweat-stained padded chair and spoke to the ceiling, his eyes rolled upward, smiling to himself as the timid new employees listened.

"First thing you're lookin' at here is that these are mostly hard-line hookers—they suck the chrome off a bumper for five bucks. You're up against bumper-suckers, pickpockets, petty thieves, what have you."

He looked up and nodded in my direction.

"Now, Ms. Mattox over there . . ."

He winked at me.

". . . doesn't believe in the Stanford-Binet standardized IQ test. She thinks she can raise a whore's IQ by giving her poetry writing classes."

He noted this in a falsetto tone, wiggling his little finger at me.

"*Very* therapeutic!"

I looked at him: his face reminded me of a big dull chromeless bumper—on a car about to be pushed over a cliff.

"Dr. Bognal," I said to the two ladies, "knows he could raise his own IQ by holding his breath for three minutes. It's been proven effective."

I smiled, and Bognal smiled too. The two churchly women coughed nervously. One stared at me, truly shocked.

"Ms. Mattox," he said, "likes to think of herself as funny."

I did not think of myself as funny, certainly not at that moment. I thought of myself as defending the real world of real women against the leveling force of the Bognal Bumper. If hookers were skilled at blow jobs, they were even better at wallet extraction, accomplished as the chrome was being removed. But they were best at remaining unimpressed by men. This was the actual touchy topic under discussion, I thought—that in fact women tricked men because they found them trickable. Or that women were cynical the way Bognal found me cynical—he thought that I believed the profession of headshrinking was no more therapeutically significant than the much older profession of giving head.

Either way, Bognal wasn't going to let me have the last word.

"I'll pass around some of these intake files," he said, reaching for a pile of manila folders. "And you can decide for yourselves about these hopeless cases."

I let myself drift away, ruminating about Polly, then thinking about hopeless cases in general. I was one. As my mother had long ago predicted, I pissed men off, and I knew now I always would—particularly men who assumed they had power over me. Hopeless Case Number Six Million and Two: Me. Always in trouble with men.

And once really, as they say, *in trouble.* A story I'd never told anyone—because I could not find the language to do so. This thing had happened to me, but I had no way to express it.

*A*ll my life it was there: the thing that I could never write about. It had happened to me, but I could not tell anyone.

I had gone to California from Minnesota for graduate school—by way of New York City. I'd stopped to see K.B. in med school before I flew to San Francisco. We spent an idyllic weekend, then I waved goodbye walking to the plane.

Two months later, I discovered I was pregnant. I didn't tell K.B. and I didn't tell my roommates. I did not want to be pregnant. It was right before the law changed, right before *Roe v. Wade,* and I knew that in California women had three realistic ways to approach termination. First, private physicians performed the operation—if one knew the right people and had enough money. Second, there was Mexico. Just across the border in Tijuana, it was possible to arrange an abortion—but this way was frightening and dangerous. Finally, if a psychiatrist stated that the woman would be psychologically damaged by giving birth, the state would provide the operation.

I knew no private physicians in California and didn't have a lot of money. I did not, however, want to go to Tijuana and take the chance of ending up bleeding in a back alley. So I went to a psychiatrist, a woman, who had no sympathy for me at all.

"You're a smart girl who didn't think things through," she said. "A smart girl who got herself into a pickle—and the system doesn't provide for girls like you. You're not unstable, you were just unlucky."

We had used birth control, but something had gone wrong. I knew if I had a baby it would take away my life: no graduate school, no writing, no future. I was too young and I was not ready for a kid. I was trapped by my own body, which was now changing daily. I developed morning sickness, my breasts swelled. I knew that there had to be a doctor somewhere who believed in the right to choose and who would sign the form.

So I tried again. I went to a psychiatrist at a San Francisco hospital. In the waiting room, a thin pretty black girl was reading a magazine. She looked like a child. We began talking and she told me that she was eighteen. Her uncle had raped her one night—he pushed into her bedroom high and violent—and now she was pregnant and wanted to terminate immediately.

"I can't go this way to term or I will die," she said. "That he could do this thing and get away with it is drivin' me wild—that he make me bear his child is hell on earth."

She looked so very young. She was chewing bubble gum and as she chewed, tears ran down her face. I began to cry too. My story was nothing like hers, but our connection was the sense of being trapped and helpless. Our bodies had betrayed us. They had become prisons.

We held hands for a moment. Tears rolled quietly down her face as she quietly blew bubbles and quietly popped them. It began to rain outside and rain ran down the glass as our tears fell. There was a clock on the wall, but time had slowed down to a near-stop. We were in trouble, we were in the waiting room, waiting for a man to decide what would happen to us.

Then she was called into the office and was inside for about fifteen minutes. I jumped as she came out—she pushed blindly through the door, weeping. She didn't speak to me or say goodbye. I stared after her—I wanted to call to her, but then I remembered that I hadn't asked her name.

Then my name was called and I went in.

The psychiatrist was a professorial-looking man with glasses and unruly hair. He wore a checked jacket that was too big for him in the shoulders. He was smoking a cigarette and fiddling with his Zippo lighter, popping the top open and shut in a maddening way. He stacked and unstacked the papers, then turned to me.

He greeted me courteously enough, scratching his ear, and seemed to listen as I began my statement—about how I would be giving up my life if I had a baby, how I was not ready to be a mother—then abruptly interrupted me.

"You know," he said, rubbing an eyebrow. "I can't stand these black whores. They get knocked up by family members, then they come whining for help. The last one, just before you, was such a slut she actually stank. I had to open a window."

In my mind's eye, he began to shrink until he was the size of a tiny crocodile—in fact, he suddenly looked exactly like a crocodile as he smiled at me.

"It's pleasant to see a nice girl like yourself," he said. "After all this trash."

I sat forward—I looked into his tiny darting eyes.

"Tell me," I said. "How does it feel to combine the energy of a whippet with the IQ of a concrete slab?"

I left with his signature on my form. I was granted an abortion because I was "hostile, aggressively unstable, and unfeminine." I hadn't planned it this way. I may be the only woman ever granted a medical procedure on the grounds of lack of femininity.

But I told no one—and I did not tell K.B. And I would never know what happened to the gentle girl who cried and blew bubbles in the waiting room. I had taken the form and I had done what needed to be done, but I never did try to find my friend from the waiting room. All of my life, I have wished that I had.

As my poem grew, line by line, a sense of clarity and resolve about Sam Glass grew in me simultaneously. "If the snow grew/ steeped in blood, they raised a Court. But no one/out-thinks the two-in-one." I made up my mind—for good.

I met Sam Glass, as planned, for a drink.

"I don't want to see you anymore," I said to him. "I mean, except professionally. As poets. As editors."

"That's groovy with me," he said. "I'm getting a little tired of all the ambivalence. I want someone who is into me unequivocally."

"The way you can't be into anyone," I noted.

"The way *you* can't," he returned in a schoolyard taunting tone. "You are incapable of even *liking* a man. Why don't you face it?"

He then set forth a list of qualities he expected women with whom he spent time to possess—all qualities I lacked, like "excellent cook," "understands wine," "hip to design," "literary but not competitive."

We were back at the Irving Place bar. Billie Holiday was singing in the background again.

"Still, you'll be back," he said, and sipped his drink smugly, though he looked a little unsure, a little battered. Sam Glass had been on a rough ride too. He was used to an easier time of it with women, I thought.

"Not if I can help it," I said.

A sad pause descended and I looked fondly at him, slumped a little, across the table. I swallowed some of my martini and coughed.

"But I have to admit, Sam. I have learned a lot from you."

He perked up.

"About editing," I added, too late.

He laughed. "I am an amazing teacher," he said. "Utterly amazing. I'm good at what I do—if I'd chosen any other field I'd be the top executive, no question. You know, head of IBM or something. As it is, I have to be content with being the best literary editor ever."

He lifted his glass and toasted himself, his Artful Dodger grin on his face. Looking at him, I thought: *I will always remember Sam Glass this way.*

I went back to our apartment to collect my mail. There was a letter from Kyrilikov, who'd gone to Venice for a quick vacation. In the letter, he wrote (in near-perfect English—the clarity of his writing exceeded that of his speech at this point) how the work of the best poets seemed to be written by beings who were no longer people. Later in the letter he wrote that a writer is himself "a superb metaphor of the human condition." I put down the page and thought about how a writer could be herself a metaphor. Kyrilikov's final thought was that because a writer was a metaphor for other humans beings, what he had to say about prison "should be of great interest to those who fancy themselves free."

I was still in our apartment, sitting at my desk, when K.B. called. I picked up the phone and I knew he was there, on the line, though he was silent. Then he cleared his throat. I could hear him trying to decide how to tell me, what words to use. I felt the planet, the star, shift. *"They have made this star unsafe." This is the silence,* I thought, on the slaughterhouse floor, *this is the silence after the bloodbath.*

"It's okay," I said. "Please, just say it. Jesus Christ, Kenny. Say it."

"I was there, I was right there, Holly. Five minutes earlier and I might have been able to save her. I stopped to check on one inmate at C-76 and then I went right over to the Women's House. I got inside and there was a lot of commotion. Everyone shouting that there'd been a hang-up.

"Holly, she took the classic out—she tore up her bedsheets and tied them to a ventilator grate. I talked my way in—I was her physician, I'd treated her previously. When I entered her cell they were just cutting her down. Her neck had just snapped. We tried mouth-to-mouth. She was gone. They're holding the body in the hospital morgue now. There's apparently no one to claim it, so I asked, as her physician, to be involved in any decision about the disposition of her remains."

There was a very long silence.

"I knew," I said. "I knew what you were going to say."

Then, as I knelt down on the floor, still holding the phone to my ear, I slid against the table. As I fell, I dislodged the papers on top, a stack of poems. I let poems fall all around me: poems by my Columbia students, poems by the Rikers Island students, my own poem, a copy of Auden's poem "First Things First," and Kyrilikov's letter—every written paper I carried around in my schoolbag. I heard myself crying out, but then I stopped the sound, stopped myself.

"Jesus Christ," K.B. said, and his voice was raw. It sounded as if he'd been crying too. "The truth is, there are so many goddam suicides out there, they can't keep up. The shrinks and the social workers are incompetent and so they institute what they call Inmate Watch, but one inmate can have up to thirty or forty others to watch. Holly. This is not the way it was supposed to turn out."

I couldn't speak, I couldn't find a way to words. Where was language, where were we on this unsafe star? I held my breath, sobbed again, willed myself to stop crying.

"Holly?"

"Kenny?"

"Her face was young, but her hair was so white."

"I know. Her hair was white."

"Can you tell me what she was in for?"

It took me a long time to get my breath, but I finally found a way to speak. *Her wounds came from the same source as her power.*

"She was in for channeling Mark Twain," I said. "I'm pretty sure that was her only crime."

Poem of Navigation

North Brother lies due southwest of Hunt's Point
As the crow flies. Small craft from Rikers Island:
Turn the wheel starboard as the current will
Pull you port. Mark you the tide rips, they hit you
Aft, but there are seven whirlpools that seem
Constant on the path. Stay steady in neutral as you
Come up to the old pier wall. Go under port side and down-
shift into a cove. Bow in middle of hidden cove and tie up
    starboard.

Climb the south facing rock wall and head Up Island.
At the north end the plain field, the meadow will shine.
Below is a diagram of the field. Beware marshes on
East side. Clear landing space, three hundred yards.
Don't forget the weeping willow. You can waltz across
That landing space like a ballroom floor. Look below
For the arrow's path. Look for markings of tide rips and
Side-winding currents. Look for names of who've come before.
Destroy this when you have found your way. Destroy the map
And all signs of writing about the body of North Brother.
Do not bother the birds. If you are quiet, they will show you
                    All you need to know.

fourteen

The day after Polly died, on a hunch, I'd stood outside Bognal's closed office door waiting to talk to him. He was on the phone and I could hear occasional flickers of his conversation.

It hardly seemed possible, but it sounded as if he was having phone sex. I stood there outside his door, crying a little. I was not ready to let Polly go and I was deeply defensive about anything said about her in the prison—yet it seemed to me, oddly, perversely, that Polly wouldn't have minded what I was hearing from old Bognal on the horn. Polly approved of any sad passionate thing—even a furious self-pitying shrink holding a phone receiver, longing to re-create something resembling intimacy for himself. His hoarse, altered voice, baying for love, a kind of diminished love, into a plastic receiver.

"You want it? You want my rock-hard . . . down your throat? You want it [inaudible] your wet pussy . . . just like before, you were wearing some [inaudible]— Baby: beg me! Say it, baby! Tell me!"

I knocked loudly and there was a sort of muffled, choked cry, then silence. After a bit, I knocked again.

When he finally opened the door, he looked dazed. I brushed back my tears and nodded to him.

"I wanted to ask you about Polly Lyle Clement again," I said. He frowned at me.

"Who?"

"The inmate who . . . killed herself. Two Main."

"The hang-up?"

"Right. The hang-up. Am I interrupting something important?"
He looked startled.

"Conference call. I just got off."

I insisted that he find Polly's file and that he let me read it, stand-ing there in front of him as he dazedly rearranged his desktop. And there, sure enough, was what I was looking for. There were a few, a very few, scrawled notes—reports on Polly's health and state of mind. Polly had mentioned, after she'd been given a lot of tranquilizers, in an intake interview, something no one had picked up on. She'd re-ferred vaguely to the "State place" just once, in passing—but I imme-diately knew what she'd meant and what to do next. Manhattan State Hospital was on Wards Island, right under the Triborough Bridge.

The following day I sat before a member of the nursing staff at Manhattan State Hospital on Wards Island. Wards Island is at the northern end of the East River and is sometimes considered to be part of Manhattan. I'd taken a bus from 125th Street, reading a bit about the island as I traveled there. Its history, like that of the other is-lands, was shadowed. At first it had been a potter's field. Then a site for a hospital for destitute immigrants. Then asylums for the insane were built. City Asylum became Manhattan State Hospital. The Tri-borough Bridge shot right over it, and landfill connected it to Ran-dalls Island—people walked over a footbridge to get there. It was covered with chain-link fences. The windows on the buildings were barred and shuttered. An exit off the FDR Drive that might have been called the Island of the Mad.

Still, my hunch had paid off. The nurse's name was Brenda Michiko, and I had found her by asking questions over the phone about specialties at the hospital. As a psychiatric nurse, her subspe-cialty was epilepsy. She wore harlequin glasses and a very starched crackly-white uniform, and she immediately remembered Polly. Her hands rested on a thickish file with Polly's name on the lip. We sat in her tiny windowless office, its walls covered with *Peanuts* comic strips—and she ignored her phone, which rang every so often. Just as in the Women's House, I could hear shouts in the halls somewhere in the hospital's interior.

Why, I asked, hadn't anyone tried to locate Polly Lyle at the Women's House and bring her back?

"City services don't seem to talk among themselves," she said. "We sent out bulletins about a missing patient—but they were probably never picked up and read. We don't pool information. Lots of confusion and bureaucratic miscommunication, I guess you'd say."

She smiled at me, a little dazedly. She had very bright, very sad eyes behind the wing-shaped lenses.

"To tell you the truth," she said, "we assumed that Polly had drowned."

"So you knew she was out on the water? Was there a search for her?"

She looked down, then up again at me.

"There wasn't a very big search," she said. "The City doesn't allocate much in the way of rescue budgets."

"But how," I asked, "did she manage to get away from here, to get out on the water—how did she travel?"

"You see," said Brenda Michiko, "Polly built a raft."

She opened Polly's file and turned some pages.

"She was a member of a reading group," Brenda said, and glanced up at me. "They read the Great Books, classics—you know, there are some very intelligent patients here. They read all the time and they want to talk about what they read."

She looked down and then up at me again and smiled.

"They read Mark Twain."

I smiled back at her.

"I've never seen anything like it," she said. "You know that Polly believed that she was related to Twain?"

"Yes," I said, "I knew that."

The phone rang again and Brenda glanced at it, then turned back to me.

"She talked the other patients in the reading group and the nursing staff into mounting a play. A play about Mark Twain—all of his writings. Polly wrote the script. The play centered on Huck Finn and Jim and their travels down the Mississippi on a raft. Polly was set on building a real raft for the play. Something that would look really authentic onstage. We could not provide the actors with much splash-water or fake waves or smoke or much in the way of lighting—but Polly Clement found a way to build a raft down in the basement here with a former employee who was the janitor. His name was Jericho Daston and he loved listening to Polly recite lines from Twain. She memorized everything, all of Twain—I truly believe the girl had a photographic memory! It might interest you to know that she ended up here because she had been wandering the streets, homeless, talking to herself. When she first arrived here—you know, filthy, disheveled—you would never have suspected the intellect on that girl!

"Anyway, Jericho handled the garbage detail down in our underground plant here. Part of his regular job was to load the plastic bags and bins onto a small barge that is picked up by a tug from our 'port' and sent to Hunt's Point sewage plant. So, the staff believed that she was building a prop. Something for the actors to stand on, onstage. It seemed therapeutic as well as an artistic effort. Well, it was that and something more, if you know what I mean.

"The play took place in the auditorium here, and it was a big success with staff and patients—Polly stood on that raft and was a ringer for Huck Finn!—and then, after the standing ovations and the reception here, all the props, including the raft, were taken downstairs for storage. At that point, Jericho and Polly made a plan. We think he agreed to open the garbage float doors for her and put her out on the Hunt's Point barge on her raft, and she must have cast off from there—and got herself all the way from here to Rikers Island. You know, the staff all thought that raft was made of cardboard and twine—but Jericho had helped her build a seaworthy kind of float, made of material to withstand wind and current."

"And she knew about the currents, too," I said.

"Yes." She glanced at the file in front of her again. "Her history was, well . . . tied up with that."

"With . . . ?"

"The sea." She flipped through some more pages, then looked straight at me.

"Polly Lyle came to trust me. She told me the truth about her life. She did not trust the psychologists, but she put faith in me. Perhaps because I have daughters and I felt so badly for her—what she'd been through. And I do not believe in heavy medication. So she told me: her mother was Mulatto and her father was"—she opened the file and flipped a page—"yes, German. He was a member of the merchant marine and the family lived in New Orleans. The mother was a prostitute and died when the girls were small. The mother came from a family who owned a brothel in New Orleans—they'd been there a long time. There was a family legend about Mark Twain and how he used to visit the brothel way back before the Civil War."

I started to ask a question, but she went on without hearing me, as if she'd been waiting to tell Polly's story for a very long time.

"Polly was a twin. The sisters were very high-strung and the father talked often of them being psychic. Polly was epileptic, as was her sister, and he believed that the condition gave them special powers, you know. But he was an unscrupulous man. He actually sold his daughters into prostitution."

There were more shouts in the hallways and the telephone rang again.

"She was abused physically—she and her sister were beaten and sexually assaulted. When the father drank, he became violent. His father or grandfather, I can't remember, was a survivor of a terrible ferryboat accident here on the river on one of the islands—and he apparently spoke of it and terrorized the girls with the idea of fire."

"The *General Slocum*," I said.

"I think that was it."

"Polly got to the island where the *General Slocum* crashed," I said, "all alone on that raft—and she stayed there for quite a while before she landed at Rikers."

It was Brenda Michiko's turn to smile.

"I believe she could have done that. Polly was a very resourceful person. And she said her daddy taught her one sure thing: how to sail."

I spent two hours with Brenda Michiko and I left with Polly's story in my head. Or most of it. I'd asked how I could find Jericho, the janitor who had helped her build the raft, but she shook her head. The administration had fired him after Polly disappeared. They'd discovered his role in her escape and they'd let him go, after threatening to charge him with a criminal act.

"I have no idea where he could be," Brenda Michiko said. "He left no trace of himself here. It's the bureaucracy—it allows people to vanish, nobody bothers to check on anything."

We looked at each other and I thought if I began to cry, she might begin to cry as well—a situation it seemed wise to avoid.

"Polly told me how she lost her sister," said Brenda Michiko. "Are you sure you want to hear?"

I nodded.

"The father was a merchant marine, as I mentioned. He took his daughters on board one of the vessels he worked on. It was night, there was a party—and he ended up offering his daughters to the other seamen. There was a fire on the boat that night. No one ever knew how it was started, but Polly's sister and father died in that fire and Polly's face was burned. It's possible that Polly was responsible; she said strange things about the fire, but I don't know. She also hinted that her sister knocked over a torch or a lantern and set a fire on purpose—to get back at the father. But there are no definite answers to that one."

She looked at her watch.

"I have to go now," she said. "We have back-to-back meetings all afternoon."

I was about to ask her for a copy of Polly's file, but then she opened a drawer in her desk and took out a battered leather-bound book with a broken gilt-stamped binding and placed it on the desktop between us.

"I thought you might want this," she said. "I cannot locate any of her kin, here or in New Orleans, who might be entitled to it. Maybe you could keep it as a memento of her. She always told such big stories."

She smiled at my confused look.

"It's just an old Bible," she said. "Polly always carried it with her and talked about it being handed down to her from her mother's family. She said they kept it on a stand in the brothel and the women wrote in it. I haven't bothered to open it up. I don't put much stock in the Bible myself."

I waited until I was back in the lobby to open it. I walked through one of the long winding dark tunnels that connected the various hospitals and the reception area and I sat down in a plastic chair and held it gingerly in my lap. Gilt powder fell from the page edges as I turned them, noting the scrawled handwriting in the margins, the "Blessed are . . ."s and the jokes. And then I flipped back to the flyleaf and there was the ladder of names, most of them in the same spidery hand. But there, at the top, the swooping straightforward cursive, readily identifiable: SAMUEL LANGHORNE CLEMENS.

fifteen

It was a clear morning on the river. I wrote these words in my notebook, then stowed the tiny notebook away in my jeans pocket and pulled my leather jacket more tightly around me. The river was moving too fast, and the day was too bright, to look away.

K.B., Benny, and I, and in a broader sense Polly Lyle Clement, were on a small hired craft, a boat piloted by a shortish man named Bob Torginruud, who looked a great deal like a fireplug in a watchman's cap. We were in Hell Gate, on the East River. We stood on the wooden deck, the wind blowing so hard that it was impossible to talk to one another. So we stayed in our separate places, looking out at the brightness—those successive flashes like gunfire off the bridges and pylons and high-story windows. The fast-moving air smelled of garbage and jet fuel, just as it did on Rikers Island. It was a winter day, but it was sunny and not too cold at all.

There were a few black-and-red tugboats around us, some hauling long lines of construction barges—but we kept to the middle of the river, holding our own. The boat's radio beeped and spoke periodically in snarls of static. Bob T. was busy in the pilothouse and appeared to have no interest in anything beyond the river, which I found reassuring. The world on either shore was urban, jam-packed with buildings—or, in a very few places, green as gems, as emeralds coming toward us, parklike.

K.B. pointed out whirlpools to me, just off the bow, but Bob-at-the-wheel steered impressively through them. We were bouncing around pretty hard now, hitting the wakes of other boats, the tugs, and a large smelly garbage scow. We swung in one direction and then the other, making quick turns in the fearsome currents. I held on to the rail and shot a thumbs-up to Benny, who was sitting down on a coiled pile of old rope, smiling weakly. None of us had gotten seasick so far. Traffic was not bad now—the currents were sweeping us past Randalls Island and then past the Triborough Bridge, under the thundering of a thousand cars—I gazed above the bridge to the grim sentinel figures of the Wards Island mental hospitals as K.B. pointed them out, rising high above the bridge-way. Planes hung overhead awaiting landing instructions, then they bore down over the streams of cars.

Bob T. had told us before we shoved off that Hell Gate Passage ended not much beyond the Triborough Bridge—then, he said, there were the "tide rips" and strong currents guarding the Bronx and Queens shores. The wind filled with the smell of the Hunt's Point sewage treatment plant, on an ugly stretch of the Bronx shore, where the sludge barges were loaded up. Benny held her nose and waved to me. I held my nose and waved back—then pointed ahead. We were heading straight downriver from the arch of the Hell Gate railroad bridge toward North and South Brother islands. We'd passed the Sunken Meadows section of Randalls Island (Bob T. pointed it out) and the industrial sections, Stony Point.

Now we could see Rikers Island coming up on the other side of the river. I could make out the razor-wire fences and the gray blocks of the prison buildings, the sun glinting off the vehicles on the bridge heading onto the Island. I squinted into the dazzling light off the water—I was trying to see if there were any pimps gathered on the far side of the bridge so early in the day, but I couldn't make out any big hats. Planes circled down, then over the Island—on their way to the La Guardia runways.

There were gulls everywhere, shrieking and following the boats. I thought of Polly and the birds on North Brother and I glanced over at K.B. He smiled back at me. *All the poetry in my head,* I thought, *and I can't think of a word for this moment.* Nor a word for K.B., except *friends,* we would be friends always. Then I thought, *Maybe we won't stay apart, maybe we'll come back to each other. Maybe the path will be clear.* (The night before, I had finished my poem called "Twin Cities." The last lines were "City and City and / river and river of this, my Ever-Dividing Reflection.") My reflection divided again and I thought about Sam Glass, how we were bound to make more trouble for each other, then maybe also end up as friends. I would not understand passion or love—what either meant to me—not for a very long time. I was going to have to suffer some more, enter despair, come close to giving up on my life, close to the end-of-the-line despair Polly Lyle Clement had felt: then out the other side. Then I looked away from my own visions— I thought about Polly again and what we were about to do in her name. "Truth is, I'm a seer," she had said, and I felt her gaze upon us now.

Then I remembered the immortal lines of poetry: "But you don't understand how to think about the dead. / . . . There are nothing but gifts on this poor, poor Earth."

She had been a gift, she had been given to us by some strange profoundly articulated power. She had persuaded me that these gifts, distributed among us, made sense, made joy. I remembered the end of Kyrilikov's letter from Venice: "Poetry is not an art or a branch of an art, it is something, we think, more. If what sets us apart from other species is speech, then poetry—the supreme linguistic accomplishment—is our anthropological, even our genetic, goal." I remembered that I'd said something like that to K.B. once, over dinner at the French bistro (I glanced over at him again), but I'd gotten the observation wrong. The woman had needed a shawl, not linguistic light. If Polly's great gift had come from a wound, it was also a power, an astonishment, a coincidence of love and language and terror—deserving of great honor.

Far beyond us floated buoys that marked the channels into Flushing Bay and the Whitestone and Throgs Neck bridges. We were coming up now on North Brother Island—Bob T. had told us that there were the ruins of a pier and a ferry dock on the Bronx side of, as he put it, "abandoned North Brother Island." I could see it now, the crumbling, half-attached pier—Polly Lyle's pier; the gulls flew all around it, their wings glinting in the sun, their cries fierce—alternating between falsetto and bass. Their raucous male-and-female shouts reminded me of Gene/Jean. How her voice changed register mid-sentence. Then I paid close attention as Bob T. maneuvered the boat, turning expertly back and forth, closer to the shores of North Brother.

It wasn't as hard as I thought to get permission to bring more teachers in. Superintendent Ross signed off on our program, which at first was called Free Space, then Writing Without Walls. Writers took turns coming out to teach, and the Columbia students assisted as interns. There was a workshop in fiction and another poetry workshop and a playwriting class. But there was never again a workshop like that first one. Aliganth agreed with me—and she knew, because she kept requesting guard duty for the poetry workshops, complaining all the while.

It happened slowly, but first Billie Dee was sent upstate to a psychiatric facility. Then Never got hard time, about seven years, for being a drug runner and was sent to federal prison. Gene/Jean served less than a year in the Women's House and completed her sex change when she got out. S/he sent me a photo of her/himself in an Elvis getup: gold and white lamé with a huge rhinestone-studded belt and codpiece. Baby Ain't got back on the calendar and her pros charge was dropped for time already served. Roxanne Lattner was convicted of cocaine possession and sale; she was sent to a medium-security jail

somewhat upstate—she never turned state's evidence. Dar-
lene's charge was softened to a Class E felony—closer to
manslaughter than murder—and she got off with a year's
served time. I don't know if she ever got her children back. Aki-
lah Malik took up permanent residence in Cuba, where she
wrote her autobiography. The family of the New Jersey state
trooper who was shot, and others, posted a reward of a million
dollars for her return to the United States to stand trial. Sallie
Keller disappeared not long after Polly Lyle Clement killed her-
self. I never heard what happened to Sallie and her unforget-
table ruined face.

*B*ut now the future was in the future. Now we bumped hard
against the pilings of the tumbledown pier, and birds, what
seemed like thousands—gulls, cormorants, egrets, and storklike
winged creatures—descended upon us from the air, shouting out
their fevered petitions and complaints.

We walked down the broken cobbled streets under the wild
growth of trees near the vine-covered redbrick contagious hospital—
and there was the old clock stopped dead on a Tuesday in the fifties
and the buildings left with their doors gaping as if the inhabitants had
just gone out to lunch. The birds followed us, some flapping overhead, some waddling along, insultingly imitating our manner of walking and talking.

I told Benny and K.B. that I wanted to go back to the shore, to the
lighthouse ruin we'd passed climbing up out of the broken boards
and pilings. I'd noticed it as I stood teetering on the dock. So we
rounded back and climbed down the rocks to the lighthouse itself.
The huge octagonal light, as Polly had said, was long gone from its
turret, but the old lightkeeper's house still stood fair and sturdy.

We ducked under a fallen beam and were inside: a terrible musty smell and mud-crusted walls everywhere, but a shelter with a kind of cove in the kitchen, broken furniture, and ripped wallpaper—roses and teapots—still peeling away. I walked out onto a little deck that had slowly lowered itself onto the rocks and I shrugged out of my backpack.

Her ashes were in a small earthenware jug, stenciled to make it look like an Athenian black-and-red-figured funerary urn. K.B. and Benny joined me and we climbed down the rocks and opened the urn, and I put handfuls of Polly's remains into each of their hands. Then we stood on our separate stones and committed her to the river. As I reached out and opened my hand, I called out, not caring if I sounded ridiculous, to Polly: "Light out for the territory, Polly Lyle Clement, light out!" The ashes flew out of our hands and up into the wind, then straight out over the water, sparkling in the bright moving air. Like falling stars in a wilderness of stars.

It took me a long time to find the weeping willow tree, but I did. It was shrunken, overgrown, sunk into the rocks a few yards up the beach from the lighthouse. Perhaps it was dying—but its gnarled roots looked so set into the earth, its branches drooping so timelessly into the water, that it could also have been simply easing into its immortality. It was winter and there were no leaves on its branches, but I could suddenly see it in full leaf: that breathtaking light light green color—the color of a seer's eyes.

Then I saw the names: one of the inmates' signatures was almost obliterated by overgrown bark, but the other, LEWIS B. JAMES, stood out in relief, still. Below those names, in hastily cut but clean letters: AKILAH MALIK. I took my pocketknife and I added Polly's name. I carved it deep, in order that it would last: POLLY LYLE CLEMENT, and just below that:

BELOVED DESCENDANT OF SAMUEL L. CLEMENS,

A.K.A. MARK TWAIN

It took me a long time and I cut myself a little but I felt no pain—I kept working till her epitaph was in place.

Then I gently took out the Whorehouse Bible and began to follow the instructions that Polly Lyle had given to me about her personal effects the last time I saw her alive. She had told me that she "saw" that the Bible would come to me and she had asked that I set it afloat on a small raft in the East River and let the Holy Word travel where it would. It was what she'd wanted, her last request—and I knew I had to honor it.

I'd made a small float out of sticks and rubber bands, and now I pulled it out of my pack and I kissed the Whorehouse Bible and fastened it to the stick-float with a rubber band and knelt on the rocks, then pushed it out into the water. It dipped a little, then began to bob away.

I immediately had second thoughts about what I'd done: about the delicate pages filled with the whores' variations on scripture and the signature of Mark Twain himself on the first gilt-edged leaf—floating away on the river, destined to end up as fish food—and I couldn't bear it. So I lay down on the rocks and stretched my arm out and pulled the Bible-raft back just as the current was about to sweep it away. I fetched it up, a little damp but whole and entire for posterity.

Or, Reader, I did not. I put out my hand but then let it go, as Polly had instructed.

I won't say which choice I made. So all right, then, I'll go to hell for not telling. But Polly and the old man would want me to keep the secret, I know.

K.B. and Benny stood on the rocky incline above and called to me. "Time to go, Holly, it's late!"

And the birds flying over echoed their call, "Late, late." Not as if they were registering a complaint, but as if they'd been waiting patiently there on North Brother—waiting for me, waiting for Polly Lyle Clement, for a very long time.

Twin Cities

I come from Twin Cities, where
the river between, surging, stands.

I believed once that what I called desire
flowed in that confluence between twins,

capitol and columned future. I come from
twin cities: Dark and Light. But the river

was dammed, managed for miles above the locks:
even at the source where the god's mouth opened

and what we call belief thundered down in
every synonym. Two mirrored cities:

their symmetry invented as my own present,
twinned to a past to which it is now forever

subordinate. Twinned to a future, stunned
in its white eclipse. They killed the white

foxes, brought their pelts to market in the one
named for the Saint pierced by lightning.

The richer Sister prospered on the threshed tons
near the shared slaughterhouse. If the snow grew

steeped in blood, they raised a Court. But no one
out-thinks the two-in-one. The river was dammed, the moon

afloat, an animal face, in the crossed ambivalent tales
of my people and those of the suffering ancients.

Our gold domes on earth imitating the gold clouds
of the Ojibway, their vision-figures who doubled and

doubled but remained apart. Like this single mind, forever
unable to refuse its over-statement: blood on snow,

the gnawed bars of the trap, crack after crack in the
courthouse floor. And one irrefutable truth after another—

obliterated by the irrefutable dual: City and City and
river and river of this, my Ever-Dividing Reflection.

—HOLLY MATTOX, POET

ACKNOWLEDGMENTS

The list of people to whom I owe thanks is long. First, to my inspired, steadfast, and supportive Random House editors, Laura Ford and Daniel Menaker, and to my agent, Molly Friedrich—there's no way I could have written this book without you! And all my gratitude to the amazing Jynne Martin and Laura Goldin.

There are also friends and family to whom I quite literally owe my survival during a year of moving and enormous change and upheaval— Laura Baudo Sillerman; my sister, Michele Mueller; April Gornik and Eric Fischl; Elizabeth Bassine; Michelle Latiolais; my daughter, Annie; Luis Caicedo; Grace Schulman; Amy Schroeder; Bill Handley; Jim and Kathy Muske; Erik Jackson; Jason Shinder and Sophie Cabot Black; Bruce Lagnese; Mary Karr; and the Minnesota Muske family (thanks especially, Mike and Chris!). I will never forget what you've done for me.

And special thanks to Mark Doty, Billy Collins, Clare Rossini, Jonathan Galassi, Nanci Lee, Sylvie Rabineau, Sara Davidson, Jody Donahue, Susan Halpern, Marion Ettlinger, Debbie Gimelson, Cleopatra Mathis, Lisa Russ Spaar, Sheryl Bellman, Pam Macintosh, Megan Fishmann, Quincy and Margaret Porter Troupe, Mark Strand—and Mae Jackson.

I am also grateful to the University of Southern California, my L.A. "home."

To my mother—thank you for "growing me up" within poetry. And to my father—thank you for my stubborn mind.

As always, in memory of David. And in memory, too, of Fletcher Marie.

Channeling

MARK TWAIN

CAROL MUSKE-DUKES

A Reader's Guide

A Conversation with Carol Muske-Dukes

Rachel Rowe is an editor for the website A Gaggle of Book Reviews, where this interview originally appeared, in somewhat different form, in 2007.

Rachel Rowe: *Channeling Mark Twain* is filled with multilayered characters and topics from pimps and prostitution to mental illness and social activism. What made you decide to give the novel that title? Were you trying to direct the reader's attention to one area of the book?

Carol Muske-Dukes: I couldn't write this novel for years. I tried it as a long poem (I'm a poet) and as a kind of journalism, but no go. My difficulty in finding its center or nucleus was caused by a conflict I felt in my own life which colored my initial attempts to write this novel. The novel is set in a time I remember well. I was teaching poetry at the Women's House of Detention on Rikers Island (and in other prisons) during the seventies (the "present" of *Channeling Mark Twain*) and I discovered that I could not seem to bring together, in my mind, the world of prison and prison poetry—and the world of the literary life of Manhattan and its traditional aesthetic of poetry. This division of sensibilities, of language, tortured me for years. Finally, I realized that I could write about the conflict itself, what that felt like at the time. And what helped me realize this was a moment of inspiration: I suddenly thought that, along with writing about a time period I knew from my own experience, I could invent a character who was a version of Mark Twain's Huck Finn, contemporized—and I tried to imagine what it would be like if Huckleberry Finn "came back" as a young African American woman in prison on Rikers Island. Thus, my character, Polly Lyle Clement, is at the center of *Channeling Mark Twain*. This young woman, a mysterious wayfarer and self-described blood descendant of Samuel Langhorne Clemens, channels him—just as I tried to channel her.

RR: As I read the novel, the characters that stood out to me were not Holly's friends and colleagues outside the prison, but the prisoners and prison employees. The vibrancy of the prisoners contrasted to the more muted personality of her husband. It seemed to keep the reader's attention on Holly's activism rather than her other activities. Was this contrast intentional?

CMD: I'd hoped that the characters on both sides of the bars would hold equal interest and weight, but I do understand that prison inmates, will, almost by definition, given their extreme circumstances, be more intriguing than "civilians." The prison poetry writing workshops I taught were filled with fascinating women. Some were "ordinary," at least in terms of their crimes. (So many women go to jail for so-called "victimless" crimes, prostitution, drugs, shoplifting, etc.) So a streetwalker like Baby Ain't had a "regular" job, but a wild and funny street personality. Others, like Akilah Malik, were personally charismatic and notorious.

RR: I understand that this novel is somewhat autobiographical— why did you choose to fictionalize your experiences rather than write a memoir?

CMD: Because of the reasons above, having to do with imagination and inspiration. As I was saying, it was my imagination that saved me, my ability to conjure up people and events never exist-ing before—which finally freed me up to write this book. We live in a time that seems to give tremendous value to the "it really hap-pened just like this" memoir sensibility. I wanted this story to be told in the most powerful way possible—to do justice to the char-acters I created and to the time in which they lived. As Picasso said, "We lie in order to tell the truth" in art. Like all novelists, I draw to some extent on my experiences in the world, but the world I evoke is the "real life" of fiction—invented characters and events that, at their best, approach the "truer" truth of art.

RR: Holly and Polly have very similar names, as well as similar lit-erary interests. They are also very different—one a young, white, social activist poetry teacher and the other an older, black, men-tally unstable inmate—and yet they are drawn together. Were their names a conscious choice to tie them together? Was Polly based on any inmates you encountered?

CMD: No, she was not. And their names were not a conscious choice—I only realized that their names rhymed when my editor or my agent pointed it out to me!

RR: You continue to be involved in teaching poetry to prison inmates—how much do you think has changed in the thirty years since the setting of *Channeling Mark Twain*? Could the story have been as effective if you set it in the present day?

CMD: I'm just struggling with the plausibility of resetting this story in the present—as there is TV interest in the book—which I will not address till after the Writers' Strike is over—but I really don't think the narrative could have the degree of emotional power it perhaps has now. Maybe I'm wrong. But it seems to me that the consciousness of the sixties and seventies would be very hard to "translate" into our consumer-oriented fashionista times. Maybe Martha Stewart could star?

I haven't been involved in teaching in prison for a long time—but recently I started a workshop at Bayview Correctional Facility in Manhattan—the only remaining women's prison in the city! A lot has changed, a great deal has remained the same. Women still go to jail for "victimless" crimes on one hand, with very little "middle" crime like burglary, breaking and entering, grand larceny, etc. However, women's crime tends to leap from stealing a Twinkie to blowing a pimp's head off, as it always did.

More depressing is that corporations have taken over prisons and there is even less rehab than before. And suicide rates are up. In early 2003, a woman hanged herself at the Women's House on Rikers Island (I wrote a city op-ed piece regarding this for *The New York Times*)—she'd been arrested for stealing several lipsticks. Depressed since early adolescence, she nevertheless was not seen by a psychiatrist during the months she was incarcerated. She finally gave up. An inmate-run suicide watch could not catch her in time. When I was at the Women's House of Detention on Rikers Island in the seventies, women were routinely "off the calendar" like this, which meant that they were arrested but not officially charged with a crime before a judge. A woman busted for holding a small amount of drugs could sit in prison for several months, even a year, before being charged. Routinely, women would lose their children, who would be given to foster care as wards of the state. This is supposedly better, but in reading about the suicide rate, which is as bad as it was before and worse, I wonder.

RR: You don't make income or finances a plot point for Holly and her husband, K.B. Holly has enough time to do volunteer and paid nonprofit work, in addition to freelance poetry writing. Could Holly, or anyone, be as socially active if she needed to earn a living wage?

CMD: Holly is teaching at Columbia University, plus she is working as a kind of social worker, or AfterCare worker at the Women's House, for which she is paid. It is not volunteer or nonprofit work, I can assure you, as I did it. It's very tough work. And teaching is wonderful, but very demanding as well. And I love the expression "freelance poetry writing." There ain't any other kind—and you know, poets regularly make in the high two figures.

RR: I grew up in a very socially liberal family, and I followed Holly through the disappointment of realizing that the protesters and inmates aren't always right, and the institutions aren't always wrong. Has that shift in perspective altered your outlook on protesters and institutions in general? Has it changed how you work inside the prisons?

CMD: This is a coming-of-age novel, I guess—and therefore a novel about growing up. I guess we all go through periods of idealism accompanied by great naivete, but in writing the character of Holly, my hope was that a sense of her idealism as "tempered," not destroyed, would come through. No person or institution has cornered the market on "right" and we must be thankful for that, I suppose.

RR: Fiction with a political message is not always engaging, and yet your novel is engrossing while covering prisons, socialism, and prostitution. Did you edit the political messages inside *Channeling Mark Twain* to make it more readable?

CMD: Well, that's what I was talking about when I mentioned the process of the imagination fictionalizing some of the more obdurate political realities—also, I hope, making them funnier, more poetic, more human. Thus, I hope, a character who channels Mark Twain can perhaps convey a political message by implication (and by humor, as he, the Great Old Man, did) more effectively than an ideological rant would. We're all on the same raft, as Polly says, and we'd best, therefore, get along.

RR: Thank you for your time—I loved your novel.

CMD: Thank you so much for reading my book and asking such terrific questions.

Questions and Topics for Discussion

1) How does Holly change over the course of the narrative? What kind of self-awareness does she gain?

2) How has Holly's upbringing informed her perspective and outlook on everything from politics to art to love? What does she in particular take away from her mother?

3) On page 33, Holly thinks, "Teach what you read . . . the great haunting voices. Teach what stays in your memory. What runs in your veins." How does this idea apply to her own teaching, both in the prison and in a university setting?

4) Why do you think Holly is so conflicted about many elements of her life? She describes herself as full of "angry contradictions." Have you ever felt similarly? Do you think one can have two different selves?

5) What draws Holly to Sam Glass, especially when she has a loyal, kind husband? What is their attraction based on?

6) How would you describe the different styles of poetry that appear throughout the novel? Which speaks most powerfully to you?

7) What do you make of Polly's claim that she is a descendant of Mark Twain, and able to channel him, and that she was present

during the *General Slocum* disaster? Do you believe her? Were you able to take a leap into the supernatural, or do you think there's a rational explanation?

8) What makes Holly different from the other young women she meets with in the Bail Fund? How do their philosophies differ?

9) Why does Holly pose such a threat to Aliganth and the other corrections officers at the prison? Are their attitudes toward her justified?

10) What risks have you taken in your own life for something you believe in? What were the consequences?

11) What is the significance of Polly's Whorehouse Bible? What does it symbolize?

12) "Like a thumbprint, a mug shot, I was on record. I was a whore too. And all this, I saw now, for an idea of Justice, sold to whoever bid," Holly states after her tumultuous confrontation with the warden (p. 158). How does their conversation change Holly's perspective? Where did your sympathies lie during this scene?

13) Why do you think Muske-Dukes introduces the character of Joseph Kyrilikov into the narrative? What similarities does he have in common with Holly, with her prisoner students? What perspective does he add?

14) Akilah tells Holly she believes that in order "to teach poetry—you have to have lived" (p. 193). Do you agree with her statement? Is Holly justified in writing poetry—does it mean anything? Is any poet's voice ever justifiably disregarded? What do you think makes a true poet?

15) How can a poem be, as Holly describes, both "a shawl wrapped around them—and a gun held to their heads" (p. 208) at the same time?

16) Discuss Holly's final poem (p. 251). What is she saying in this piece? What image or idea stands out the most for you?

CAROL MUSKE-DUKES is the founder and former director of the Ph.D. program in literature and creative writing at the University of Southern California. Her last collection of poetry, *Sparrow,* was a finalist for the National Book Award, and she has been the recipient of many other awards, among them an Alice Fay Di Castagnola Award from the Poetry Society of America, and National Endowment for the Arts and Guggenheim fellowships. She has published seven books of poetry, three novels, and two collections of essays, including *Married to the Icepick Killer: A Poet in Hollywood.* A former columnist for the *Los Angeles Times Book Review,* a regular contributor to *The New York Times,* as well as founder of the Free Space/Art Without Walls prison arts program, Muske-Dukes lives in New York City and Los Angeles.

www.carolmuskedukes.com

ABOUT THE TYPE

This book was set in Bulmer, a typeface designed in the late eighteenth century by the London type cutter William Martin. The typeface was created especially for the Shakespeare Press, directed by William Bulmer; hence, the font's name. Bulmer is considered to be a transitional typeface, containing characteristics of old-style and modern designs. It is recognized for its elegantly proportioned letters, with their long ascenders and descenders.